THE
CARSON C
CHRONICL
BOOK O

JUDITH and
the JUDGE

STEPHEN & JANET BLY

VINE
BOOKS

SERVANT PUBLICATIONS
ANN ARBOR, MICHIGAN

OTHER BOOKS IN THE SERIES:

Marthellen and the Major
Roberta and the Renegade

For a list of other books by Stephen & Janet Bly
write:
Stephen & Janet Bly
Winchester, Idaho 83555

© 2000 by Servant Publications
All rights reserved.

Vine Books is an imprint of Servant Publications especially designed to serve
evangelical Christians.

Published by Servant Publications
P.O. Box 8617
Ann Arbor, Michigan 48107

Cover design and illustration: Hile Illustration and Design.

00 01 02 03   10   9   8   7   6   5   4   3   2   1

Printed in the United States of Americ
ISBN 1-56955-158-8

Cataloging-in-Publication Data on file at the Library of Congress.

For
Judith Kathryn

For we brought nothing into this world,
and it is certain we can carry nothing out.
And having food and raiment
let us be therewith content.

1 Timothy 6:7-8, kjv

CHAPTER ONE

Carson City, Nevada … August 1880

H is silk top hat fashionably cocked, Governor John Henry Kinkead flashed a politician's smile as he stood in a receiving line and introduced some of Nevada's leading citizens to the bearded, balding congressman from Ohio.

Kinkead turned to his guest. "If this crowd is any indication of support, you should do well in Nevada come November, Mr. Garfield. Or should I say, Mr. President?"

The Easterner's friendly eyes stayed poised on the milling crowd as he replied, "General Hancock might take exception to that term."

"Well, Congressman, perhaps you'd like to …" Governor Kinkead tugged the presidential candidate toward the middle of the Alaskan marbled floor of the reception hall where people were still filing in.

The energetic James Garfield brushed past his bewildered host to embrace a short lady with curly dark brown bangs and long hair neatly stacked on the back of her head. She wore a hunter green taffeta dress with velvet cuffs on the long sleeves. A gold butterfly brooch decorated her high black lace collar.

"Judith and Judge Kingston," Garfield's voice boomed out. "What a delight to see you!"

All conversation stopped in the crowded capitol rotunda. Heads craned and eyebrows lifted as Garfield's hand shot out to the tall, distinguished, arrow-straight man standing next to the lady. The man seemed as startled as the woman looked pleased.

"You, eh, … you know the Kingstons?" the governor sputtered, his top hat now in his hand.

"My word, Governor! Everyone in Washington knows Judith and the judge." Garfield stared into the woman's penetrating brown eyes. "Judith, did you ever get enough funding for that orphanage asylum?"

A gracious, easy smile broke across Judith Kingston's face. Her features were small and delicate, but the congressman knew from experience how well defined and strong were her opinions. "Yes, we did, James. And I want to thank you and Lucretia again for your more than generous contribution."

The congressman spread out his arms as though to include the whole room as his audience. "I have to admit it was because of your excellent presentation … and Crete's insistence. My wife has a very sensitive nature."

Judith's eyes took in the stylish notched, broad collar of his topcoat as she said, "I have the impression Lucretia is also a strong-willed woman."

"Ah, yes. Crete grows up to every new emergency with fine tact and faultless taste."

The judge grinned. "Well said, James. I learn much about a man's character by the way he speaks of his wife."

Judith took a deep breath, then blurted out, "I do trust you will join the judge and me for breakfast in the morning?"

Governor Kinkead tried to scoot between them, but the congressman's strong left arm got in the way. "We have Mr. Garfield scheduled to meet with the mine owners for breakfast in Virginia City tomorrow," he said. "His time with us is so short, and with the Republican State Convention in full session …"

"Nonsense," Garfield roared. "I can meet with the mine

owners later. Besides, most of them are here tonight." He turned to Judith. "Of course I'll have breakfast with you and the judge." Then he turned to the governor. "You don't think I came all the way to Nevada just to campaign, do you?"

Governor Kinkead looked a bit crestfallen as he led the presidential candidate to a cluster of eager handshakers.

Judith Kingston slipped her arm into her husband's as they strolled across the crowded room. She laced her small fingers into his large, calloused ones and squeezed his hand. Then she stood on tiptoe and whispered in his ear, "I told you."

Judge Kingston stroked his mustache and goatee as if he were brushing off loose hairs. "You win, my dear Judith."

"Thank you."

"But, I do think your breakfast invitation put our industrious governor into a dither."

"The governor is a dear man. He'll get over it." She smiled sweetly as she glanced around the state capitol lobby, studying the crowd of Carson citizens. She found herself noting the materials of the women's dresses. She knew exactly how much each ensemble had cost and where it had come from. She took some small satisfaction that her dress had been sent to her by her daughter, who was at college in the East, then immediately felt ashamed because of this indulgence of pride.

Judith Kingston watched the warmhearted and genial presidential candidate trying to please everyone, working the room. "Did you know that James Garfield writes poetry?" she asked. "Lucretia told me he can write a poem in Greek with his right hand while he writes the same poem in Latin with his left."

The judge glanced down at his wife's dancing eyes. "While of dubious value to a president, I have to admit that's quite impressive." He fussed at straightening a perfectly straight black bow tie as he thought, *How in the world does Judith know so many details about so many people?*

"You look impeccable, as always, Judge Kingston," Judith said, as she patted the front of his three-piece charcoal gray silk suit.

"And you bring radiance to an otherwise dull evening," he replied.

She tilted her head. "Oh, Judge, you are such a flatterer."

"I most certainly am not!"

Judith stood on her tiptoes and brushed a kiss across his blushing, clean-shaven cheek. "And that, dear Judge, is one of the reasons I love you so."

The judge stepped away but didn't release her hand. "Private affections should not be displayed in public places," he intoned, as if giving a ruling from the bench.

They promenaded toward a linen-covered table supporting an enormous punch bowl filled with a liquid of a deep orange hue. Open-faced sandwiches, stuffed mushrooms, large green olives, shortbread cookies, and dark chocolate cake filled silver plates. "Look around, Judge Kingston," Judith challenged. "Is there anyone in this room paying any attention to us?"

From his six-foot, two-inch height he surveyed the capitol lobby, including the sweep of the polished wooden staircase to the second floor. "No one's looking at us at all."

"Then I would say we're practically alone."

The judge's hawkish gray eyes locked onto hers. "In that case …" He leaned down and kissed her lips.

Judith clutched her husband's arm, eyes closed, enjoying the warm touch of his mouth on hers. *Judge Kingston, at times you are absolutely, wonderfully, and so completely unpredictable.*

A rough voice rasped behind them. "Oh good, I'm glad you

two ain't tied up with anything important!"

The judge pulled away and Judith opened her eyes. "Levi! How are you this evening?" she asked.

Levi Boyer rocked back on worn boots and tugged at the hastily knotted black tie that flopped across his soiled, collarless shirt. "I was doing fine until a few minutes ago. Doc couldn't come. He sent me in his place."

Judge Kingston retrieved two crystal glasses of punch. He handed one to his wife, the other to Levi Boyer. "How is your new racehorse?"

Levi plunked a black cowboy hat on his head, making short dark brown curls spring out at the forehead. His eyebrows shot across the bridge of his nose, a replica of his mustache. Judith had the urge to trim both. "That nag is a total waste of money," Levi said. "You was right about her, Judge. Listen, the Doc wanted me to—"

He broke off speaking when Judith suddenly said, "Did Doctor Jacobs give you some of that walnut pie Marthellen and I made for him?" She sipped the punch, detecting the taste of cloves, black tea, and apricots.

A scar on Levi's right cheek made his smile seem wider than his face. "That was a delectable delight! The crust was the best I've ever had since I was at my granny's. Now, the Doc said I should—"

"Have you met Mr. Garfield yet, Levi? He's running for president, you know. Come on, I'll introduce you to him," the judge offered. "I trust you've registered to vote."

"This ain't my crowd and you know it," Levi protested. "Now, will you two stop being so nice and let me say somethin'?"

Judith laid her hand on Levi's soiled gray wool coat. "Is

something wrong, Levi?"

"Doc Jacobs needs your help ... bad."

Judge Kingston rubbed the back of his neck. "He still can't find a full-time assistant?"

"I don't know about that." Levi gulped down his punch and wiped his mouth on the back of his hand. "He told me to send Judith over to his place."

Judith leaned her head close to his. "You mean, he wants me to stop by in the morning?"

Her penetrating stare made most men squirm. Levi was no exception. "No. I mean he wants you over there right now. There's an emergency."

"What happened?"

Boyer took a step forward. "It's Mrs. Adair. She's been beat up real bad ..." He looked down, his voice laced with sorrow.

Judith gasped. *Oh dear Jesus, not Audrey. Not again. That poor, poor woman. Have mercy on her soul. Have mercy on her body.*

"Was it her husband?" the judge demanded. *This has to stop, Lord. The battle rages down here, and the innocent take the brunt of the pain. Lord, bring him before my court. That's all I ask. Give me a chance at justice.*

Levi peered around the hall, his eyes darting from one staring face to another. "That's what Doc said, but Milton ain't nowhere to be found and Mrs. Adair ain't up to talkin' much."

As Judith glanced up at the judge, he reached over and squeezed her hand, saying, "You go on. I'll apologize to the governor and Congressman Garfield, then be right over. Levi, have you notified the sheriff?"

"Yes, sir. He and the others are searchin' all over town for Audrey's husband."

The gas lamps burned brightly from almost every window by the time Judge Kingston arrived at the two-story Adair home on the southwest corner of King and Ormsby. Even after ten years, its Victorian elegance dwarfed the landscaping of the yard. He could see the outline of trees and shrubs cast by the shadows of globe lamps on top each fence post. The low, hand-carved and engraved wooden picket fence dramatically defined the boundaries.

Judge Kingston stooped down to open the gate. He had just reached the fanned staircase to the front door when Judith burst out into the warm Nevada night.

"Have you seen the sheriff?" she asked.

"No. How's Audrey?"

"She looks like a stagecoach ran over her. Doctor Jacobs says she has a broken jaw, a broken left arm, and probable cracked ribs. Audrey says Milton did it."

The judge pulled off his top hat and paced back and forth on the porch. "This can't be. It's inconceivable. No woman on earth should have to put up with this. Why didn't she bring charges against Milton last spring? I begged her to. I would have sent him to prison for years."

"You mean, after the jury convicted him you would have sent him to prison," Judith corrected.

"Yes, of course. These types must be withdrawn from society. Milton cannot be allowed to strike her or any woman again. Surely she will bring charges against him now."

Judith stood still in the doorway and hugged herself as if the warm summer night had suddenly turned cold. "Audrey isn't talking much."

The judge continued to pace the porch. "Weren't there any servants at home to stop him?"

"He gave them the day off. Mrs. Coffee returned to the house early and discovered Audrey on the floor of the parlor. Judge, I believe this is a sign of the end times. Satan is getting the upper hand."

"It's always been his business," the judge added. "'The thief cometh not, but for to steal, and to kill, and to destroy....'"

"I can't understand how a man can efficiently run a bank during the day and shamefully treat his wife this way at night," Judith commented. "I don't know if such people push the Lord to the limits of his grace, but they certainly test me."

The judge shook his head. "Audrey kept trying to cover up his problems, a fact that did neither of them any favor. We all knew Milton got wild when he drank. The dance hall girls that come before my court have told me that for years. I'll never understand why Audrey Adair married Milton Primble."

Judith rubbed her shoulders. Her dark green dress looked almost black in the evening shadows. "Poor Audrey. But this isn't the time for 'what if?' questions. It's time to doctor a woman with a wounded body and spirit."

"Quite so ... and we've got to find a criminal and see that he's arrested. Perhaps I should go assist the sheriff."

"Doctor Jacobs asked if I could sit up all night with Audrey," Judith said.

"What about Mrs. Coffee?"

"She's so distraught ... Dr. Jacobs gave her some calming syrup. The other servants aren't due back until morning."

"Then I'll stay with you," the judge offered.

"You need your rest. I saw your docket ... you have a busy morning tomorrow."

"Nonsense! I'm not going to desert you here and then have Audrey's husband show up drunk."

Judith cracked a smile that barely moved her narrow, tense lips. "I was hoping you'd say that."

"Shall we go inside?"

"There's something I want to do first." Judith slipped her arms around his waist. She held him tight and laid her head on his strong chest. His arms returned the hug.

"Now, Mrs. Kingston, what's this all about?" His naturally stern voice softened into what she called the "Judith-tone."

"For thirty years, Judge Kingston, you have loved and protected and cherished me. And never laid a harsh hand on me."

He continued to hold her tight. "For thirty-*three* years," he corrected.

"We have only been married thirty years, and you know it."

"Yes, but I was quite smitten by you on the first day you walked into my chambers as a seventeen-year-old clerk."

"That's only because you had never seen a female clerk."

"That's because I had never, and still have never, met anyone so absolutely captivating."

"Well, dear Judge, when I looked at poor Audrey, I couldn't help thinking about how protected and safe I have felt in your company, every day, for thirty years."

"Every day?"

"Except that afternoon two weeks after our wedding when I busted your award gavel trying to kill a rat in our tiny little kitchen. I was afraid you'd either have a heart attack or strike me."

"My temper has cooled over the years. But I could never harm you ... I could never harm any woman."

"Well, there is a much-harmed woman upstairs who needs us." She let go of him. "Shall we adjourn this discussion on the porch?"

"We will postpone it," he declared, "but not adjourn."

"Yes, Your Honor." She tugged his hand and led him into the two-story white clapboard house.

First District Judge Hollis A. Kingston sat on the front step of the Adair home. He watched the Nevada sun slowly ease over the Pine Nut Range. *So different watching the lift and sink over the various mountains that completely surround this Eagle Valley ... the multishaped ridges make such a rocky veil of teasing light and shade, as Judith would say.*

The charcoal sky slowly turned to pale blue. A soft peach glow outlined the rocky rim of the eastern range, with a sudden brightness of deeper rose peach toward the center. A flock of V-lined geese veered south. The judge turned his gaze toward the Carson Range of the Sierras. A pallid, full morning moon sat in the sky like a dull dime on a pale blue floor.

It was a clear but slightly cool morning. The judge had reluctantly abandoned his topcoat and hat, but not the black bow tie, charcoal gray vest, starched white shirt, wool trousers, and polished black boots—his attire from the evening before. It was about as informal as the judge ever got in public.

Even after a sleepless night, his back was straight, his shoulders squared. It was as if he expected at any moment for the bailiff to shout "All rise!"

Doctor Jacobs shuffled up the sidewalk from Carson Street. He looked like a man who had just ridden shotgun for one of Hank Monk's stagecoach rides from Placerville. His suitcoat and trousers were wrinkled. Breakfast coffee stains covered the previous night's supper stains. Disheveled hair stuck out over his ears.

Carrying his leather satchel in one hand, he opened the gate with the other. "How's the patient, Judge?"

"As of an hour ago, both Audrey and Judith were sound asleep."

"That's good. Sleep will bring healing to Audrey's bones and her spirit." He plopped down on the step next to the judge. "I could use a little more sleep myself. You won't believe this, but I slept on my couch." He covered his mouth to suppress a yawn. "When I got back to my room last night, Duffy Day showed up with a deep knife wound in his left hand. When I got him sewed up, Sheriff sent word for me to hustle down to Jack's Saloon."

The judge rested the palms of his hands on his knees. "Did the sheriff find Milton Primble?"

"Nope. And he searched ever' rented room and rathole in town. But while he was looking, an old boy from Arizona, named Orson Kendall, decided the law was lookin' for him. He got spooked and pulled out a .45 and started scatterin' bullets like Johnny Appleseed plantin' trees. Fidora, the crib girl with the scar on her neck … she took a bullet in the foot and I was patchin' her up most of the night."

"How about this man, Kendall? Will I be seeing him in court?"

"The only place you'll see him is the cemetery. Nothin' I could do for him except call Kitzmeyer's."

"Oh. But who in the world would stab a harmless man like Duffy Day?"

"You know crazy Duffy. He done it to himself. He said he was sittin' by his campfire whittlin' when some hombres rode up and started shooting. He jumped up and cut himself."

"Someone actually shot at him?"

"He thinks so. But you know how the sound echoes along

the river. Could have been a half mile away. Duffy's jittery that way. Whenever he hears a gunshot he'll mount up that ol' sway-back and ride the opposite direction."

"I presume Duffy was camped up by his hog pens at Rocky Point?"

"You bet. He still claims that ten acres belongs to him and his brother Drake. He ain't goin' to leave it until Drake comes back." Dr. Jacobs peered up at the second-story windows. "Did Mrs. Adair say any more during the night?"

"Judith said Audrey talked for a while, but she wasn't sure if Audrey was conscious enough to be coherent."

"What did Mrs. Adair say?"

"She said she chased Primble off and she wouldn't have to worry about him again."

"Why's that?"

"Because Primble said he was leaving town."

"Leaving town? You mean, he'd just ride off from the bank job?"

"She claims Primble just got on a horse and rode off to Mexico."

Dr. Jacobs leaped to his feet. "Mexico! You mean, just like C.V. McKensie, her first husband?"

Judge Kingston fiddled with the gold cufflinks on his starched, crisp cuffs. "I figured she was delusional, getting the two mixed up in her mind."

Jacobs plopped back down on the step. "I reckon you're right. She must have a slight concussion and is having a tough time rememberin' one husband from another."

Judith Kingston burst out the door with one of Audrey Adair's knit afghans around her shoulders. "Dr. Jacobs, your patient is asleep and the judge and I had better hurry home. I just remembered that we have a presidential candidate due at our house for breakfast in an hour, and he and I will both be disappointed if I don't have biscuits and gravy ready."

The judge looked at her and said mildly, "I'm sure Marthellen will be up and—"

"Judge, our housekeeper is in Sacramento, awaiting the birth of her first grandchild. Remember?"

He scratched the top of his head. "Quite so."

"Mr. Garfield will have to put up with my cooking, I'm afraid."

"That, dear Judith," Dr. Jacobs added, "will be the highlight of his Western campaign."

The biscuits were tall and flaky. The elk sausage gravy was thick and hot. The eggs, seasoned with hot peppers and onion, were moist and fluffy, garnished with thin slices of tomato and fresh parsley.

"So," the judge guided the conversation, "how are the New York newspapers weighing the election? Our daughter, Roberta, attends college there and basically keeps us informed, but she must be distracted lately."

"Even though my running mate, Chester Arthur, is from there, they say it will be close," James Garfield muttered as he chewed eggs, then latched onto a crystal water glass. "But who knows? My word, let's not talk about politics for a moment. Tell me again about this lady who was savagely beaten and kept you two up all night."

Judith refilled the thick porcelain coffee cups as she said, "Audrey Adair has been a friend of ours for almost fifteen years." She returned to her mahogany chair with its forest green needlepoint cushion.

"She's married, yet she goes by her maiden name?" Garfield asked. "Is she an actress?"

"Oh, no," the judge mused. "It's rather a long story. She came out here in territorial days ... I believe it was '62, a year or two prior to when Judith and I moved out. She had just sold her parents' farm in Illinois and decided to open a bookstore."

"In Carson?" Garfield probed.

"It wasn't too successful," the judge said, "but she bought some books from some prospectors. Turned out one of 'em had a dozen mining certificates folded between the pages. When she tried to return the deeds, she was told the man had been killed by Paiutes or Shoshones out in the Ruby Mountains. Anyway, Audrey ended up owning a controlling interest in what she called the Tiny Tim Mine."

Garfield raised an eyebrow. "I presume the book that contained the stock was by Dickens?"

"Exactly," Judith said. "Audrey found herself very wealthy."

The judge cleared his throat with a "don't-interrupt-me-when-I'm-telling-a-story" inflection, then said, "She built a beautiful home in town."

"I surmise there were many suitors?" Garfield added.

"Yes. And that, I believe, was a new experience for Audrey. She's rather ..." The judge turned to his wife. "How exactly would you describe her, dear?"

Judith sipped her tea and rolled her eyes. "Now you need my commentary?"

The judge frowned. "I am not sure I can ..."

"Audrey is a wonderful woman with a heart of gold. She is quite pleasant and ... very healthy," Judith explained.

Garfield nodded. "Say no more."

"Perhaps you'd like me to continue this story, dear?" Judith pressed. "You seem to be rather lost for words."

"I'd hate to see my gravy grow cold," the judge mumbled.

Judith set down her teacup. "Mr. C.V. McKensie was a very handsome man who had already run through several fortunes when he met Audrey."

"You mean he'd struck it rich repeatedly?" Garfield asked.

Judith pursed her lips. "You might say that. He had a way of running through other people's fortunes. Audrey married him and changed her name to McKensie."

"And then he started spending her money?"

"Precisely."

The judge wiped biscuit crumbs off his mustache with a white linen napkin. "Then she cut off his funds."

"That was frightfully slack," Garfield grinned. "I presume he didn't care for that feature."

The judge banged down his coffee cup as if it were a gavel. "No, he just saddled a horse and rode off. That's what Audrey reported. She said he went to Mexico."

"Wherever he went, he didn't come back. So dear Audrey was finally granted a divorce for desertion," Judith explained.

"Then McKensie wasn't the man who did this to her last night?"

"Oh, no. That was her second husband, Mr. Primble. He was a bank manager over in Eureka, Nevada. She got him a similar position here in Carson," Judith said.

Garfield waved a biscuit over his plate. "And managed her funds, no doubt?"

"Yes, and a flask of whiskey most of the time, as well," the judge said.

Garfield rubbed his forehead. "She married exactly the same kind? That does seem strange."

"They were quite different in looks and personalities, but both took advantage of poor Audrey. The really strange thing is, she said that Milton Primble, her second husband, told her last night he was riding off to Mexico. We presume she was a little confused," the judge remarked.

"She repeated it this morning, dear," Judith confided. "She said that Milton rode off to Mexico just like C.V., and she hoped they would be happy together."

The judge brushed his mustache with the tips of his fingers. "I suppose in her battered condition she could have imagined that's what he said."

"Yes." Judith paused. "But still, I worry ..."

"About what?" Garfield asked.

"It's probably nothing but rumor."

"But what?" Garfield prompted.

The judge sighed. "What Judith is hesitant to say is, many folks have assumed that Audrey did away with C.V."

"My word, you mean, she may have murdered him?"

"C.V. was a crook. He was legally married, and part of the wealth certainly belonged to him. But he rode off without a penny. Some think that is incredible," the judge offered.

"Not only that," Judith said, "but no one has ever seen him again. He has a sister in Tucson who's been looking for him for years. Tucson is right on the way to Mexico and she can't understand why her brother didn't stop by."

"The sister even searched down in Mexico," the judge said.

Judith rose from her chair, a napkin in her hand, and dusted off the glass door of the carved china hutch whose countertop was of Italian marble. "There was enough suspicion that the sheriff looked into the matter," she said.

Garfield waved a gravy-laden fork. "Did he find anything?"

The judge shook his head. "No, but his heart wasn't in it. McKensie had committed no crime and we figured Audrey was better off without him."

"Well, I know Audrey Adair ... and she could not have murdered anyone," Judith said. "Not even under the physical duress of being beaten by her husband would she do such a thing."

"But she can drive them off to Mexico?" Garfield posed.

"I admit it does seem like a strange coincidence," Judith commented.

"An almost unbelievable coincidence," the judge said. "Extremely circumstantial evidence for suspecting murder."

"Her wounds are believable," Judith said.

"Objection sustained."

"Thank you, Your Honor."

"So, here's a woman who seems to attract men who squander her money, then have a penchant for disappearing to Mexico," Garfield mused. "It's intriguing."

The judge scooted back his chair. "It's life on the frontier, Mr. Garfield. This land won't get properly civilized for another hundred years."

"That brings to mind another subject—back to politics," Garfield said. "I've heard a number of men mention your name as nominee for Judge of the Supreme Court. I personally encourage you to consider it. That's one reason I came over this morning."

"I'm greatly honored," the judge replied. "But the other aspirants are men of integrity and ability. And they really want it. I don't."

Judith looked out the window toward Musser Street. "Looks like you have company, Judge."

When the judge stood, his head barely missed the crystal chandelier that hung from the dining room's twelve-foot ceiling. "Looks like Duffy. Did you hear Dr. Jacobs say that someone spooked Duffy while he was whittling last night? He got so flustered he stabbed himself."

The judge watched the man with the bandaged left hand approach the side entrance on Nevada Street. "I presume it was the Washburn brothers. It's as if they have no other purpose in life but to torment poor Duffy."

"My, for a small town, Carson does have its share of characters," Garfield commented.

"You have to be a character to live in Nevada," the judge said.

Garfield grinned. "Present company excepted, I presume."

"Oh no, not at all. Judith has taken on legendary characteristics out here."

"Me?" Judith protested. "The judge has men stop him on street corners to settle disputes. Whatever this man says, everyone does."

Judge Kingston raised his sweeping eyebrows. "Not everyone. I'll get the door."

"Tell Duffy I'll bring him out some breakfast."

"Judith, do you feed the whole town?" Garfield asked.

"Only those whom the Lord brings to my door," she said as she scurried to the kitchen.

"Duffy won't come in to eat," the judge told Garfield. "He had a mine shaft cave in on him up at Gold Hill. He was buried for almost three days before he was pulled out. He hasn't quite been the same since. He won't enter any building."

Judge Kingston slipped on his suit coat but left his hat on the peg as he stepped out on the back porch. "Duffy, how's that hand this morning? Dr. Jacobs said it was a nasty cut."

"Yes, sir, Judge, it was a beastly slice. I jist cain't take folks slippin' up on me like that. That's why I camp out on our place alongside the Carson River. I like bein' alone. Ever'body knows that."

The judge examined the wrapping on his hand. "Who was it, Duffy?"

"Cain't say, Judge. It was mighty dark." He leaned forward and the garlic on his breath caused the judge to blink. "I think it was Wild Bill Hickok, comin' to get me."

"Duffy, J.B. Hickok was murdered four years ago out in the Dakota Territory."

Duffy Day stepped back. "Hah! That's exactly what he wants you to think. No, sir, Judge. I seen him in Genoa just last month, and he took a shot at me then, too."

Judith stepped out on the porch with a plate of steaming food. James Garfield followed right behind.

"How about some breakfast, Duffy?" she asked.

"I'll have to decline, Judith. My mama told me it was impolite to show up at folks' houses at mealtime."

"Your mama must have been a wonderful woman. Did she also tell you it was impolite to reject a lady's offer of biscuits and sausage gravy?"

He gulped audibly. "Sausage gravy?"

"And scrambled eggs with peppers and onions."

"Yes, ma'am, you're right. She, she ..." he stammered as he licked his lips. "She taught me to be polite to the ladies."

"Good. Would you like to come in?" Judith offered.

"If you don't mind, it's such a glorious day I think I'll eat outside."

The judge winked at Garfield. "These two have exactly the

same conversation every time. Don't you, Duffy?"

"Yes, sir. That's right." Duffy scooped the plate from Judith's hand and plunked down on the step, ignoring the others.

Garfield shook the judge's hand and bowed to Judith. "It has been a delightful morning. Thank you so much for the home cooking and a chance to get my mind on something else besides the Republican State Convention. It might be the last time I can relax before the election."

Judith laid her hand on Garfield's arm. "James, I pray you will have God's strength and know his will. As for us, we are quite sure how we will vote."

"Thank you. It's the support of good folks like you that make me think I'm doing the right thing. But I'm not at all positive one's life is made better because he is elected president. I'm afraid I'm bidding good-bye to private life and a long series of happy years. Right now I'm off to a charming rendezvous with mine owners who want the government to miraculously rejuvenate the silver industry."

Garfield strolled down the sidewalk on Nevada Street, then turned east on Musser.

"Please give our love to Lucretia and the children," Judith called out. "We will expect her to come West with you next time." Then she turned to the judge and Duffy. "Now, if you men will excuse me, I'll clean up inside. Then I need to go check on Audrey … and I have no loyal and able Marthellen to help me out."

Judge Kingston sat down next to the man in tattered, suspendered ducking trousers and grimy cotton shirt. "Duffy, I have a feeling you came by for some reason other than Judith's biscuits and gravy."

The thin, lanky young man wiped gravy off his scraggly chin

onto his sleeve. He looked a worn-out forty, but his eyes were much younger. At the moment, they were serious and probing. "How's that boy of yours, Judge?" he asked.

"Fine. Thanks for askin', Duffy."

"Is he still in Afrikey?"

"He's still in India."

"Preachin' the gospel and raisin' them grandbabies?"

"That's right. We're very proud of David and Patricia. We miss them dearly. However, that's not what you wanted to talk about, is it?"

"And Miss Roberta? How about handsome Miss Roberta?"

"Our daughter has all of her mother's charm and none of her mother's wisdom," the judge said with a sigh. "Yet, she's maturing. I think college in the East has been good for her. It certainly keeps me praying every day. Now, that's all the children we have, Duffy, so why don't we get down to what you really wanted to discuss?"

"There was something funny about them that shot at me last night."

"Them? You mean there was more than one?"

"Only one shot at me. I cut my hand and went runnin' off into the sage. But when I hid in the bushes and looked back, I could see their shadows in the night sky. We had a harvest moon hangin' behind their heads. It was as if they was posin' for me."

"Could you recognize them?"

"That's the thing, Judge. It was way too dark to see 'em in the face. But I got me a good view of their outlines."

"And was it Wild Bill Hickok?"

"Wild Bill? Shoot, Judge, he died four years ago at the No. 10 Saloon in Deadwood when Jack McCall shot him in the back of the head. It was on a Wednesday, about 3:00 in the afternoon, as I recall. I thought ever'one knowed that."

"So, who did you see in the night shadows, Duffy?"

"A she gal, it was."

"A woman?

"Judge, sometimes my mind just blacks out. But I can surely tell a woman when I see one. She was ridin' sidesaddle."

The judge rubbed his chin whiskers and stared across the street. *Sidesaddle ... just as Audrey Adair does when she goes for her afternoon ride?* "And the other rider, Duffy? Who was that?"

"A man, but he was sleepy or hurtin'. His shadow was leanin' way over the saddle horn."

"Where did they go?"

"Down toward the rock quarry at the prison, I think. I was tryin' to saddle my horse one-handed and ride to town before I bled to death. I stomped out my fire and was about to mount up. Then I heard them horses comin' back, so I tucks myself down. I didn't want to get shot at again."

"Was it the same two?"

"It was the same two horses ... but the man was gone ... just the lady ridin'. And she stopped them horses so I could see her shadow again. Now don't that seem strange?"

"Duffy, was she anyone you knew, say ... Audrey Adair?"

"Shoot, Judge. I told you I couldn't tell. But I do believe I'd recognize that shadow again."

The judge stretched out his long legs in front of him. "Well, Duffy, maybe it was just some gal from town takin' a drunken drifter home."

"Ain't no houses out that way."

The judge rested his hand on Duffy's shoulder. "A person doesn't need a house to live by the river, do they, Duffy?"

Duffy's eyes lit up. "No, sir. I reckon you're right about that.

I don't need no house, myself." He set down the plate and folded his arms on top of his head. For a moment he was silent, then his dark brown eyes grew wide. "Why, I'll bet it was some dance hall girl takin' Wild Bill Hickok to his camp. When he saw it was me, he reckoned he could eliminate the competition. Probably had that there gal ride back to see if I was dead!"

Judge Kingston stared at the expectant expression on Duffy Day's face. "Well, Duffy, that Wild Bill always has been a tricky hombre, hasn't he?"

A wide smile broke across Day's face. He began to rock back and forth on the wooden step. "Ain't that the truth, Judge? Ain't that the honest truth!"

CHAPTER TWO

J udith Kingston gazed across the road to the massive sandstone Nevada state capitol building. She stood at the north-
west corner of King and Carson, with a shopping basket
looped over her arm, waiting for a water wagon to pass. It made
slow progress as it sprinkled water on the wide dirt street. As she
watched pairs and groups of men and women in tailored suits
and hats mill in and out the doors and down the walks of the
capitol, she recognized the governor walking with Alf Doten,
secretary of the Republican State Central Committee. Several
gardeners trimmed young trees and planted new shrubs.

*Someday, Lord, those trees will tower above the building. The
plaza grounds will be shady. The black iron fence will look more
like a scrubline than a barrier to keep the wandering cattle and
creatures out. It's your way, isn't it? Everything we build is locked
into time and space. Everything you create is constantly changing,
growing, renewing itself. Everything we produce is finished ...
completed ... dead. Except our children.*

*Father, thank you for our children. How I miss them! They are
too far from us. Called to serve in India. Away at college. I ask
you to provide a means to bring them all home this Christmas.*

*David, so sincere in his faith ... ever since his childhood friend,
Jenny Clemens, died of spotted fever. Patricia, so strong-willed, so
different from sweet Jenny, yet so right for David. Thank you,
Lord, for her partnership. I know my David's being cared for. And
Alicia and Timothy ... I still remember them as babies. They're
growing up. We're missing so much of their lives.*

*And Roberta, my darling Roberta. She's as stubborn as her
father. But not nearly so wise. So playful, too playful at times.
Please protect her, Lord.*

A constant worry. A constant blessing, all of them.

Thank you, Jesus.

"Mrs. Kingston! Is that you?"

Judith spun around to see a man with a foot-long, unclipped
dark brown beard, wearing an old suit coat several sizes too
small. His dark eyes peered out from under a slop hat, a muddy
horseprint stamped on the felt brim.

"Yes, I am Judith Kingston."

"You don't recognize me, do ya?"

"Your eyes look familiar. Perhaps last time I saw you, you
were clean-shaven?"

"I didn't have a whisker on my face when I was seventeen.
That was ten years ago next spring."

"I'm sorry, you'll just have to introduce yourself."

"I'm Bence Farnsworth … Marthellen's boy."

"Bence? Young Bence! My word, look at you!"

He dropped his eyes. "I know I'm kind of rank. I've been up
in the Sierry peaks for a while and—"

"No, no, I meant how grown up and filled out you are."
Judith set her basket on the wooden sidewalk and threw her
arms around the young man, clutching him tight. He smelled
somewhere between a dirty bearskin rug and an unshoveled
stable. When she stepped back, she noticed tears welling in his
eyes.

"Oh, Bence, I trust I didn't hurt you in my enthusiasm."

He wiped his eyes, then looked down at the recently
sprinkled and still muddy street. "Jist got a little dust, that's all,"
he mumbled. "Mrs. Kingston …?"

"Judith."

He finally looked up. "Ma'am, I ain't been hugged tight by a righteous woman since that day I said good-bye to Mama at the jail. You caught me by surprise."

"Where have you been, Bence? What are you doing in town? Why haven't you written to your mother? I know you can write, Bence Farnsworth. I taught you myself."

The young man glanced around them, and Judith noticed a certain tension in his voice. "Yes, ma'am. I ain't got a nice story to tell. I was waitin' for good news. But I did hear all about how you and the judge got Mama out of prison and took her in. Is she all right?"

"Marthellen is one of the dearest people in this entire state. Judge Kingston and I consider it a privilege to have her employed in our home."

"I've been walkin' the streets since I got to town, tryin' to get the nerve to go over to your house and see her. I don't blame her for hatin' me. I jist up and rode off, leavin' her in jail. I ain't proud of my life, Judith."

"You have a lot more years to go, Bence. Plenty of time to straighten things out. The Lord is gracious to us in that way."

"I might not have as many years as you think."

"What do you mean by that?"

"Nothin'," he said quickly. "I'm just ramblin'. Would you go with me to see Mama? I'd feel better if you was standin' there with me."

She reached out and put her hand on his soiled jacket. "Marthellen's not here. She's on a little trip. She's in Sacramento with Charlotte."

The disappointment in Bence's eyes faded at the name of his sister. "Charlotte lives in Sacramento?"

"Yes, her husband works at the Wells Fargo Agency there."

"Little Charlotte's married?"

"She's twenty-two, Bence."

A wide smile broke across his face. "Yes, ma'am, she surely is. How's she doing?"

"Long about now she's probably in a lot of pain."

"Did she get hurt?"

"She's having a baby. Marthellen went to be with her."

"A baby? Lil' sis is having a baby? But, but … that means I'm … "

"You're going to be an uncle."

Bence Farnsworth yanked off his dusty brown felt hat and slapped it against his trousers. "Well, I'll be … " The smile immediately left his face. "But I need to see Mama."

"Yes, you do." Judith Kingston retrieved her basket. "While I finish shopping, you go over to my house. I want you to take a bath and wash your hair. The judge has some old clothes in the closet by the back door; you help yourself to anything that fits. Trim your beard and get yourself spruced up. Then you'll have supper with the judge and me and spend the night with us. You can sleep in your mother's room. In the morning, we'll put you on the Virginia and Truckee Railroad with a ticket clear through to Sacramento. By tomorrow evening you can see your mother and your sister."

"But … but … I ain't got any money," he stammered.

"Bence Farnsworth, did you hear me say one word about money?"

"No, ma'am, but I'm not a beggar."

"Your mother has rewarded the judge and me with kindness and service beyond all remuneration. It is her loyalty and graciousness that will pay for the train ticket. You can thank her personally when you see her."

"You don't know what kind of trouble I'm in, Judith. I cain't just … "

"Bence, is there any legal or biblical reason why you can't travel to Sacramento?"

His eyes got a worried look. Then he grinned. "No, I guess there ain't."

"Well then, don't just dawdle. Go on to our house and clean up."

"Yes, ma'am."

Cheney's grocery store, in the Adams block on the corner of Carson Street and Telegraph, was not the largest in Nevada, nor in Carson City. But Judith Kingston was convinced that it provided the best staples and quality foodstuffs. And they stocked unique products not found elsewhere. John Cheney seemed to take it as a personal goal to carry every item that could be found in any store west of the Mississippi.

The whole town was full of campaign ads, state and local. Cheney's store was no exception. A huge poster on the outside window, next to one promoting James Garfield and Chester Arthur for national office, announced John E. Cheney running for a second term as county commissioner. Inside the store, a toddler wearing a small red sombrero was being chased down the main aisle by a young girl wearing a plaid cotton dress. Two male clerks were pulling down canned fruits, lard, and grain from the shelves at some customers' requests.

Judith squeezed through to the far end of the store. She placed some tins in her basket, then read the label on a jar of airtight pickled asparagus spears and pimento. "You won't find that in any of Leland Standford's stores," Mr. Cheney called out.

"But do you have much call for them?" Judith replied.

"As a matter of fact, I haven't sold a one. But once they catch on, I'm sure they'll be quite popular."

"Well, why don't I try them?"

Mr. Cheney pulled off his gold-frame glasses and lightly rubbed the bridge of his nose. "Thank you, Judith. I predict the other six jars will be sold by Saturday."

"But how can you say that?"

Mr. Cheney wiped his glasses with a handkerchief, then carefully tucked the wires behind his ears. "All I have to do is get the word around that Judith Kingston purchased a jar and there will be thirty women in town clamoring to buy them."

Judith shook her head. "John Cheney, you overrate my endorsement power."

"Oh no, I'm completely accurate on that account. There are a number of women in this town who have recently become wealthy. They're trying to live up to a standard of society to which they are not accustomed. You've become their paragon, their epitome of culture. Surely you must know that."

"What I do know is that there are at least a hundred families in town who make more money than the judge and I."

"That might be true, but no one displays more class and grace than you."

Judith plucked another jar off the shelf. She squinted her eyes at the label. "Wine-pickled Sicilian artichoke hearts?"

"Ah, I can make you a very special price on the artichoke hearts." He tapped his finger on the lid. "I've had them on the shelf since Christmas."

"That's only a few months."

He pulled down his glasses and peeked over the rim. "Christmas 1878."

"Oh my, the wine should be quite strong by now. I'm afraid the judge would never allow anything in our home like that."

"That's not real wine, Judith. It's wine vinegar. It hasn't fermented."

"After two years on your shelf?"

"Well ... you just might be right."

Judith plopped them in her basket. "I'll take them, but only if you promise not to tell a certain court official that I purchased them."

"I can keep a secret," he assured her. "That's essential in any business, even the grocery business."

"Grocery secrets?"

"One learns a lot about people by the food they eat ... and the beverages they drink."

"And one can certainly learn a lot about a person's income by the budget he or she follows. And I've about spent mine. But I do need several large potatoes."

"I've got the finest, from Carson Valley."

"Are they a new crop?"

"No, ma'am. New ones don't come off for two weeks. But these are tender and tasty."

"Mr. Cheney, you are quite a salesman. And I want you to know I appreciate your personal service, what with the store so crowded."

"My clerks know that when I'm here I wait on Mrs. Judith Kingston. As owner, I get the privilege of choosing whom I serve."

Rising voices coming from one of the white-aproned male clerks and a woman wrapped in a black wool shawl caused them both to turn around. Three children clung to the woman's black cotton dress.

She looks like she just returned from a funeral. I don't remember there being one today. "I think you are needed, Mr. Cheney," Judith said. "I'll select the potatoes on my own."

There was still a heated debate going on when Judith reached the counter. "What's the problem?" she asked.

Mr. Cheney smiled grimly. "This woman doesn't speak much English and it seems she hasn't enough money for the groceries she has picked out."

The woman pointed to the small children clinging to her and said, *"Tengo siete niños."*

Judith scanned the lady's appearance. *She's very light-skinned to be Mexican, and so are the children. But she sure seems desperate.* "This woman says she has seven children," Judith said, "and as you can see, she is dressed in widow's weeds."

"Judith, I have to run a cash business for transient customers. That's the only way I can make a living."

"I understand, Mr. Cheney. But I was wondering … how many pounds of last year's potatoes do you have?"

"About five hundred more pounds down in the cellar."

"What will you do with the leftovers when the new crop comes in?"

"I sell the whole lot for about two dollars to anyone who needs them to feed to their hogs."

Judith straightened her back and grabbed her basket with both hands. "Then I'd like to buy some potato futures. I'll purchase your leftover ones in advance, two dollars for the lot."

"But I won't know how many pounds are left until next week," Mr. Cheney protested.

"My offer stands."

The grocer crossed his arms. "I'll take it. But what does this have to do with this woman?"

"Well, don't you think some of those pounds of potatoes in her basket look an awful lot like some of my leftovers?"

Mr. Cheney peered over his glasses again, looking hard at Judith. "I suppose they could be."

"Good. I'd rather give them to this lady than some hog. So reduce her bill by that amount. Does she have enough money now?"

"She's still sixty-six cents short," the clerk replied.

Judith plunked her basket on the counter. "Well, if I put back this jar of Sicilian artichoke hearts, I'll save enough to give her the sixty-six cents. Mr. Cheney, will you please return this jar to your—"

John Cheney held up his hand, his stern face melted to resignation. "I'll stand for the sixty-six cents, Judith. You made your point."

"Thank you, Mr. Cheney." Judith put the jar of artichoke hearts back into her basket and patted the young boy on the head.

When Judith buzzed into the post office, grocery basket still in hand, the postmaster said, "The sheriff's looking for you, Judith." His eyes were gleaming. "I don't suppose it has to do with that strange fellow who accosted you earlier on the street? I saw him startle you and handle you some."

"Lemuel, that was Bence Farnsworth, Marthellen's boy. We were greeting each other after ten years apart. Don't be so quick to jump to conclusions."

Lemuel picked his teeth with a splinter of wood and handed her the Kingston mail. "Yes, ma'am."

Judith stepped away from the counter. *My, two letters in one day. One from David, Patricia, and the children. Thank you,*

Lord. You know how melancholy I've been over them. And one from Martina Swan in California. I really should wait patiently until I get home and then leisurely ...

"The sheriff seemed persistent," Lemuel called to her. "You might check down at Benton's Livery. He was headed there to find one of the deputies. You don't have any idea why he wanted you?"

Judith set her basket down on the polished wooden floor and ripped open the thick brown envelope from India. *It must be frightfully boring standing behind that counter all day.* "No, Lemuel, I have no idea at all."

She pulled several papers from the envelope. *Oh, my ...* She pulled out a homemade card. Above a black polka-dotted orange drawing was scribbled the word "tiger." *Alicia drew us a picture! She's so artistic at six. Just like her mother.* Judith felt a sting of tears. *Lord, this is hard. Real hard. I want to see my grandchildren. I want to see them today, not ten years from now when they're fully grown. They simply must come home this Christmas.* She turned the card over and studied the perfect penmanship.

Dear Grandmother Judith,

Thank you for the book. You are right. *The Adventures of Tom Sawyer* is the best book I have ever read in my whole life! I've read it six times. Does Mr. Twain's brother still live in Carson City? A crocodile ate my dog, Tahoe. Alicia cried. But I didn't. Boys don't cry. Specially nine-year-old boys. I love you. Hug Grandpa for me.

Yours sincerely,
Timothy A. Kingston

The last few words blurred. Judith retrieved a cotton handkerchief from her sleeve and wiped her eyes, then took a deep breath.

I've got to wait until I get home to read the rest of this. The judge would not approve of such a public lack of emotional control. I'll read Martina's instead.

She neatly ripped open a green, three-cent-stamped envelope that bore a Wells Fargo and Company insignia. The rich black ink stood out clearly on the crisp white paper, the writing curled and twisted in ornate Victorian script. *My word, her daughter, Christina, is sixteen. She's practically grown. And, oh dear ... the judge will want to know this sad news.*

Judith scooted down the brick stairs of the post office to the sidewalk. She glanced across the street at the most imposing structure in town, the huge sandstone U.S. Mint building situated beside the state capitol. *I suppose the judge is knee-deep in the silver stock litigation. Maybe this letter from the children will cheer him up. I wish it cheered me up.*

The reflection from a crescent-shaped Ormsby County badge caught her eye.

"Judith, thank goodness I found you." The man had large ears and small eyes. Sweat dripped from his nose and mustache.

"Sheriff Hill, Lemuel said you were looking for me."

He tucked his arms behind his back and peered around her and beyond. "I'm really sorry to pester you, Judith, but I've got trouble at the cribs. I need your help."

Judith's heart sank. "Don't tell me one of the girls got beat up or knifed. I don't think I could handle another scene like we went through with Audrey."

"It's Willie Jane. She got depressed, took too much laudanum, shot up the walls, and is threatening to kill herself. No one can get near her. She won't put down her gun for anyone. Won't talk to anyone. Says the only one she'll talk to is you."

Judith studied his face. His eyes seemed anxious and sincerely concerned. "Poor dear," she said. "Willie Jane almost died last winter with cholera."

"Well, she's going to die of lead poisoning if we don't talk her out of it."

"I'll go, Sheriff, but you know we should close the crib district."

"They'd only move out to Dayton where they won't have a doctor ... or a patron saint like you. Besides, a number of the ladies have already left, what with the Comstock starting to decline."

"Patron saint? What on earth do you mean?"

"Judith, let's face it. You're the only decent woman in this town who has ever befriended one of them girls."

"Yes, well, the judge doesn't need to hear that. He's convinced that if I come within a block of the cribs I'll be assaulted."

At mention of the judge's name, the sheriff's face blanched. "Judith, I don't want to endanger your health."

"Nonsense. I'm certainly willing to go where I'm needed."

They waited to cross Carson Street while twenty horse-drawn freight wagons hauled mining equipment on their way south to the boomtown of Bodie. Behind them, two loaded wagons lumbered past. Judith thought she saw the lady from the grocery store poke her head out of one of them, then quickly pull back.

"I'm happy to see that bunch leave town," the sheriff said as he led Judith across the street.

"What 'bunch'?"

"A couple of them claim to speak Spanish, but they only

know a few words, just enough to bilk a store owner."

Judith looked sharply at the sheriff. "What do you mean?"

"They hit town this morning, then begged, borrowed and stole their way up Carson Street. I sent Lucky over to run them out of town. There's not an honest one in the lot of 'em."

"They look extremely poor."

"Well, they ain't now. Couldn't catch 'em stealin', but they're a pack of sneak thieves and footpads for sure. The lady with the black shawl seems to be the ringleader. I just learned they did the same thing in Virginia City and Gold Hill yesterday. I sent word ahead to Genoa. I reckon they're headed that way. Kin I carry that grocery basket for you?"

Judith Kingston handed the basket to the sheriff. *Well, Judith Kathryn ... I'm glad you donated some potatoes and Mr. Cheney's sixty-six cents to the cause. I can't believe it was a ruse. They were so convincing. And that darling little boy with the sad face ... Lord, you know I gave with a generous heart. I trust you will lead their hearts toward righteousness ... and mine away from resentment.*

Several blocks from the Carson City Mint, there were eight identical one-room cabins on Ormsby Street. Each shared a common wall with the next and was about ten feet by ten feet. Each had a door facing the alley and a single blanketed window that faced the street. Each had peeling white paint on the clapboard siding. Each boasted a "Sewing Wanted" sign and was decorated by a red railroad lantern hanging by the door.

And each cabin housed a woman who was known for one thing.

Three girls huddled by the shotgun-wielding deputy in the alley. They all stared at the bullet-ridden door of #6. Several men loitered in the shadows.

"Any change?" Sheriff Hill asked.

"Nope, she's still in there, cryin' and screamin' holy murder." The deputy tipped his hat. "Good morning, Judith."

"Good morning, Tray. How's Haven's cough?"

"It's gettin' worse ever' day."

"Did you try that juniper extract I sent over?"

"We don't know how to use it."

"Boil a teaspoon of it in a cup of water. When it begins to steam, have Haven breathe in the fumes."

"Yes, ma'am."

The sheriff drew out his gun and hunkered down behind a stack of busted wagon wheels. "Willie Jane, this is the sheriff," he hollered.

The blast of a bullet ripped through shingles. Everyone in the alley ducked behind trees or the nearest cabin.

"Go away or I'm going to shoot myself," a woman's voice wailed.

"I brought Judith Kingston with me," the sheriff yelled back. "Judith?"

"I'm here, Willie Jane. Let me come in so we can talk."

"You can't go in there," the sheriff protested. "She's armed and on morphine."

"I'll shoot you, Judith. Or me. Or both of us," Willie Jane echoed.

"You'll do nothing of the sort," Judith called back. "I'm coming in."

"I've got a gun."

"Well, I don't, and you know it."

"The door's locked."

"Unlock it, dear. We need to talk."

"We can talk like this."

"Nonsense, Willie Jane. There are some things women need to discuss without loafers and bummers hanging around and listening. Are you hungry? I'll send someone to bring us something to eat."

For a moment, every creaking wagon wheel and summer sparrow was silenced. Then Judith heard the latch click. The door swung open a few inches. "I ain't hungry," Willie Jane said hoarsely. "Well, maybe just a little."

Judith set her basket of groceries down and stepped slowly across the alley.

"Be careful, Judith, she's a deranged woman," the sheriff warned, his weapon aimed at the door.

"Sheriff Hill," Judith lectured sternly, "she's a depressed woman. That makes her a little erratic, but certainly not deranged." She turned to the deputy. "Tray, would you please trot down to the Ormsby House and retrieve us two cups of eucalyptus tea, a plate of English butter crackers, and a small wedge of white cheese?"

"Yes, ma'am. Who shall I charge it to?"

Judith glanced at the sheriff and raised her eyebrows.

"Charge it to our office," the sheriff replied. "I suppose it's a small price to pay to keep someone from gettin' shot."

The cabin was filled with gunsmoke and the smell of strong lilac perfume. The combination made Judith's stomach churn. Numerous items had been knocked off a single shelf that circled the room. Bedding was strewn from wall to narrow wall. Two beat-up leather bags and a trunk sat by the door.

Willie Jane wore a black, low-cut gown with long sleeves ripped at the right shoulder. She sat cross-legged on a bare, soiled mattress, rocking back and forth, as she loosely held a single action Colt Peacemaker and a handful of bullets. There was a gold bracelet on her left wrist and a gold cross around her neck. She was pretty and round-faced, neither smiling nor frowning, but her black hair was as wild as her glazed eyes.

"It's a mess in here," she said, her voice quieter, almost like a little girl's.

Judith stepped over the crumpled comforter and sat on the edge of the dingy gray mattress. "Think nothing of it, dear. Some days there are more important things than keeping house. What happened, Willie Jane?"

The young woman's skin was soft and fair and she was about twenty-four years old. She always dressed neatly and took special care with her hair and makeup and nails. "I'm going to kill myself. I really want to do it," she blurted out.

"Let's talk about that later. I have Tray running all the way to the Ormsby to bring us some tea and English butter crackers. We'll discuss the options after we have a little bite. How about you telling me what happened?"

Willie Jane's dark eyes were stormy. "He jilted me. He promised to take me away from all this, then he forsook me in the wilderness." Her arms crumpled and the bullets fell across the mattress. "I don't want to live anymore."

"Are you all right, Judith?" a male voice called out from the alley.

"Sheriff, we are both fine. We're just talking girl talk," Judith called back. "Now don't interrupt us again." She turned back to Willie Jane. "Men don't understand how we need private times to talk, do they?"

Willie Jane rocked back and forth on the mattress again, the gun hanging from one finger.

"Why don't you just lay that gun down, dear?" Judith calmly suggested. "Your poor hand looks all cramped and white."

The girl sat straight up and raised her gun arm to the roof. "He told me he would come for me. I waited and waited." A shot rang out and splinters fell down from the roof. Judith heard the scuffle of boots outside the door.

"We're all right, sheriff," she yelled. "Give us some more time."

"Willie Jane," the sheriff shouted. "I want to remind you that's the judge's wife you've got in there."

"She's my friend," Willie Jane said. Her words came out flat and monotone.

"Give me the gun," Judith said quietly.

Willie Jane let the gun slip from her fingers and it banged to the floor. Judith finally felt herself relax as she kicked the weapon into a corner.

She reached over and began to rub Willie Jane's back. "Who was the man? I didn't know you had a beau."

"It was a secret. Milton said to tell no one."

"Milton?"

"Yeah. It don't matter now. He took off without me. It was gonna be me and Milton Primble."

"But he's married to Audrey Adair."

"He don't love her. He just married her for all that money. He told me so. He said he was pullin' out. He was goin' to take his share of the money and come and get me and we'd move to Santa Barbara."

"That's what he said? Santa Barbara?"

"That's by the ocean in California. I was goin' to quit the cribs and we was goin' to watch the waves from our window every day. Don't that sound peaceful?"

"It certainly does. When were you going to leave?"

"Last night. We've been plannin' it for nearly two weeks and we was going to get two horses and ride south during the night. I like ridin' horses. All he had left to do was tell that Adair lady he was leavin' and get his due."

"His due?"

"He said she owed him a lot of money for managin' her affairs."

"How did your dress get torn?"

Willie Jane shut her eyes. "I done it myself. I was hurtin' so bad. I really thought he loved me."

"Judith," Tray called from the alley. "I've got the tea and crackers."

Willie Jane jumped off the mattress and grabbed up the gun.

"Careful, dear," Judith cautioned. "You don't want to hurt me or Tray, do you?"

Willie Jane dropped the gun again. "No, ma'am," she said.

Judith took in the platter from Tray's hands and nudged the door closed with her foot. She slid the tray onto the mattress.

Willie Jane straightened her dress and pulled back her thick, black hair. "I ain't never drunk no eucalyptus tea. What is a eucalyptus anyway?"

"It's a tall tree from Australia, I believe. It's a very calming tea. Perhaps it will offset some of that horrible stuff you drank. One thing for sure, it will speed everything through your body, if you understand my meaning."

A smile spread across Willie Jane's full lips. "I ain't dumb. I know what you mean."

"So Milton Primble said he was coming for you, then didn't?"

"I sat right here on this mattress all night long with my stuff packed. I didn't have any men come over or nothin'. Then about daylight Stone Julie said that Primble beat up his wife and lit shuck for Mexico."

"So you took some laudanum and went to sleep?"

Willie Jane rolled her head and neck against her shoulders. "Yeah. Did he kill her?"

"No, but she's been battered severely."

"I've been beat up before. More than once."

"You should never put up with it. Mr. Primble is certainly not the type of man you want to be around. You should have known any man who would betray his wife is not a very desirable suitor."

"But that's about the only kind I ever meet."

"Willie Jane, you need to start setting your sights higher."

The young woman bit off a piece of white, extra-sharp cheddar cheese and chewed it slowly. "I do, don't I?"

"You certainly do."

Willie Jane began to cry, as though an incredibly sad story had just been told. "What am I going to do, Judith? What am I going to do?"

"Do you have any funds saved up?"

"A little bit."

"Do you have family somewhere? Perhaps you need a short vacation?"

"My mama lives in Texas, but I cain't go back there as long as she's with that new husband of hers. He don't keep his hands off me."

"Do you have any other kin?"

"My sister teaches school in Traver."

"Where's that?"

"In the Tulare Valley of California."

"Why don't you go see your sister?"

"We don't have much to talk about."

"Is she married?"

"I don't think so."

"Well, you can discuss how difficult it is to find a good husband."

Another smile broke across Willie Jane's face, then disappeared. "But if I leave, I'd lose my crib."

"Maybe you'd enjoy trying some other kind of work."

"I ain't very good at anything else. I'm good at this."

"I'm sure you are, dear, but as you said yourself, it's not a very good place to meet a kind, loyal man."

Willie Jane scooted off the mattress and began to pick up the bedcovers. Judith reached down to help her with the sheets. "Maybe I should go see my sister."

Judith patted her arm. "Good. Now, how about you letting me take that gun with me?"

"I can't do that."

"But you must. If I don't come out of here with that pistol, the sheriff and deputy will be hanging around your door all day and night, worried about you shootin' yourself. Let's just let everyone go home and give you time to sleep this off. I'll come around in the morning and take you to the depot. You can ride the train to Sacramento, then get a stage down to the Tulare Valley."

Willie Jane handed Judith the pistol. "Can I keep the cheese and crackers?"

"Certainly. Would you like anything else?"

"Just some sleep."

"I'll see that your lantern is off all night." Judith retreated to the door, keenly aware of the cold metal in her hands. The acrid smell of gunsmoke still hung in the air. "You know, I have a brown dress that I haven't worn in a year, and it's still nice. I believe it will fit you. Shall I bring it over in the morning? You could wear it on the train. It's not very nobby. Rather modest, I'm afraid. But you're welcome to it."

"I got clothes of my own."

Judith smiled. "I know you do, but they're all packed away and what you had on last night looks pretty worn for travel."

Willie Jane gave her a look of gratitude. "That really sounds nice. Thank you, Judith."

"I'll see you in the morning."

"Judith?" Willie Jane was back on the mattress, rocking back and forth again, but this time her chin was up. "Thank you for not preaching at me. I know what I do is wrong. I know I'm a sinner."

Judith felt a shiver down her back. "And I am, too, Willie Jane. But the wonderful thing is that Jesus came to save sinners just like you and me. Did you know that?"

Willie Jane slumped down on the bare mattress. "You don't know all the things I've done."

"That's the beauty of forgiveness, Willie Jane. Only God knows all that any of us have done, and he loves us anyway."

"I know it … I heard the story … my mama used to tell me all about Jesus ever' Christmas." She stood and stretched and yawned. "I'll see you in the mornin', Judith."

"Yes, you will, dear. Now finish your crackers and sleep this off."

"Yes … Mama."

Judith handed the gun to the waiting sheriff and retrieved her basket. "Everything is fine, Sheriff. Willie Jane's going to take the night off and get some rest."

The sheriff shook the remaining bullets out of the pistol. "Fine? She's fired holes through buildings and terrified the neighborhood. I need to arrest her for reckless endangerment."

"Are you telling me you arrest every person who discharges a firearm or pulls a knife in the crib district?"

"Of course not. I cain't stop everything."

"Well, you certainly stopped Willie Jane. You have her gun, don't you?"

The sheriff tapped the gun in his hand. "Yep. I reckon you did disarm her."

"You disarmed her, Sheriff. I merely assisted. I believe that's the proper way to list it on your report."

The sheriff's eyes opened wide, then narrowed. "Well, then, I appreciate your, eh … assistance, Judith."

Bence Farnsworth sprawled on a three-legged stool in the pantry, shucking sweet green peas as Judith fussed in the kitchen.

"I'm surprised you shaved off your entire beard," she said as she buzzed by the open doorway.

"Me too. I just started trimmin' and got carried away. You surely did a good job at cuttin' my hair, too. Do you do much barbering?"

"You're my first," she said with a laugh.

"You're kiddin' me! You never cut hair before?"

"Oh, I trimmed up my children's hair when they were little, and I clipped my own, but the judge won't let me touch his at all."

"Well, you surely did a good job with mine."

"Bence, the way it looked earlier, I could only improve it."

"I surely appreciate your kindness. I didn't expect to have a fine home to spend the night in."

"Well, I don't see why you thought you'd stay anywhere else.

You should consider this your mother's home as well as ours."

"I ain't too sure she'll be as happy to see me as you are."

"Nonsense."

He carried the bowl of peas into the kitchen. "Well, at least there ain't goin' to be no one lookin' for me in this part of town."

"Is someone looking for you, Bence?"

"I reckon they are."

"Do they have a good reason?"

"Yes, ma'am, I reckon they do."

"Is this something you need to talk to the judge about?"

"I'm not sure … but I do need to keep on the move."

Judge Kingston showed no surprise whatever at entering his home and finding a strange man in the kitchen, holding a huge bowl of uncooked green peas. He quietly hung his hat on a peg and neatly draped his topcoat alongside. He straightened his black tie, tugged down his white shirt cuffs, then waltzed over to Judith and kissed her on the cheek.

"Mr. Farnsworth," the judge said, "what a pleasure to see you after all these years."

"You recognize me, Judge?"

"You have filled out some, but you haven't changed all that much. Has he, dear?"

Judith winked at Bence. "He did scrub up fairly good."

The judge shook the young man's hand. "Sorry Marthellen isn't here. I'm sure Judith explained. You are spending the night, aren't you?"

"Yes, sir, I am."

"Splendid. Well, where are you headed? Looking for a new gold field?"

"Bence is going to take the train to Sacramento in the morning."

"Oh, yes, of course. I'm sure Judith will help you with all that. I'm afraid I'm tied up on this silver business."

"How did things go in court today, dear?" Judith asked.

"It was a battle between two teams of self-deluded, imprecise, and greedy lawyers."

"Rather boring, I presume?"

"Yes. And you, dear Judith? Other than having Mr. Farnsworth drop by for a chat, how was your day?"

"Rather routine. But we did get a letter from David, Patricia, and the children."

"Well, this is a glorious surprise! I pray all is well."

"There is some rebellion in south India. The British won't let them return to the Bible school until the turmoil calms down. Why don't you bring the letter in and read it aloud? I'd like to hear it again, and Bence knew David."

"What is this other letter?" the judge called out from the table in the entryway.

"It's from Martina Swan in California." Judith dried her hands on her long apron as she sidled up next to the judge. "Her father died."

"No! Wilson Merced gone?" The judge looked away. "It's like the end of an era."

"Poor Alena. She will miss him so."

"All of California will miss him. I must write my condolences tonight," the judge announced. "And I'll have to get word to the Republican State Convention while they're still convening. He had many friends there, including the governor and James Garfield."

"Not until you come in and read the letter from our children." Judith led him back to the kitchen where Bence

Farnsworth was washing the peas.

"That's a nice-looking wool vest, Bence," the judge remarked. "Had one like that myself, once. Didn't I, dear?"

"Yes, I believe you did."

"I haven't seen that vest in years."

"Oh, it probably hasn't been that long. Now, sit down and read us the letter before I pitch a fit," Judith insisted.

The judge eased into a straight-back wooden chair and carefully unfolded the letter as if it were a jury's verdict. "That reminds me, did you hear about the trouble down in the crib district?"

"What was that?"

"One of the girls got morphined up and started shooting. It took the sheriff and a deputy a couple hours to disarm her."

"And how is the young lady?" Judith inquired.

"How is she? I, eh, believe she's all right. We're fortunate she didn't shoot herself and a few others. I'm certainly glad we don't live near that part of town. I praise the Lord every day that he's given us a home where you don't have to be exposed to such violent and dangerous elements."

CHAPTER THREE

In 1860, Major William Ormsby began construction of a huge two-story adobe house in Carson City. He intended it to be a multipurpose residence, place of business, general store, and hotel. But he rushed off on an ill-planned attempt to put down a Paiute Indian uprising near Pyramid Lake and died in an ambush.

The establishment was completed that summer.

At 12:06 P.M., the Honorable Hollis A. Kingston, First District Judge, State of Nevada, sat down at the front window table at the Ormsby House, on the southwest corner of Carson and Second Streets, and ordered liver and onions ... the same as he did every Wednesday.

Same time.

Same table.

Same three friends.

Same menu selection.

William Cary, the man his friends fondly called "the mayor," spooned into his grits, chitlins, and cooked cabbage with his usual vigor. "Judge, did Mary Curry come see you today?"

"No, I haven't seen Mrs. Curry in over a week, mainly because I've been tied up in court. What did the honorable lady want?"

Mayor Cary quickly swallowed a mouthful of cabbage. His balding forehead and slightly wavy white hair clashed with the sudden red flush of his face. "She discovered another of Abe's missing invoices. She claims the city owes her additional funds."

"She's probably right. For all that Abraham Curry did for this city, the least we could do is help out his widow or buy the man a stone for his grave. He did more in fifteen years for Carson than most men hope to accomplish in a lifetime. And he envisioned Nevada's statehood long before its time."

The mayor sunk his head down to scoop up more grits. He avoided the judge's glance. "Yes, but when will this be completed? I do believe Abraham Curry took the easy way out. He died living high on the best cigars when he should have made provision for his family. He could have been one of the richest men in Nevada with a little forethought."

The mayor finally looked up. "Anyway, Mary just smiled sweetly and said, 'Perhaps you should let the judge study this matter?' Now it's your turn, Judge."

"If you ask me," Doctor Jacobs said, "she needs some of that Tennessee Southern charm and beauty like Elizabeth Ormsby had. After the Major was killed in that Paiute altercation, Elizabeth sweet-talked the legislature into helping raise her daughter, and she eventually became quite wealthy on her own."

The mayor waved his fork at the judge. "That makes more sense than what the Supreme Court did in that Pritchard case. What do you think of that, Judge? A lot of the delegates at the Republican Convention have been complaining about it, including, I hear, James Garfield."

"They acted on a perfectly legal proposition in granting a new trial," the judge replied.

"But a convicted killer gets what amounts to a discharged jury and acquittal. The law is supposed to punish crime, but it more often serves the purposes of criminals than the interests of society."

The judge carefully wiped his mouth. "We're often caught

between justice and fairness."

Ormsby County Sheriff Loyd Hill studied the brown gravy that flooded the thin sliced roast beef on his plate, then he piled it with salt. "I'll tell you what worries me. That young man who pulled a gun on me the other night."

"The one named Orson Kendall?" the doctor asked.

"Yep. His compadres say he has several brothers down south of here who are even meaner than him. They all got run out of Arizona Territory last spring. All I need is a gang on the prowl, sneakin' up behind me."

"If they're a gang, how come he was here alone?" the mayor inquired.

"I was told he slipped into town lookin' for someone."

Doctor Jacobs pointed a knife at a green object on his plate. "I hate to change the subject so abrupt like, but what is this?"

"Looks like pickled Sicilian artichoke hearts," the judge replied.

Doc Jacobs studied the object intently. "You don't say! Why in the world would a respectable place like the Ormsby House serve such a thing?"

"Now, be patient," the mayor said. "You know Ormsby's is going through a change of management and proprietors. Maybe they're trying to entice new customers."

"Entice? This looks like something the dog coughed up."

The mayor briskly wiped his mustache. "The hotel and restaurant business is hard, thankless work. You got to keep trying something new. I had two different places in Placerville. Yep, I'd much rather have a nice quiet dry-goods store and serve as city magistrate than run a hotel."

"Personally, I've never had any complaints about the Ormsby's menu," the judge offered.

The doctor grimaced as he bit into the artichoke heart. "Easy for you to say, Judge. You always order that foul-tasting liver and onions. No cook on earth could make it any worse than it is to start with."

"I happen to know about those Sicilian artichoke things," the mayor added. "Estelle says they're quite the rage around town this week. We've already had them at home."

"Well, I say it's Pompeii's revenge. I prefer my food plain and simple ... and American," Dr. Jacobs added.

The judge savored a large bite of sweet liver meat. "I agree with the good doctor." *Now, Lord, that's one thing I'm thankful for ... Judith never feels the need to follow the crowd. She knows what I like.*

"Judge, did you ever hear of a Kendall gang in Arizona?" the sheriff asked.

"No. But, if it's hounding you, telegraph someone down in Prescott or Tucson and ask if they've heard of them."

"Who should I telegraph?"

"If it were me," the judge replied, "I'd wire Stuart Brannon. He's run up against most every hard case in the Territory."

"You mean the dime novel hero?"

"I thought he was a lawman over in Colorado," the sheriff said.

"I heard he's back in Arizona," the judge added. "I read a report about a conflict he was having over a Spanish land grant. He's a good man. He'll tell you what he knows."

"Are we talking about a real person?" the mayor blurted. "My nine-year-old, Eugene, has gotten started on those Hawthorne Miller books. The stories are quite unbelievable. I assumed it was all fiction."

"The stories might be fiction, but the man's real," the sheriff said. "Anyway, maybe I'm worked up over nothin'. I've just never seen a man so anxious to get in a gunfight as that Kendall hombre. It's obvious he was feelin' mighty worked up over something."

Dr. Jacobs stared out the window. He pointed to a tall, thin man with a crisp new bowler and neatly trimmed short beard. "Who's that man coming down the street? I've never seen him before."

"Maybe he's another stock speculator," the judge offered.

The mayor kept his eye on the man's slow, even gait. "I believe it's the man they brought in from Virginia City to examine the books at the bank. All the trustees are nervous, what with Milton Primble suddenly gone."

The sheriff stabbed a slab of gravy-covered beef. "There's got to be a glitch in the accounts, someplace. I can't imagine a man riding off like that without taking sufficient funds."

"I can," the judge added. "Some men don't know how depraved they really are until they face an event that demonstrates it clearly. They actually shock themselves. When it hits them, they either run away—"

"Or put a bullet in their brain," the doctor said.

"I know one thing," the sheriff hooted. "The next man that decides to marry Audrey Adair better like living in Mexico."

The sheriff grinned, then said, "Did you ever hear about Jorae Renault over in Plumas County?"

The judge nodded. "A quite celebrated case in some circles."

"They found all six of her husbands dead and buried in her rose garden, and she insisted that every one of them died from natural causes."

The mayor chuckled. "A couple of women like that could depopulate the entire state."

"What happened to her?" Dr. Jacobs asked.

"She was acquitted. There were no witnesses, no known motives, and no obvious signs of foul play."

"I trust the line of suitors has slowed," the doctor mused.

The judge broke open a hot biscuit and slathered butter and strawberry preserves on it. "I don't know about that. She up and moved to Idaho."

The mayor genteelly picked his teeth with his fingernail. "Are you suggesting that Audrey Adair has C.V. and Milt buried in her rose garden?"

"Nope. I can guarantee she doesn't." The judge rubbed the bridge of his nose. "She doesn't have a rose garden." He managed a sort of grin. "But I don't think we'll see Milton Primble in this town again."

"I reckon Audrey will give away all his personals like she did with C.V.," the sheriff said.

Tray Weston scurried across the polished wooden floor of the Ormsby House dining room, his boot heels signaling concern.

"Tray, you know I don't like to be interrupted during my Wednesday lunch meeting," the sheriff said.

"Yessir, but this is important." Tray shoved his brown felt hat to the back of his shaggy brown head. Three wisps of hair served for a beard below his unkempt mustache. His usually droopy eyes were alive with either excitement or fear. "I think you might want to come to the office. They showed up already, asking for you."

The sheriff laid down his fork and knife. "Who?"

Tray slammed his hand on the grip of his holstered revolver. "Them Kendall boys."

The mayor scooted back his chair. "Well, so much for contacting Arizona."

The judge glanced out the window. "How many are there?"

"Four of 'em. What are we going to do, Sheriff?"

The sheriff glanced slowly around at the judge, the mayor, and the doctor. They each nodded back in silence. "I'm going to finish my meal, that's what."

Tray's eyes grew wide. "What should I tell them?"

"Tell them that I'll meet with them in my office at 1:00 P.M."

"You're takin' this mighty collected for a man who's been stewin' over this since you shot that feller the other night," Tray commented.

"I was stewin' 'cause I didn't know how many there would be and where I would have to confront them. Now I know."

"You quit worryin'?" Tray quizzed.

"No," the mayor said, "but now he can worry smart."

"What do you want me to do, Sheriff?"

"Tray, just deliver the message, lock the office, and ride around Carson. Find out if the Kendalls have any compadres scattered around town. Then meet me back at the office at 1:00 P.M."

"Don't you figure there will be some trouble?" the deputy insisted.

"Did they look happy?" Dr. Jacobs asked.

"Nope."

"Are they wearing guns?" the judge probed.

"Yep."

The sheriff sopped a biscuit in the dark brown gravy. "Then I reckon they have a point to make."

Tray pulled his hat nearly over his eyes. "So I jist tell 'em you'll be at the office at 1:00?"

"Yep, and tell 'em I'm eating lunch at the Ormsby House and do not wish to be disturbed."

"You want me to tell them where you're eatin' at?"

"By all means."

The deputy shuffled out of the hotel dining room. They watched him trudge down Carson Street.

"I don't think they'll wait for you, Sheriff," the mayor cautioned.

"They don't sound like patient men," the judge added. "I think I'll go check at the desk in the lobby. I'm sure they have something besides umbrellas under the counter."

Doctor Jacobs searched around the room. "Say ... isn't that a rare Winchester '73 Carbine over in the corner? Why, it could be one of those 'One of a Thousand.'"

"You better go check that out, Doc," the judge said.

"Sheriff," the mayor piped up, "do you still carry that pocket revolver as well as your Peacemaker?"

The lawman patted his chest. "Right here in my vest."

"I'd like to look at that. You know, I just might like to get one of those myself sometime."

The sheriff handed the mayor the small pistol as Dr. Jacobs retreated to the carbine in the corner. The judge exited to the hotel lobby, where a young clerk was staring out at the street.

"Mr. Kelly, have you got a shotgun under the counter?" the judge asked.

The blond, clean-shaven clerk shook his head as though in a daze, then looked around. "Excuse me, Judge, I was tryin' to figure out those four old boys on horseback. I can't figure if they're coming in or not."

The judge glanced out the open double doors in the corner. Four men in dusty duckings were dismounting. One of them, a redhead, was bossing the others around. "They're coming in," the judge said. "Kelly, do you have a Greener shotgun under the counter?"

"Yessir. Do you expect trouble?"

"How many shells do you have?"

"About a dozen, I reckon."

"Then I don't expect any trouble at all. Would you take the shotgun and shells and lay them on the counter between us?" the judge instructed. "Quickly."

The judge kept his back to the door. "Are all four coming into the hotel?"

The clerk nodded. "Looks like they're going to have some dinner," he whispered.

The judge cracked open the shotgun, checked the chambers, then stuffed the remaining shells in his pocket. "Kelly, when the men go in, I want you to go out there and untie those four horses and lead them to the livery. Go down the alley."

"Now?"

"Yes."

The hotel clerk scooted toward the front door. The judge followed the four men into the crowded dining room, about ten steps behind them, as they marched toward the window table. Only the mayor and the silver-badged sheriff remained there, both of them with right hands under the table. The crowd around them sensed conflict. All conversation died.

The redhead stepped out in front of the rest of his cohorts. "Are you the sheriff that murdered my brother?"

Sheriff Hill sipped his coffee. "Nobody's been murdered in this town recently. And I'd be the first to know." He calmly rubbed the mug against his cheek. "However, I did run into a crazy man who tried to kill everyone in sight the other night. I asked him three times to lay down his gun because I wasn't lookin' for him. But he grabbed a girl and threatened her life. So, I did like any of you men would do; I protected the girl."

"You killed our brother. So now it's your turn!" Before the redhead could pull his gun, the judge laid the barrel of the shotgun alongside the man's neck.

All four men froze, guns not fully drawn. The diners scrambled to the safety of the hotel lobby.

"Who are you?" the redhead hollered.

"Why, that's the judge," the sheriff announced. Both he and the mayor pulled out their guns from under the table. "You'll probably be seeing more of him later."

"I was rather hoping these boys would pull their guns, Sheriff," the judge reported. "Very seldom do I get to carry out the sentencing. I thought it might be an interesting respite."

Dr. Jacobs stalked the men, the cocked carbine at his shoulder. "I was wrong, this isn't a 'One of a Thousand.' It's just an ordinary .44-40." He stuck the barrel of the gun in the ribs of a second man.

"Who are you?" the man gasped.

"That's Dr. Jacobs," the sheriff announced.

"And look, boys, I want to tell you something," the doctor began. "I am very, very tired. I haven't had good sleep for over a week. So I've decided to take the day off. I'm not patchin' up anyone today. I just don't have it in me. If you four boys fool around and get yourselves shot, don't come crying to me. I'm not working on any gunshots till ten o'clock tomorrow."

The mayor stood, gun in hand, and approached the four. "Raise your hands while I remove your guns."

"And who do you think you are?" the spokesman growled.

"I'm the justice of the peace and city magistrate."

The redhead punched his fists above his head. "What kind of town is this?"

"A peaceful one," the sheriff said. "We aim to keep it that way. You boys aren't planning on staying in town too long, are you?"

"We need to bury our brother and locate an … old acquaintance."

The sheriff nodded. "That's good. I believe every man deserves to be buried by family. I'll just keep your weapons until you're ready to leave town. That way I won't have to figure out your next of kin."

"What man are you lookin' for?" the judge asked.

"His name is Bence," the redhead replied.

"What would you want with Mr. Horace Bence?" the mayor asked. "He's our county surveyor and assessor. You boys speculating in land or struck a vein?"

The redhead shook his head. "This fella's no county nothin'. He's a cheatin' bum."

"I don't believe we have anyone else in town with the last name of Bence," the mayor said. "And I ought to know. I shook hands with every voter six times last spring."

"We'll find him if he's here," another of the men growled.

"Our dinner's gettin' cold, boys," the sheriff lamented. "So, if you'd go on out and take care of your affairs, we'd appreciate it."

"We're free to go?"

The judge lowered his shotgun. "Certainly. You haven't committed any crime … yet."

"This whole town is crazy," the man whined.

"You know," the mayor said with a grin, "I've had other

people tell me that. If I were you, boys, I'd get my business done in a hurry and go find some town that's more hospitable."

The sheriff waved his gun-wielding hand. "Go on! Let us eat in peace."

When the four men slumped their way through the lobby, most of the diners quickly returned to their tables.

The judge laid the shotgun on the floor by the window table and sat down, straightening his tie and placing the linen napkin across his lap. "Mayor, I believe this coffee's cold," he said.

"It's a sad commentary when a man can't keep his coffee warm for the duration of his meal," the sheriff concurred.

The judge didn't look back as he heard bootheels pounding into the dining room once more.

"Somebody done stole our horses," one of the Kendall brothers shouted.

"This is the worst town I've ever been in," another grumbled.

"Obviously, you four have never been to Bodie," the sheriff said.

"I think your horses were confiscated and taken to the livery," the judge announced, never turning to face the men.

"Confiscated?"

"Yes, I believe you tied them off illegally."

"Sheriff, you'd better give us back our guns now, because we're leavin' town as soon as we can find our horses," the redhead declared.

"What about burying your brother?" Dr. Jacobs asked.

"The county can pay for it!"

"Well, I'm not going to return your guns until after I finish eating," the sheriff said.

"When will that be?"

"I'll meet you boys down at my office about 1:00." He

turned to Dr. Jacobs. "Or are we havin' pie today, Doc?"

"Yep, it's Wednesday … that means it's apple pie day."

The sheriff turned back to the four frustrated gunmen. "Make that 1:15, boys. I like to have my pie heated with just a little cheese on top."

Judith Kingston strolled south from the train depot at the corner of Washington and Carson Streets. She could hear the scrape of wheels churning. The deep blast of the whistle signaled they were pulling out. She couldn't refrain from looking back. The eruption of white steam from the engine rolled over the cars behind. She could imagine Willie Jane and Bence Farnsworth seated near each other, exchanging polite comments about their good friend, the judge's wife.

Now, Lord, I don't want to meddle. But this could be Willie Jane's only chance to get out of this quicksand of sin. I don't know if she can give up the morphine or not. I don't know if she really wants to quit this lurid business. She hasn't been able to pull away from this life for years, so I think it's going to take a miracle. Now, that's your department, Lord. I'm not telling you what to do, but if a miracle doesn't happen, that girl is lost.

Of course, if a miracle didn't happen, we would all be lost.

She stopped in front of the U.S. Mint as a man on a long-legged black horse rode to the curb.

Her straw hat shaded the noonday sun. "Levi, is that your new horse?"

"Yes, ma'am."

"He's quite handsome."

"Yeah, but he's all show. I've had wide-rumped ropin' horses that was faster than him. I think he could run fast if he wanted to. He jist don't want to. How's Mrs. Adair doin'?"

"She improves a little every day. Thank you for asking."

"I heard that ol' Primble done run off for good," Levi announced.

"That seems to be the consensus."

"I don't blame him for hittin' the willows. Any man that would do that shouldn't be allowed to live in polite society. A man shouldn't even treat an animal that way, let alone a lady." Levi paused a minute, "Except maybe if it was a lazy racehorse that a man spent his last eighty-five dollars on."

"Are you going out to the track, Levi?" Judith asked.

"Not with this nag. I'm going out to the orphan asylum and give the kids some rides."

"That's a very generous thing to do, Levi."

"I certainly hope Marcy thinks so."

Judith felt warm all over. "Marcy Ciprio?"

"Yes, ma'am. Ain't she got the sweetest smile you ever saw?"

"You have a good eye for smiles, Levi."

"Thank you, Judith."

She watched Levi gallop south past the capitol. Then she waited at the corner while four tough-looking men, one a redhead, rode past her toward the sheriff's office.

Bence said someone was after him. I wonder ... Lord, keep him safe and let him see his mother and sister while he's all cleaned up. And oh, I do pray for Charlotte. Maybe she's in labor today. Keep her strong and safe. May Bence's arrival be a time of joy, not sorrow. Marthellen has gone through so much. She needs some good things to happen to her little family.

And Bence needs to ...

"Good morning, Judith dear," a woman called from a half block away.

Judith watched every move as the woman stalked straight for

her. She studied the taupe gabardine jacket and skirt that fit snugly, nipped in at the waist and slightly flared at the hips. Black Spanish-style braid in hearts and flowers lined the jacket's front and ends of the sleeves. There were flashes of satin trim and nickel buttons. A very deep burgundy georgette scarf was sprinkled with delicate black beadwork in some sort of tapestry pattern. The woman twirled a black silk umbrella to shade herself from the harsh Nevada sun. "Hello, Daisie Belle," Judith said, "what a striking suit!"

Daisie Belle Emory gushed with delight. "Oh, this old thing? Do you really think so? Actually, it's an antique. It belonged to my grandmother. But it hung well on my mother and now, me too."

"It's … lovely." *Daisie Belle, everything about you "hangs well." And I certainly knew that wasn't a Carson department store outfit.*

Daisie Belle's free hand fluttered a black gauze handkerchief. "Have you seen Governor Kinkead?"

"Not today. Did you check his store?"

"No, but I certainly will. I simply must talk to him. I had such a marvelous idea about how to celebrate Nevada Day this year. I thought we should have each county send a representative dressed up in a costume depicting the local geography. For instance, each of the children at the orphanage could be costumed like a nugget of gold or silver."

"Dressed like nuggets?"

Daisie Belle pulled down her umbrella. Her dark brunette hair was parted deeply in the middle. Soft, thick waves, piled high, met on each side with ringlets of long curls. "Isn't that cute? Can't you just see the little cherubs' smiling faces?"

"That would be quite a sight." *Mrs. Emory, you might be the only woman in Nevada who thinks of orphans as little gold nuggets.* ✓

Daisie Belle frowned, then quickly relaxed with a smile. "The state will have to appropriate more funds, of course, but think how splendid it will be. Imagine a woman dressed like the Humboldt River."

"That would be quite a costuming challenge. But I think you'd make a lovely Lake Tahoe."

"Why, thank you, dear. However, I'm sure a younger woman will probably want to be Lake Tahoe."

I can't think of any woman on earth who would want to dress up like a lake. "I really believe you'd be perfect in the role."

"I must say I've given it some thought. I think it could be done with hundreds of tiny mirrors laced together like a cloak. But I must go see the governor immediately. Nice chatting with you, dear. Say hello to that handsome judge for me."

As Judith continued her stroll toward home, she thought about Daisie Belle Emory's voice. It was neither too high nor too low. It was just constant, unrelenting, especially at events like Estelle Cary's tea parties or Farmer Treadway's picnics, where you could be trapped for hours. But most of the women persevered with her because they'd rather a widow like her be talking to them, instead of to their husbands. *Lord, sometimes I do believe you created humans for your own private amusement. Of course, some of us are more amusing than others.*

Judith Kingston turned west on Musser and nearly got run down by two identical brown dachshunds being chased by a large black cat. *Why, they look like part of the trained dogs and monkeys act the judge and I saw at the Opera House a few weeks ago.* When she noticed the tails of the dachshunds tied with red bows, she was sure of it.

She began to run after the animals, then stopped. *What are you doing, Judith Kingston? You can't save everybody and every critter in Carson. Besides, you're going to fall flat on your face, or worse. And what are you going to do with them, if you capture them?*

Judith whirled around the other way and bumped into a panting, limping woman with a deep scar on her neck. "Fidora! I'm so sorry. I was distracted by a cat chasing two dogs."

"Those are my dogs," the woman panted. "I've got to get them back."

Judith glanced back down the alley. "I thought they were from that animal act at the Opera House, so naturally I—"

Fidora abruptly cut her off. "Well, they ain't. At least, not any more. Say, have you seen Willie Jane? She borrowed my pistol and didn't bring it back. Do you know where she's gone?"

Judith felt a sudden protectiveness for the girl. "I believe she went to her sister's in California."

Fidora limped on down the alley. "If you hear from her, you tell her I want to talk to her."

Judith returned to Musser Street. *Now, Lord, concerning Willie Jane and Bence. There must be a reason why you and I both decided to sit them side-by-side all the way to Sacramento. Neither are refined, but both have gone through the fire. I don't believe either has had very many happy years, and it seems to me it would be an economic use of your divine power to … but, I don't want to tell you what to do.*

I'm beginning to sound like Daisie Belle Emory, aren't I?

May you have mercy on both of us.

After Judith polished the silver and copper trim on her black wood stove and played some sonnets and hymns on the piano, she sat alone at the dining room table, poking at the jar of pickled Sicilian artichoke hearts. Beside her was a short stack of salt crackers, a cucumber and chives sandwich, and a cup of steaming green tea.

Not exactly to the judge's taste, but nice for a change for me. So cool, so delicate. So delicious. Ah, my sandwich and artichoke days, when I was green in judgment. Shakespeare's sentiments, I believe. Or should I say, Antony's? Or Cleopatra's?

She lifted the thinly sliced bread and poured a little salt and a few drops of olive oil and vinegar from the artichoke jar.

Wednesdays are so boring when the judge eats at the hotel. Especially when Marthellen is gone. I should just go and eat at the hotel, too. Not with the men, of course. I could just sit at a table nearby. How would that be? Daisie Belle Emory would do it. And maybe Estelle Cary ... or Audrey.

Poor dear. At least I have a husband and know where he is.

She ate the sandwich and crackers, then stuck her finger into the marinated wine vinegar of the artichoke heart jar and licked it.

Two husbands who ride off to Mexico? It's so strange it has to be true. Anyone who was trying to cover up something would think of a much more plausible story.

However, no one ever accused Audrey of being creative. She's certainly no Daisie Belle Emory.

Someone pounded on the front door. Judith jumped to her feet and dashed down the hall. She flung open the door so quickly she startled the round-faced, dark-haired man. "Levi, I thought you went to the orphanage."

"I did, but I rode right back when Marcy gave me this." Levi Boyer handed her a long-stemmed clay pipe.

Judith took it and twirled it in her hand. "What does this mean?"

"One of the orphans found it on a hike this morning."

"Which one?"

"Jesse Zake."

"Where was little Jesse hiking?"

"I guess the whole passel of them had a picnic and bird-watching trip down by the river."

"Levi, why is this of interest to me?" Judith asked. "Two-thirds of the men in Carson smoke clay pipes."

He reached over and ran his finger along the stem of the pipe. "Look at the engraving."

She studied the tiny letters. "To M.P. from A.A .... Milton Primble? Audrey Adair? So, you think this could be Milt's pipe. Where did you say little Jesse found it?"

"Just upriver from Duffy Day's place."

"I suppose Milton could have dropped it as he galloped out of town."

"If he headed out there, he wasn't on a straight line to Mexico."

"No, but perhaps he only told Audrey he was going to Mexico to confuse anyone who might try to follow him."

"You might be right, Judith. Or maybe it's an old pipe and a dog carried it out of town."

She leaned her head closer to his. "A pipe-smoking dog?"

Levi cracked a grin. "Sort of a silly soundin' theory. Anyway, I thought I should bring it to town, but I didn't want to return it to Audrey. Thought maybe it would rile her."

"Levi, I'll see that she gets it at an appropriate time."

"Thank ya." He waited a moment, leaning on one foot then another.

"Is there anything else?" Judith asked.

"I was wonderin' ... you know ... if maybe Primble lost a few other things out there along the river. I think, perhaps, I'll ride out and take a look."

"We'll need a carriage," she announced.

"We?"

"You, me, and young Jesse."

"Yes, ma'am. I'll borrow Doc Jacobs'. But what shall I tell him?"

"Tell him the truth, Levi. Tell him you're driving me out to the orphanage asylum so I can visit Jesse Zake."

The hot August sun blazed down on the brown sandstone blocks of the Nevada State Prison as Judith, Levi, Marcy Ciprio, and a stick candy-sucking five-year-old named Jesse Mariweather Zake passed by.

"We get our shoes and boots from there," Jesse reported. "The prisoners is real nice."

"Some of them are. I received a present just last week from one of them," Marcy said.

Levi frowned. "Why'd he do that?"

She avoided Levi's eyes and looked at Judith. "It's a very beautiful work box, a foot square, finely veneered and inlaid." She turned and smiled at Levi. "It was a thank-you for taking the children out there to sing."

They rode east to the Carson River, then turned south at the sandy trail that led to Duffy Day's camp. Levi parked the carriage in the shade of a cottonwood grove. Trees lined both sides of the river.

There was a strong scent of wild sage, sweet and pungent, like oily sugar. Sunflowers and blue lavender aster-like flowers sprouted in the decomposed granite. In between the sage were round clumps of rabbit brush. Fields of cattail stalks revealed where the swampy places hid. The cool, sparkling waters of the Carson flowed easy on the desert valley. Ducks and geese flew and grazed all along the river.

"Are we going to have another picnic?" Jesse asked.

"Not this afternoon," Marcy said. "Judith wants you to show her where you found the pipe."

Jesse hopped down and skipped along, in and around the sage and brush, clutching Miss Ciprio with a sticky hand. Judith and Levi followed.

"That's not all I found either," Jesse announced.

"Oh? What else did you find?" Judith asked.

"I found two red rocks that I skipped in the river … and I found a J."

"A blue jay?"

"NO!" he protested. "A 'J'. It was a stick shaped like the letter 'J'. I took it back to our room. I know all my letters. Miss Marcy taught me."

"That's nice, Jesse. Now where did you find the pipe?"

"Over by that sage. Do you want to hear my letters?"

"Yes, I do … which sage was it?"

"A - b - c - d - e - f - g - h - i - j - k - l - m - n - o - p - q - r - s - t - u - v - vv - x - y - z." His face beamed when he finished.

"Double 'v'?" Levi asked.

"Jesse insists that a w does not look like two u's, but rather like two v's," Marcy explained.

"Can't argue with you there, young man," Judith said. "Whoever drew up the shapes and named them goofed a little bit. Now where did you find the pipe?"

"Right down there." He pointed to a clump of blue flax flowers in a slight indentation. "I can count to five hundred. Miss Marcy taught me. Would you like to hear me count to five hundred?"

"Jesse," Miss Ciprio advised, "save something back to tell Judith next time she comes out to the orphanage. What exactly are we lookin' for, Judith?"

"If Mr. Primble was riding out of town in a hurry, maybe he dropped some other things."

"What difference does it make what he dropped?" she asked.

"Perhaps it would give a clue about where he went. Then we could locate him."

"And bring him back to face charges about whippin' Audrey Adair," Levi blurted out.

Judith Kingston strolled slowly around scattered knots and masses of Eagle Valley sage. *And if we find him, it keeps people from suspecting Audrey of eliminating her husbands.*

This one, at least.

The quartet hiked for nearly a half mile south, parallel to the Carson River. Marcy found half a head of a porcelain doll buried in the mud. Levi found a rusted snaffle bit. Judith and Jesse found a "1" stick and a "7" stick. They circled around and returned to the carriage by a different path but added nothing to their collection. A slight breeze had softened their task, but their faces were hot and sweaty.

Judith adjusted her straw hat. "Well, thank you all for the lovely walk. Jesse, you are a delightful young man. Will you go on a walk with me some other time?"

"Tomorrow?" he quizzed.

"Well, maybe not tomorrow … but soon."

"Can I have a butterscotch next time?"

"Jesse Zake, you know better than that," Marcy scolded.

Jesse's eyes widened. "I'd be pleased to eat any old candy you brought me," he amended.

Levi drove the carriage back along the river. Just as he turned west, the gaunt, disheveled form of Duffy Day popped out from behind a tall sage, one hand wrapped in a dirty flour sack. Boyer abruptly stopped the carriage.

"Duffy," Judith called down. "You startled us."

"What are you doin' out here?" he asked.

"We went on a little hike."

"Did you find anything?"

"Oh, yes," Jesse said with a squeal, "we found wonderful rocks and sticks and everything."

"The property on this side of the road belongs to me and my brother Drake, you know," Duffy called out.

"How is your brother?" Judith asked.

"He got in with the bad crowd."

"Where is he?" Marcy probed.

"He's runnin' around with Wild Bill Hickok and that bunch."

"But," Levi protested, "Wild Bill is ..."

Judith's hand on Levi's arm silenced him. "Duffy, are you headed into town?" she asked. "We'd be happy to give you a ride."

"Nope. And I ain't comin' by for supper, neither. It ain't polite. My mama taught me good."

"She certainly did. You probably wouldn't like scalloped potatoes with cheese and ham, would you?"

"Yellow or white cheese?" he asked.

"White cheese."

"I don't like yellow cheese," he said.

"Would you like a ride to town now?" she asked again.

"Nope. I aim to walk. I want to try out my brand-new shoes."

Judith looked down at a pair of highly polished, new leather boots. Even though the shafts were short, Duffy wore them on the outside of his grimy ducking trousers.

"They're beautiful," Judith exclaimed. "Where did you get those new shoes, Duffy?"

"The Lord brought them to me."

"That's nice. He takes care of us, doesn't he?"

"'For we brought nothing into this world, and it is certain we can carry nothing out. And having food and raiment let us be therewith content,'" he quoted.

"You're right about that, Duffy."

"That's in the Bible, you know."

"Yes, it's in First Timothy."

"My mama used to read me a Bible."

"Do you have a Bible now, Duffy?"

"No, ma'am."

"I think we have a few extras at the Presbyterian church. Next time you're in town, let's go over and get one. But you still haven't told me how the Lord gave you those new shoes."

"He tossed them to me right out of heaven."

"They jist fell into your hands?" Levi pressed.

"I was down there where you all was walking. I come around the corner and these shoes was standing right there by the sage."

"Really?" Marcy exclaimed.

"How did you know they were from the Lord, and not just bounced off someone's wagon?" Levi asked.

"'Cause they was a sittin' right side up, lined up next to each other, just like you do at night when you go to sleep and put your shoes next to your bedroll. Not only that, they fit me perfect … sort of."

Judith glanced at Levi and Marcy, then back at Duffy. "So you're sure you want to walk to town?"

"Yep. I'm sure."

"Will I see you for supper?"

"If my new shoes get muddy, kin I eat on the steps?"

"Certainly," she said.

Levi drove slow until they passed the state prison, then they raced the dust cloud they generated as they rolled toward the wide two-story Nevada State Orphan's Asylum. Some of the shades were half open at the thirteen rectangular top windows and Judith could barely see children's heads peering out.

"Judith, those surely didn't look like country shoes," Levi said.

"You think they look like banker's shoes, Mr. Boyer?"

"Yes, ma'am, I do. Do you know if Mr. Primble had short-legged boots like those?"

"I know he had brown dress boots, but they were always tucked under his trouser legs, so I can't really identify them."

"Duffy said he found them right down by where we were looking."

"Maybe Mr. Primble camped out there for the night," Marcy suggested.

Judith raised her sweeping narrow eyebrows. "And then rode off the next morning barefoot?"

Judith Kingston was at the kitchen sink when she heard the back door open. She didn't turn around, but began to count. *Fifteen ... fourteen ... thirteen ... he's hanging up his hat ... twelve ... eleven ... ten ... he's hanging up his topcoat ... nine ... eight ... seven ... he's straightening his tie, vest, and cuffs ... six ... five ... four ... he's walking into the kitchen ... three ... two ... one ....*

She felt the stiffness of his whiskers and the softness of his lips on her cheek.

"And how's my favorite girl in all Nevada?"

Judith returned his kiss. "Only Nevada?"

"My word, you're right. My favorite in all the world."

"I was wondering," she teased. "Just what woman is in second place?"

The judge peeked under the lid of a stew pot on the stove. "Oh, there's a college girl in upstate New York who's running a distant second. At least, I certainly hope she's in college. It's been two weeks since we had a letter from Roberta."

"Relax, Father dear. Your daughter still worships you."

The judge stiffened. "That's hardly what I meant."

"Now, now ... none of that keeping up judicial appearances at home. How was court today? I trust it was not as boring as yesterday."

He stepped behind her and began to rub her shoulders and neck. "There was a slight improvement."

Judith closed her eyes and relaxed. "Perhaps you'll get a nice perplexing murder case one of these days."

He stopped rubbing. "Oh? Do you know something I don't?"

Judith opened her eyes. "I was speaking hypothetically, of course."

"Yes ... quite." He strolled across the wide kitchen. "How about you? Did you get young Mr. Farnsworth off on the Virginia and Truckee?"

Judith wiped her small hands on her apron. "Yes, I saw them off this morning."

"Them?"

"Eh, there was a whole trainload of people. It seemed like each one stopped to say good-bye." *Dear Judge ... you do not need to know about Willie Jane. It would only cause you needless concern for my safety.*

"I'm glad he scooted out of town. I understand some brothers named Kendall were looking for him."

She stared into his eyes. They were deeper gray than usual, almost blue. "Where did you hear that?"

He glanced away. "From the sheriff ... at lunch." *Dear sheltered Judith. There are violent situations in the world that your tender soul should never have to face. May the Lord graciously continue to keep you from such confrontations and worry.*

"Well, I'm glad you take once a week for a relaxing meal with your friends. How was your food? I presume you had liver and onions."

"Oh yes ... you know how routine I am."

"Did you have apple pie and cheese?"

"Yes, but I'm not sure the new baker is as good as Mrs. Tankersley. It looks like you've cooked plenty for me tonight."

"We're having stewed lamb and a little cheese on the potatoes. I had planned a light supper, but I invited Duffy to stop by. He's looking thinner than ever. I wanted to fix him something hearty."

"Is Duffy in town? A surveyor was looking for him."

"I saw him in the valley. I went out to the orphanage for a visit—didn't I tell you?"

"I probably forgot."

"We took a walk and ran across Duffy out at his place," she reported.

"You walked all the way from the orphanage to the river? That's over three miles."

"Oh, no ... Levi Boyer was sparking Miss Ciprio. He had Dr. Jacobs' rig, and little Jesse and I rode along."

"Always playing the chaperone." The judge opened a

cupboard and pulled out a crystal glass. "And how are things at the orphanage?"

"Splendid. Miss Ciprio seems to be doing a wonderful job. Little Jesse is a darling."

He poured water into a glass. "Will this be another discussion about how we should adopt every child in the orphanage?"

Judith laughed. "Oh no ... I cried myself through that phase years ago."

He held the glass high and peered at it as if his glare would remove all impurities. "And how's Audrey today?"

"Recovering slowly. Perhaps you can stop by sometime soon. She had a legal question or two about filing for desertion."

The judge swished the water in the glass and then took a deep gulp. "But Milton Primble's only been gone a few days."

"I know, I know. However, dear Audrey's quite convinced that she will never see him again."

CHAPTER FOUR

The deep circles under Audrey Adair's eyes had turned yellow-green. She was perched on the brown leather divan that graced the east wall of her parlor. Beside the divan was a large Italian tapestry depicting gauze-draped young girls dancing around a sleeping lion. Audrey's navy blue, lace-trimmed cotton robe was buttoned high on her neck, making her face look even wider.

"Judith, did I tell you I'm thinking of moving?"

"Oh my, that would be drastic."

"You know how much I love this home."

"And all your friends are here." Judith gazed around the Adair mansion, one of the largest dwellings in Carson and one of the first to be piped for gas lighting. Consisting of fifteen rooms and seven marble fireplaces, it was constructed of clear sugar pine and cedar.

"That's part of the problem."

"What do you mean?"

"I'm afraid I'm getting quite a reputation. People in town don't know whether to feel sorry for me or to fear me."

"Audrey, all those who know you, appreciate your consistent wisdom and loyal friendship."

"Loyalty, perhaps, but wisdom? I can imagine the jokes about the rich old lady who can't tell a gigolo from a decent man."

Judith examined the full, round face, still bruised. The nutmeg brown hair was neat, three rolls pinned above the forehead, the rest drawn into a bulging bun at the nape of Audrey's neck. "I have heard no such talk," Judith said.

Audrey managed a weak smile. "Judith, dear, your ears are much too delicate to hear such disparaging comments."

Audrey's housekeeper and maid, Sylvia Coffee, entered the parlor with a silver tea service. She wore a long black apron over a dull white pinafore the color of her straight hair. Sylvia adjusted the large Pompeii red velvet pillows at Audrey's head and gently patted her cheek while Judith poured orange spice tea and buttered slices of saffron cake dotted with raisins and candied citrus peel.

"Judith, the doctor said I should get some sun, but I'm not about to have people in Carson see me like this."

Judith admired the gold-trimmed cup and saucer. "Everyone understands, and the air will do you some good."

"The air, yes, but I just couldn't endure the stares."

"Now, Audrey, you can't go through life worried about what people say."

"Oh, Judith … sweet Judith … when one looks like I do … well, I'm constantly aware of what people are saying about me. I know it's strange for you to think about. I have no doubt that you were darling as an infant, lovely as a young lady, and beautiful as a newlywed. And everyone in this state knows you look pleasing at middle age. You don't look much past thirty, yet you have a son who is twenty-seven."

"You flatter me, Audrey." *What does she mean by "pleasing" at middle age?*

"Don't be foolish. I would have sold my gold mine to look as you do now when I was twenty-five, let alone fifty."

"Thank you for your kindness, but I believe people in this town accept us for who we are, not what we look like. They're more concerned with a person's character, what they say and do, and forget our wrinkles or ... or ... "

"If only everyone saw the world through your eyes, my dear." Audrey picked at her cake. "The fact remains, I'm an embarrassment to Carson ... and to myself. I was raised by an old maid aunt who tried to pound Proverbs 4:23 into my head, 'Keep thy heart with all diligence; for out of it are the issues of life.' I allowed my resentment to cause me to ignore her good advice. I am ashamed that my heart is so easily led astray by rascals. I really do think I should move."

"Where would you go? You don't have any family left."

"I was thinking of moving to San Francisco."

"But you don't have any friends there, do you?"

Audrey lowered her eyes. "No, not many. But that's the point. I could have a fresh start."

"But surely you aren't thinking of doing anything right away. You've got to heal and think things through. After such a trauma you need time to weigh alternatives."

Audrey took a deep breath and looked Judith in the eye. "I've decided to take a preliminary trip on Monday."

"This Monday? Are you well enough to travel?"

"Mrs. Coffee has agreed to go with me. I've already made the arrangements through Mr. Fitzgibbon. Do you know him? He used to work with Mr. Ralston at the Bank of California. A widower, I believe. Not that it makes any difference. He's in real estate now and has volunteered to show me some available properties."

Judith heard music from the front of the house. Audrey Adair owned the only mechanical Swiss chime in Carson City. One twist on the handle at the front door, and three measures of one of Bach's Brandenburg Concertos rang forth in the parlor.

Sylvia Coffee hurried across the polished wooden floor of the entry. As Audrey and Judith sipped tea, there were muffled tones of conversation at the front door. Then the heels of Sylvia's lace-up black shoes hammered a path to the parlor.

"Miss Adair, you have company at the door," Sylvia announced. The crow's feet around her bright eyes were drawn tight.

Audrey grimaced and held her side as she tried to stand to her feet. "Who is it?"

"It's Eliza Conroy, ma'am."

Audrey's face lost all color save the bruises. She clutched the arm of the divan. "Milton's sister?"

"Yes, she said she was on her way to San Francisco and wanted to pay a surprise visit to you and Mr. Primble."

"*Shock* would be a better word than *surprise*."

"Where does she live?" Judith asked.

"In Pennsylvania."

"I didn't know Milton had a sister."

"She's his only living relative. A widow, without children. We've received only a few letters from her."

"You've never met her?"

"My heavens, no. She and Milton never seemed close. Oh dear, Judith, what am I going to do?" Audrey's hands began to quiver. Her speech was thick and halting.

"Tell her the truth."

"That her brother was a drunk, a womanizer, and a wife beater, and that he took off to Mexico? I can't say that."

"Well, I could."

Relief slowly flooded Audrey Adair's face. She reached out for Judith's hand. "Oh, thank you, dear. If you could attend to this unpleasant matter, that would be the sweetest thing anyone has ever done for me. Sylvia, if you'll help me, I'll go up to my room to rest." Audrey swung her legs to the floor. "Judith, after you've explained things to that woman, come up and say good-bye."

Judith Kingston stood up and stared across the parlor at the departing Audrey Adair. *But I ... I didn't mean I would ... I meant I would if I were you, but I'm not you ... and that is not my sister-in-law, or former sister-in-law, and ... Lord, I'm not sure how this happened.*

I should have gone out to the orphanage today and brought caramels to the children and taken Jesse for a long walk. Or I could have visited at the prison, exhorted the residents to righteous living, and handed out Marthellen's handwritten tracts.

Anything would be better than this.

All right, Mrs. Kingston, be truthful ... and merciful.

Judith swung open the eight-foot-tall carved wooden door that separated Audrey's parlor from her entry hall. A tall woman wearing a peach-colored French silk dress with full bustle and cream lace collar and cuffs stood with her back to Judith. Sandy blonde hair was tucked trimly under a straw hat that sported three peacock feathers.

Her back still toward Judith, the woman began to speak. "This crystal swan looks so lovely here on the entry table. That's exactly how I imagined it looking in your home the day I purchased it at Tiffany's." She spun around. "There's nothing like ... oh, my ... Milton was rather slack in describing you. You're nothing at all like ..."

"I'm not Audrey," Judith said.

A wide smile broke across the woman's face. "Of course you aren't. I'm just a little nervous. I haven't seen my brother in years, and I've never met his wife. Are you one of the servants?"

Judith tried to relax her shoulders but could feel most of the muscles in her neck and upper back tighten. "No, I'm a good friend of Audrey's. I'm afraid she's in bed recovering from a serious injury and unable to entertain visitors today."

The woman raised one eyebrow. "An injury, you say? Will she be all right?"

"The doctor says she just needs some rest now," Judith replied.

"Is Milton with her? Perhaps you could pass word to him that I'm downstairs. I'm his sister, Eliza Conroy. I couldn't seem to communicate with that woman who let me in. It's been a rather long trip getting here and—"

"Mrs. Conroy, I need to tell you some things that aren't very pleasant. I do not enjoy doing this, but with Audrey still recovering, there are some things you should know."

"It's Milton, isn't it? Something's happened to him. Oh dear Lord, no." Mrs. Conroy slumped into a turquoise velvet embroidered settee. "Was he killed in the same accident?" Eliza Conroy pulled out a cream lace handkerchief and began to weep. Judith noticed that the gold and emerald necklace and earrings she wore matched the greens in the peacock feathers. A large emerald stone garnished a ring on her right hand.

"Mrs. Conroy, please, don't get ahead of things. Your brother is not dead, or even injured." *As far as I know. Lord, this is getting really complicated. Judith Kingston, why couldn't you be one of those women who stay home and knit mittens and caps?*

Eliza Conroy looked up. There was not a blot or blemish from hanky or tears anywhere on her face. "I don't understand," she wailed. "What has happened to my brother?"

"I want to say this as delicately as possible. Your brother,

Milton, has had trouble over the years with drinking and—"

"Milton doesn't drink."

Judith felt her face go pale. "Well, he does now."

"He most certainly does not. Unless … unless … Audrey drove him to it."

Judith's heart raced. "Please let me finish," she insisted. "Your brother drinks heavily at times. When he gets in this condition, he becomes violent and—"

Mrs. Conroy forced a laugh. "Milton? Violent? I don't even think we're talking about the same man."

"I'm talking about the Milton Primble in the wedding picture on the wall above you." *The Milton who looks nothing like you. So little resemblance for brother and sister.*

Eliza Conroy got up and peered at the large gold-framed oil painting. "Yes, that's my brother … and this is Audrey, I presume?"

"Yes, it is."

"She looks different than I imagined."

"Let me continue. This is not the first time your brother has treated Audrey so violently, as Doctor Jacobs can confirm. Six days ago Milton savagely beat Audrey in a drunken rage and rode away, telling her he was off to Mexico."

"Milton? Mexico? He hates Mexico. He wouldn't even eat a Mexican omelet. There's something strange about this."

"I know this has hit you in a most abrupt way. Please forgive me for not knowing how to tell you in a more gracious manner," Judith explained.

Eliza Conroy glowered at Judith. "I don't believe you."

"What?"

"I simply don't believe this story. My brother is not that way."

"Maybe he's changed over the years."

"He couldn't change that much. He's always been a quiet, bookish man."

"Mrs. Conroy, please talk with Dr. Jacobs and the sheriff. Perhaps they can explain your brother's temperament better than I."

Eliza turned to face the wedding picture. "Milton was deeply in love with Audrey. He sent me letters. He had never been happier in his life. He wanted me to move out to Carson City myself." She walked over and opened the front door. "Is that the Montgomery house across the street?"

"Why, yes … how did you know that?"

"Milton wanted me to buy it and move out here. I don't know what to say. None of this sounds right. Something strange is going on here, and I intend to figure it out. I'd like to speak to Audrey now."

"I'm sorry, she's not physically able to—"

"You refuse me an audience with her?"

"I think it might be best to wait until—"

"Until I'm not upset? My only brother has vanished and all I hear is an explanation contrary to everything I know about him, and you expect me not to be upset?"

Eliza Conroy stomped toward the parlor. Judith slid in front of her.

"Please, get out of my way," Eliza fumed.

"Audrey is in no condition for company."

"You are a slight woman. I could easily shove past you."

"And you are a vain woman. I could easily break your nose with my fist." *I can't believe I said that. I'm beginning to sound like Willie Jane and the girls in the cribs. Oh, Lord, please forgive me. And deliver me.*

Eliza Conroy looked genuinely startled. "I am from the

East. I am not used to being threatened like that."

"Well, you aren't in the East now," Judith declared, "so get used to it. Dr. Jacobs has an office on Carson and Second Street. Please visit with him about your concerns. If you insist on challenging Audrey, I'm sure the doctor and Judge Kingston can arrange a meeting."

"I want to see her right now."

"No. I believe it's time for you to leave."

"Are you throwing me out of my own brother's home?"

"This is not your brother's home. Every item in this house was purchased by Audrey Adair."

"That crystal swan wasn't."

"Then take the swan."

"I don't want it."

"What do you want?"

"I want to talk to my brother."

"Then, perhaps the sheriff has some clues as to which direction he went, but I would imagine he's in Mexico by now."

"My brother would never go to Mexico!"

"Good day, Mrs. Conroy."

"You haven't heard the last of this, my dear lady."

"I'm sure I haven't."

When the front door slammed behind Eliza Conroy, Judith clutched her hands together to try to keep them from shaking. She could feel her heart racing. She tried to take deep breaths.

This is like a nightmare. I behaved poorly, Lord. I owe that woman an apology. She seemed to bring out the worst in me. She has a right to be concerned about her brother. And it's natural that she has a difficult time acknowledging Milton's faults. Audrey had a difficult time acknowledging his faults. I believe I just threatened to punch a woman in the nose. I would have done it, too. Perhaps I've been in Nevada too long.

She scooted through the parlor and up the wide staircase toward Audrey Adair's boudoir.

The four-by-eight-foot solid oak desk was littered with open legal tomes and precisely opened envelopes. An inspector would have had to look closely to see any edges even slightly torn.

The man in the oak swivel chair squinted his eyes and peered at the fine, thin script in front of him, occasionally stopping to dip his pen in the inkwell. He pressed harder with the quill, widening the flow of scribbled notes on the sheet of lined paper spread across a huge leather-framed ink blotter that covered the middle of the desk.

His hat and topcoat were draped neatly on a coat rack near the desk. His black tie hung straight. The brass buttons on his vest lined up perfectly down his strong chest, and his white shirt revealed the crease of careful ironing and starched cuffs. His thinning hair was immaculate and his mustache and chin whiskers were carefully trimmed.

Judge Hollis A. Kingston was in his office.

In his environment.

Everyone called him the judge. No one could imagine him doing anything else.

Except Judith.

And once in a great while he had second thoughts about the profession himself.

The judge laid down the ivory handled pen and sat back in his chair. He rubbed the bridge of his nose.

Lord, I have just spent two weeks of my life thinking of nothing but mining laws. I have heard the eloquence and nonsense of attorneys on both sides for hours upon hours.

All because of greed.

Everyone wants more money. The owners. The lessees. The attorneys. The miners. The millers. And they want me to decide who is to be rich and who is to be richer.

I should just rule the whole matter null and void and forfeit the entire mine to Miss Hannah Clapp, her assistant, Miss Elizabeth Babcock, and their Sierra Academy. That would shock them! And that would be a very good way to get impeached, Judge Kingston.

Maybe David's right. Go preach the Gospel to those who have never heard. That's a life well spent. But it's too late for me. I will have to continue judging until the day I retire. Meanwhile, twenty years from now the mine will be bust. And whoever walks away with the riches will be broke or buried.

I need a break. Perhaps when this case is resolved, Judith and I will take a little trip. We could go to Monterey. She loves it there. We could stop by Rancho Alazan and give our condolences to Alena Merced. Perhaps she'd like to travel to Monterey with us.

Sometimes, Lord, I believe I take life much too seriously. Perhaps the future of Nevada doesn't actually rest on my shoulders. But at the moment, there's a mining precedent I must set. And it will affect Nevada for the next hundred years. Get to work, Judge. Idleness doesn't become you.

The knock on the door caused him to sit up and straighten his already straight tie. His clerk, Spafford Gabbs, peeked into the office. "There's a woman here who needs to talk to you."

"Can she make an appointment for later? I'm still trying to run down the ruling on the Consolidated vs. Butler case."

"She, eh, needs to get back to work soon. Says it will take only a minute."

"All right, send her in."

The woman who came through the door wore a long dark dress with a scooped neckline. She stood about five feet tall. Her frame was thin, her face brightly painted. Her tawny hair was short and tightly curled.

After ushering her over to a leather sidechair near the judge's desk, Spafford Gabbs turned to exit.

"Please join us, Mr. Gabbs," the judge insisted, pointing to another leather chair.

"This is kind of private, Judge," the lady said.

"I'm sorry, miss, but I insist on having another witness present when I consult with women. I don't operate any other way."

She studied Gabbs, then remarked, "I don't mean to be rude, but what kind of accent does your assistant have?"

The judge was amused. "That's a breed of English you're hearing. Spafford spent many years in England; the British ways rubbed off on him."

She smiled at Gabbs but still talked of him in the third person. "Well, I think he's a distinguished and polished gentleman."

Gabbs' long, narrow face blushed fiercely as the woman turned her attention back to the judge. She fiddled with the twisted silver strands of necklace that draped across her mostly bare chest. "Well, Judge, I didn't know exactly who to talk to. I need your opinion on a very important matter."

The judge leaned back in his chair. "Please continue."

"Yes, Your Honor, you see, my name is … "

"I know your name," the judge interrupted. "You're Adelia Haven and you work on crib row."

She stopped dead still. "You've heard of me?"

"You appeared before my bench in April of '78 on a charge

of public intoxication and attempted murder, as I recall."

"I did?"

"Yes."

"Did I do it?"

"Public intoxication, yes. Murder, no."

She clutched the top of her head. When she lifted her hands, the tan curls sprang back in place. "I sort of remember waking up in the jail, hurtin' bad. But I never could remember what I was there for."

"What can I do for you now?" the judge asked.

"I'm worried sick about Willie Jane."

"Does Willie Jane work in the cribs, too?"

She registered surprise with a bit of wariness. "Why, yes. She's in #6, and I'm in #7. At least, she was there until last week."

"Do you surmise foul play? If so, perhaps you should talk to Sheriff Hill."

Adelia stretched her neck briefly against her shoulder. "The only time I see the sheriff is when he comes to arrest me. I just need some advice, and I know how you and Judith always listen to a person, no matter who they are."

"You know my wife?"

"Shoot, Judge, everyone in town knows her."

Wait until I tell Judith that she is known even by the girls in the cribs. That will shock her. "Tell me about Willie Jane. And do you mind if I have Mr. Gabbs write some of this down?"

"Why?"

"For future reference, in case, indeed, there has been foul play."

"Oh sure, I jist never had no one write down my words before."

"Please continue," the judge urged.

"See, here's the thing. Some girls in the cribs hate themselves for bein' there, but they don't figure they can get out of it. And some, like me, reckon it's about as good as we can do, and don't worry none. But girls like Willie Jane jist see the whole thing as temporary. They're always gettin' their hopes up that someone's gonna take them away and they're gonna live happy ever after." Adelia crossed and uncrossed her legs. "Well, Willie Jane's been plannin' for weeks on pullin' out with her beau come August. They was goin' to Santa Barbara … that's in California. He was goin' to be rich and she could jist sleep all day and dance all night. Don't that sound swell, Judge?"

She swallowed hard at the judge's stern glare.

"Where is this leading, Miss Haven?" he pressed.

"This time Willie Jane was packed up and ready to leave, but he didn't show up."

"Some men have been known to change their minds."

"Now's the point I've been aimin' at. It's been talked all over town that he was murdered on the very night he was supposed to come get her. But no one down in the cribs seems to know the facts. I figure you are the one who knows all about murders, so I was wonderin' if, indeed, he was dead."

"Just who is, or was, Miss Willie Jane's paramour?"

"Her what?"

"Her beau?"

"It was Primble. You know, the man at the bank."

"Milton Primble?"

Adelia nodded and the judge noticed Spafford Gabbs' shocked expression. "Let me review this. Milton Primble made some offer to Willie Jane?"

"He told her he had a whole bunch of money and they were running off to Santa Barbara, just like I said."

"Santa Barbara, eh? But he jilted her. She was crushed that he disappeared, and you think he might have been murdered?"

"That's what I heard 'em saying down at Johnny's Red Dragon."

"And you want me to know you don't think Willie Jane did it and you've got to find her and see that she comes back?"

A wide smile revealed straight, white teeth. "I knew you'd understand."

"Actually, I don't understand at all. I know Milton Primble has left town, but I know nothing else. I have absolutely no knowledge of his being murdered. If you have any information about such a crime, you need to talk to the sheriff."

Adelia became agitated. She squeezed the silver necklace so tightly the judge worried she'd choke herself. A crimson streak marred her smooth throat. "I ain't goin' to talk to the sheriff. Ever' time I talk to that man I get arrested. I just ain't goin' to talk to him."

"Miss Haven, until a crime has been proved, there can be no suspects. So, when you see Miss Willie Jane, tell her she need not worry. At least, about that particular crime."

"See, that's really why I'm here, Judge. I don't know where Willie Jane is."

"My word, you don't expect foul play with her also?"

Adelia Haven's hazel eyes grew wide. "No, sir, I don't expect … well, I don't know. I just need to talk to her." Adelia leaned closer to the judge and whispered as if Mr. Gabbs would not be able to hear. "If you could just tell me where she is, I'll try to contact her."

"Why in the world do you think I would know where she is?" Judge boomed.

She sat back and resumed her normal raspy voice. "You could just ask Judith."

"My wife? Ask her what?"

"Where she sent Willie Jane off to."

The judge stared at Adelia's eyes. *My word, she must be drunk. What else could cause this woman to think such things?* "What does my wife have to do with this?"

"You mean you don't know?"

"Don't know what?"

"That Judith came and talked to Willie Jane a long time that day. The next morning she hauled her off to the train depot."

The judge calmly folded his hands together. "That's absurd."

"I ain't too sure what that word means, but I'm sure I'd like to know where Willie Jane is and if she's comin' back or not. She ain't a killer, Judge. Some girls is just plain mean and look for a chance to hurt others. She ain't that way." Adelia Haven stood and tried to brush her curly bangs out of her eyes. "Thanks for listnin' to me, Judge. If you get an address for Willie Jane, I'd appreciate knowin' it. The least I could do is write her a letter."

The judge and Spafford Gabbs stood as Miss Haven left the room. "Judge, what do you want me to do with this testimony?" Gabbs asked.

"File it. No, wait, I'll file it. But first I'll take it home and show it to my wife. She will be amused at the stories that filter around town about her."

Gabbs handed him the three pages of recorded conversation. "What do you think about her suspicions about Primble?"

"That's for the sheriff and the county attorney to determine." The judge gazed across his desk cluttered with law books. "I certainly have enough work without trying to solve a crime, especially one nobody knows has even been committed."

The judge eased back down on his chair.

Spafford Gabbs strolled across the room and stood at the doorway. His narrow eyes were all business. "Judge, I'm going to take copies of the Ophir brief over to the State Supreme Court. Would you like me to lock the outside door and give you some privacy?"

"I'd be obliged," the judge said, and Gabbs exited. *Judith, what exactly have you been up to? I recall your saying something about "them" when I inquired about your sending off young Farnsworth. I'm sure you will have an explanation for all of this.*

The judge rose and walked over to the coatrack.

But I'm not very sure you will have a good explanation.

As Judge Kingston exited the train depot at the corner of Washington and Carson, he spotted Sheriff Hill crossing the street in front of the Mint and headed his way.

"Judge, have you got a minute? Something's come up on this Primble matter."

The two men strolled south on Carson Street.

"I've been thinking about that lately, myself," the judge commented.

"I just had a visit from the bank examiners."

"Did they find any irregularities?"

"Plenty," the sheriff reported.

"So Primble did rifle the bank before he left town?"

"Yes and no."

"What do you mean?"

"They found five hundred dollars missing from ten different accounts."

"He decided to spread out the deception?"

"I suppose. They were all substantial accounts. Perhaps he figured this way it would be some time before the error was discovered."

"That certainly gives him a better motive for running off to Mexico." *Or was it Santa Barbara?*

"One would think so," the sheriff said. "But they also found five thousand dollars in cash locked in his desk drawer."

The judge stopped in his tracks. "That is strange. Do you suppose he was in the process of embezzling the money but never carried it out?"

"That's what it seems like to me."

"But why would a man who had access to Audrey Adair's fortune embezzle from the bank?"

The sheriff shoved his hands in his jeans pockets. "Maybe she cut him off or something. It's one of several questions I'd like to ask Audrey as soon as she's up to discussing the matter. In the meantime, I'm thinking about sending Tray south to see if he can find any traces of Primble headed that way."

"I just telegraphed Prescott, Tucson, and San Diego, alerting them to be on the lookout for Primble," the judge admitted.

"You did?"

"I was getting curious myself."

"What did you tell them?"

"That Primble was wanted for questioning for possible assault of a woman. If I'd waited I could have added the bank embezzlement. Are the bank inspectors going to press charges?"

The sheriff pulled off his hat and scratched his head. "No. They got the accounts back in shape and figure it will be better for business to play down the whole matter. But I'm glad you sent the telegrams. The quicker we find out where Primble is, the sooner rumors will stop flying around the city."

"I heard a strange rumor myself," the judge began.

"The one about the Kendall brothers being wanted for stagecoach robberies near Murphys?"

"In California?"

"Yep. I got word of it today," the sheriff said. "They murdered all the passengers on the stage. Only the driver escaped."

"I hadn't heard about that." The judge stopped at the capitol and gazed across the landscaped grounds. "Sounds like those Kendall boys were more dangerous than we thought."

"Remember them sayin' they was lookin' for someone?"

"Yes."

"Could be they was after the driver."

The judge rubbed his graying chin whiskers. *Bence Farnsworth? Was he the stage driver?* "But what would they want with him?"

"Could be they don't want him around to identify them. Or he took something with him that they wanted. Or ..."

"Or what?" the judge pressed.

"He could have been in on it."

The judge folded his arms across his chest. "What direction did they head after they left town?"

"They rode out to Dayton, but I'm not sure where they went after that. I wasn't too particular as long as they left my jurisdiction. Now it's your turn. What rumor did you hear?"

"That Milton Primble was keeping a crib girl on the side and planned to run off with her."

"So, Judith told you about Willie Jane, did she? You never know what's going on in a man's mind, do you? Imagine Primble promisin' all of that to a crib girl?"

Sometimes one never knows what's going on in a woman's mind. Even one's own wife's. The judge leaned against the black iron fence that surrounded the state capitol. "I'm a little fuzzy on this Willie Jane thing. Perhaps you could explain."

"Well," the sheriff began, "I got word one of the girls was trying to kill herself, and anyone else who was around. On the way, I ran into your Judith. I knew I needed a woman's wisdom to keep anyone from being hurt, so I—"

"You decided to put my wife in a dangerous situation?"

"Now, Judge, I assure you she volunteered. And I tried to keep her behind that stack of wheels. Judith has a such a knack for bringing out the best in folks. All sorts of folks. You know that. Now, me … well, it seems like I have the opposite effect. It was amazin', Judge. Judith marched in there, calmed Willie Jane down, and left her all peaceful. You should have seen it. It would make your heart proud. But then, I reckon she told you all about that."

The judge resumed his walk. *No, but I can guarantee she will.*

The men had just crossed Carson Street at Second when they heard a shout from a second-story office.

They looked up. "Wait right there," Dr. Jacobs called out from an open window. "You're just the two I want to see."

As they stood on the corner and waited, the sheriff pointed across the street. "Isn't that Gabbs, your clerk, coming down Second Street?"

The judge turned around and started to wave, then changed his mind. "Yes, I sent him to the Supreme Court with some documents."

"That route is the long way around from the Supreme Court."

The judge adjusted his hat and brushed the dust off the sleeves of his coat. *I was thinking the same thing.*

Dr. Jacobs was still pulling on his suit coat when he reached them. "You'll never guess who just came to visit me."

"Milton Primble?" the judge said.

"No, but close. Mrs. Eliza Conroy, his sister."

"Primble has a sister?" the sheriff asked.

"Yes, and I think she'll be coming to see you next."

"Why?"

"She's very disturbed about the circumstances surrounding her brother's disappearance."

"So, what's her complaint?" the sheriff grumbled. "It's Primble who's acted strange."

"She thinks someone purposely did him in. She claims that he wasn't the type to treat a woman bad, and that his letters to her in Pennsylvania made her believe that he and Audrey were getting along quite well."

"I presume you explained Primble's more violent nature," the judge said.

The doctor blew out a breath of air. "Of course I did, but she didn't seem to believe a word."

"Does she have some evidence about Primble?" the sheriff asked.

"Not that I know of. But she did want to file a complaint. It seems she showed up at Audrey's house and was threatened with a thrashing."

"Audrey can be testy if she's in a bad mood," the sheriff commented.

"Oh, it wasn't Audrey who did the endangering. She said a

comely brunette by the name of Judith threatened to break her nose."

"What?" the judge gasped. "Judith threatened violence? That's ... that's ... preposterous!"

The doctor absently brushed off his coat sleeves. "I don't know, Judge, Primble's sister is a pushy sort of female. I don't think we've heard the last of this."

The judge tipped his hat. "If you two will excuse me, I believe I'm needed at home."

Judith lounged in the wooden lawn swing in the shade of the east side of the Kingston house. She had thoroughly brushed off her best calico dress and dabbed the delicate scent of homemade rose petal cologne on her wrists and behind her ears. Her nails were filed and she had soaked her hands smooth with cocoa butter and almond oil. An open letter and orange envelope lay in her lap. She twiddled with the seeds of a sunflower she'd pulled from Marthellen's garden as she peered down the Musser Street sidewalk and waited.

When she spotted the erect figure of Judge Hollis A. Kingston marching west, she met him at the side gate of the white picket fence. "Why, Judge Kingston, what a pleasant surprise. You're home early." She slipped her soft, warm hand in his and led him toward the yard swing.

"I have heard some disturbing news," he blurted out.

She continued to squeeze his hand and made him sit down next to her. "Well, I have some exciting good news. We got a letter from Marthellen today. Charlotte had her baby, a little girl. They are going to name her Judith Kathryn. Isn't that about the sweetest thing you ever heard?"

She could sense him relax just a little.

"I, eh …" the judge stuttered, "I trust mother and child are doing well?"

"Oh, yes. And so are Grandmother Marthellen and Uncle Bence. Young Mr. Farnsworth arrived the day the baby was born. Marthellen said she cried and cried when she saw him. She doesn't know all he's been through, but she really thought she'd never see him again. You must read the letter. It's quite touching."

"Yes, well, perhaps later …" His voice softened with every word.

"Oh, and that's not all," Judith didn't let go of the judge's hand. "Willie Jane … you know, the girl who was so despondent that she wanted to take her life? Well, she didn't go to see her sister in Traver after all. She decided to stay in Sacramento a while. Marthellen said Willie Jane seemed to be quite … what was the word she used?" Judith slowly scanned the letter. "Here it is, 'Willie Jane is quite perky and pleasant, a fact that hasn't gone unnoticed by Bence.' Isn't that interesting?"

The judge tried to tug his hand away, but Judith refused to turn loose. "You failed to tell me about this woman, Willie Jane," he said. "Do you have an accounting for that?"

"Yes, I do." She leaned over and kissed his cheek. He sighed, then relaxed. She now clutched both his hands. "Do you remember that time you and Dr. Jacobs were hunting up near Lake Tahoe and the doctor's horse slipped over that cliff? You climbed straight down a two-hundred-foot embankment and retrieved his saddle, rifle, medical bag, and tack."

"Yes …?"

She leaned over and kissed him again. "When did you finally tell me about climbing down that cliff?"

The judge turned away, then looked into his wife's persistent eyes. "Several years later, as I recall."

"Exactly. And why did you keep that from me?"

"My word, I didn't want you to worry, of course."

She raised her eyebrows and grinned.

The judge felt the back of his neck redden. "But that was different. I had to help a friend."

"And I had to help a girl so dispirited and at her wit's end that she wanted to take her life. I postponed telling you about it because I didn't want you worrying about me, that's all. But, if you promise never to hike down a dangerous cliff to help a friend ever again, I'll promise never to go into a bad neighborhood and help a depressed and desperate sinner."

"I can't promise that."

"Nor can I. I think we're stuck. We both have to do those things the Lord leads us to do, and we'll both have to trust in his protection," Judith said.

The judge stared out at the street. Finally, she felt the stiffness in his grip melt away. He leaned over and kissed the back of her neck.

The whiskers tickled. The lips teased.

"Oh, dear Judith, you've disarmed me again."

She let one of his hands slip out of her grip. "And I am thankful you're a man who is open to reason."

He looked her straight in the eyes. "I have another challenge for you."

"Oh?"

"And this time, my esteemed clerk, Mr. Gabbs, has not warned you in advance."

"Spafford was rather obvious when he came by the house today, wasn't he?"

"Is there anyone in this town who isn't one of your sentries?" he retorted.

"Now, Judge Kingston, I can't divulge private information like that. What is this additional challenge?"

"There is a rumor around town that you threatened to punch Milton Primble's sister in the nose. What is that all about?"

Judith sighed then began to chuckle.

"Is it that funny? Or is it not true?"

"No," she giggled. "It's funny because it is true."

"Judith Kingston actually threatened to box someone?" The judge tried to hold himself erect, but he began to chuckle. "I have a difficult time even imagining the scene. I can't believe you'd ever do such a thing."

Judith continued to giggle. "And I can't believe ..." she caught her breath, "that the Honorable Judge Hollis A. Kingston is sitting here laughing with me about it!"

Suddenly he sat up and quit laughing.

Judith quickly slipped her fingers back into his.

CHAPTER FIVE

Spafford Gabbs, his arms full of books to read, had just gone to lunch when the mayor burst into the judge's office. The mayor's tie was loosened, his top button unfastened, and sweat dripped off his forehead as he yanked off his bowler and fanned himself. "It's hot today, Judge. The thermometer at the Mint stood at ninety degrees by ten o'clock this morning."

The judge could feel his own shirt collar soaked with sweat. "It's one of those days a man wouldn't mind going down to the ice company to sit with some friends in the blockhouse."

"That's not a half-bad idea. Not only could we cool off, but then that Conroy woman couldn't find me." The mayor flopped down in a leather side chair beside the judge's desk. "That woman hasn't stopped stirring up trouble from the day she came to town."

Sheriff Hill burst through the door after one quick knock. "You two holdin' a meetin' without me?"

"We were just discussing the heat of our illustrious Nevada sun and the heat that Conroy woman is spreading around," the mayor reported.

The sheriff yanked a blue bandanna from his pocket and began to wipe his neck and face. "What do you think her motive is, Judge?"

Judge Kingston seriously considered pulling off his cufflinks and rolling up the sleeves of his white shirt. But such a thought didn't last long. "I can't decide whether she's driven by justice or greed."

Dr. Jacobs didn't bother knocking. He strolled in, suit coat draped over his arm, tie lying like a limp noodle around his collar. His top shirt button was unfastened. "There must be a shade tree or basement somewhere in town cooler than this office," he announced. "The state convention was over last week. You aren't talkin' Republican politics, are you?"

"Shoot no, Doc," the sheriff snorted. "But we'll only let a renegade Democrat join us as long as we don't have to hear any 'me and General Hancock' stories."

"You fellas ever notice how the further you get from Washington, D.C., the less important it becomes who's in the White House?" the doctor declared. "When I was in Virginia, we thought national politickin' was a life or death matter. But out here we're pretty much on our own anyway." He flopped down in a rosewood carved armchair next to the window. "The worst of it is, I just wasted a perfectly good nap time visiting with Mrs. Conroy. No matter what I tell her, she won't believe that her brother gets drunk and violent and starts beating up his wife."

The sheriff closed his eyes and yawned. "Judge was just explaining how he thought she was motivated by greed."

"Greed?" Dr. Jacobs quizzed. "What does she get out of this?"

The judge rolled his chair away from the desk and locked his hands behind his head. "She must figure if she can prove that Audrey did away with Milt, then Audrey goes to jail and the Adair estate is up for grabs."

"How's that?" the sheriff asked.

The judge could feel sweat from the back of his neck trickle through his fingers. "Milt is still Audrey's husband, so he certainly has some claim to what she has."

"But if Audrey's in jail, that means Milt's dead," the mayor said. "So if he's dead, how can the estate go to him?"

"It can't, of course. So it would go to the next of kin."

"But Audrey Adair doesn't have any next of kin," the sheriff said.

"Aha!" Dr. Jacobs waved his finger at the others. "That means it goes to Milt's next of kin."

The judge rocked his chair forward. "It has to go somewhere."

"That's a rather sinister motive," the mayor said. "Are you saying she hopes her brother has been murdered?"

The judge clamped the lid down on his bottle of black India ink. "I don't think she came to town with that on her mind, but she seems to adapt well."

The mayor leaned across the big oak desk. "Judge, just between us, do you think Audrey's telling the whole story?"

"I was wonderin' the same thing," the sheriff said. "No matter how much we like Audrey, it is strange to have two husbands disappear in the exact same manner."

The judge began to close up his law books, marking each page, and neatly stacking them in a pile. "The facts remain that the only crime we are certain of is that Milt beat Audrey."

Sheriff Hill strolled over to the window that looked out on Carson Street. "Did you hear what that Conroy woman is saying about that?"

The mayor, still sitting in the side chair, yanked up the leg of his trousers and tried tugging on his sagging stocking. "You mean, she's explaining it away?"

"She says Audrey ambushed Milt with an ax and—"

"An ax!" the doctor said with a gasp.

"Or somethin' like it. She claims Milt might have struck

back, trying to keep from getting killed. Or perhaps Audrey stumbled and fell. But, being a peaceable man, Milt wasn't used to such viciousness and was naturally overcome."

When the judge finished straightening his desk, he stood and ambled toward the coatrack. "Every crime has to have a motive. What kind of incentive is Mrs. Conroy touting for Audrey's behavior?"

The sheriff looped his thumbs in his suspenders. "She says Audrey's a vicious and possessive woman who, when she gets tired of a man, eliminates him faster than a black widow."

"Those are slanderous remarks," the judge warned. "She'd better be ready to prove them." He stared at his suit coat for a moment, then sighed and tugged it on.

Dr. Jacobs walked over to the judge. "So, should Audrey sue?"

"Probably not. It only publicizes the lies and makes them bigger than they are. Besides, one must prove evil intent, not just slanderous words."

All four men meandered toward the door. "How's Audrey taking all of this?" the mayor asked.

Judge Kingston set his hat lightly on his thinning grayish hair. "I don't know how much she's heard. She's leaving for San Francisco on Monday."

"That don't sit real easy with me," the sheriff said as he followed the judge through the door. "I wish she'd stick around long enough to get this cleared up."

Dr. Jacobs turned to the sheriff. "I don't suppose you could do anything to make her stay?"

"Not unless there's a crime being investigated and she's a suspect or a witness."

"What do you hear from your deputy, Tray?" the judge

asked as he locked the door behind them.

"He made it to San Bernardino but hasn't found anyone who knows of Milt Primble. I telegraphed him to come on back."

"Primble could have ridden south through Nevada instead of dropping down through California," the mayor suggested.

The sheriff tied a wet bandanna around his neck. "Even Primble wouldn't be that stupid. Once you get past Walker Lake there's nothing but one desert after another—Ralston Desert, then the Great Armagoza, then that worthless Vegas Valley. Plus, you've got to fight Diggers and Mojaves the whole way."

Dr. Jacobs carried his suit coat over his shoulder. "And I say he could have gone anywhere. If you had plans to run away, you wouldn't necessarily tell a woman you just beat to a pulp which way you were going. Undoubtedly, he had heard the countless stories of C.V. McKensie taking off to Mexico. Maybe he decided to cast doubt on Audrey's explanation by parroting C.V.'s story."

The judge nodded. "Now there's a provocative thought. The plots and plans of the devious mind ..."

The mayor's laugh was quick and short. "It's a slow summer day, boys, when we have nothing better to do than sweat buckets and speculate on uncommitted crimes."

Dr. Jacobs, who was shorter than the other three, scurried to keep up with the judge's long strides. "I don't want to spoil a good stroll, but does anyone know where we're going?"

The judge stopped under an awning. "I've been thinking some. It seems to me it's a right good day to hunt quail."

"To do what?" the mayor exclaimed.

The judge wiped his brow with a silk handkerchief. "I suggest we grab our shotguns, then take the good doctor's carriage up to Lake Tahoe and spend the rest of the afternoon hunting quail."

"There aren't many quail up at Tahoe," the sheriff objected. "If you want success at quail hunting, we ought to—"

"Who said anything about wanting success? If the hunting should prove marginal at Lake Tahoe, we could always take a dip in the lake before we return."

"Ah, that type of hunting trip," Doc Jacobs hooted. "Judge, that's the best idea you've had since you adjourned court for a week in the O'Riley ruling, on account of Farmer Treadway's annual Fourth of July picnic."

The judge tipped his hat. "Thank you. Now, gentlemen, I need to stop by the house and change into my 'hunting' clothes."

"Where shall we meet?" the mayor inquired.

"I need to stop by the depot when the Virginia and Truckee pulls in. I'm expecting a shipment of medicine," Doc Jacobs reported. "How about meeting there?"

The judge raised his eyebrows and nodded. "And don't forget your shotguns. This is a hunting trip."

There had been regular train service through Carson City since September of 1872. The massive engine house, freight house, and machine shops that lodged the various operations of the Virginia and Truckee Railroad in the middle of town had dominated the sights and sounds of the city ever since.

Judge Kingston left his home and hiked north on Nevada Street. In the distance he spied the Virginia and Truckee, chugging its noisy way into the station. He had purposely avoided Carson Street so he wouldn't have to explain his garb to curious citizens. It was only a close circle of friends who ever saw him so casually dressed.

He wore slightly faded tan canvas duckings, suspenders, a long-sleeved boiled cotton shirt, and an old brown tie. He draped his hunting jacket over his left shoulder and held his twelve bore, English-built, Winchester '79, double-barreled hammer shotgun in his right. On his head was a felt flop hat he had purchased from Abraham Curry on his first day in Nevada in 1863. Judith hated the hat, and he had to continually rescue it from her missionary barrel in the shed along the cobblestone alley.

Perhaps, someday, Judith and I will have sufficient funds to build a cabin at the lake. We could drive up on these hot summer days and fish or read ... or study court cases ... or do nothing at all. Now, there's a thought.

I can no more imagine her doing nothing than I can imagine me doing nothing. Lord, I do not believe we will ever retire ... until you call us Home. There's just too much to do.

But a cabin at Lake Tahoe would be a nice diversion.

I hope that's not too presumptuous.

I am content, Lord, with what you have provided.

Except, perhaps, for this heat. If you would like to provide the slight touch of a cool breeze tonight, I would deeply enjoy that.

The judge had turned east on Washington Street and just reached Ormsby's when he heard gunshots from the vicinity of the depot.

He slipped on his canvas hunting jacket and cracked open his shotgun as he trotted toward the sound. The gun was loaded by the time he crossed Carson Street. A crowd of women and children, all wearing hats, were fleeing the depot.

"What happened?" he shouted.

"There's a gang in there shootin' people left and right as they come off the train," someone yelled.

The Carson Street door was open to the depot as the judge approached. He stepped to one side to peer in just as a gun-wielding man ran out. The barrel of the judge's shotgun caught the man across the forehead, sounding like an ax handle slammed into a rock. The man crumpled in the doorway. The judge stooped down to retrieve the man's revolver. The barrel of the pistol was hot.

It's one of that Kendall gang. What in the world are they doing back in town?

A gun report rang out behind him and splinters shattered from the doorway. The judge spun around to face a man on horseback who was holding the reins of three horses. The judge raised his shotgun to his shoulder as the man recocked his pistol while trying to calm his prancing horse.

At that moment, both men were diverted by a carriage barreling toward the four horses. The three riderless animals jerked free and bolted down the street. The fourth horse bucked its rider off, then joined the others.

Dr. Jacobs slid the carriage to a halt and leaped down. He ran over to the fallen rider, who was crawling toward his gun, and crashed the butt of his Colt Breech-Loading, Hammer Model 1878 shotgun on the back of the man's head. The man fell motionless in the street.

Two more shots were fired from the other end of the depot. Then, all was quiet. Except for the sobs of women.

"Judge, is that you down there?"

"Yes, Sheriff ... and so is Dr. Jacobs," the judge shouted back.

"You got two of the Kendalls with you?"

"I believe so."

"Are they dead?"

"No, but they're out. How about you?"

"Me and the mayor have the others. Send the doc in. Somebody got shot in here."

Several men who had fled the depot when the shooting began now filtered back across the street. The judge left the unconscious Kendalls in their care and he and Dr. Jacobs cautiously entered the smoke-filled depot. They followed the sounds of the crying and met the sheriff and the mayor in the middle of the deserted waiting room.

"Who got shot?" the doctor quizzed.

"Must be out there on the platform," the judge called out.

At the sound of his voice, the sobbing ceased.

An icy chill slid down his sweaty neck as it dawned on him that one of the women's voices was extremely familiar.

Judith fastened the button of the high white lace collar on her yellow print cotton dress. She snatched the tea towel from the dresser and wiped her brow. Her curly bangs drooped with perspiration. She picked up a wide-brimmed straw hat circled with a pale blue ribbon and sprinkled with tiny yellow and blue flowers.

It's not even lunchtime and already the heat is unbearable. Lord, I believe hot days are my least favorite. Sweating is so … so messy … so unladylike. You don't have hot days in heaven, do you? That other place is the lake of fire, so heaven must have nice cool breezes.

Not too cool, of course.

Just a light drift like those across Lake Tahoe in the summer. Oh, wouldn't that be pleasant? The judge and I should drive up to the lake. We could take a picnic dinner and perhaps do a little fishing. Then we could pretend we were twenty-five ... and go swimming. I almost get goose bumps thinking of that chilly lake water surrounding me.

But, the judge swimming? I'm afraid nowadays that would be much too spontaneous for him.

Judith couldn't keep from grinning as she descended the stairs. "You were a young man once, Judge Kingston," she said out loud to the empty house. "Maybe no one else remembers you in a knit swimsuit, but I do. Oh my, how you took my breath away ..." *And you still do, you gray-haired old man.*

She walked through the kitchen, breathing in the scent of soda bread and New England baked beans, and plucked up a small notebook with lavender paper and printed pansies across the top. She tore off the top sheet and glanced at her notes.

Check on Audrey's house.

Beef chops.

Stop by bank.

Post office.

New potatoes?

Check the library for novel. (#6 in Arizona Border Ranger should be there by now.)

Visit with Duffy: Did he find anything else at the river?

Avoid Mrs. C.

She grinned at the last item on the list. *How does Hawthorne Miller put it in Border Ranger?*

She cleared her throat and spoke in a deep, gruff voice, "Eliza Conroy, this town ain't big enough for the both of us." *Then I'd whip out my single action Colt .44-40, with only five beans in the wheel, so I can safely keep it in my purse and plug her right between the eyes at fifty feet, just like Stuart Brannon.*

Judith Kingston, if the judge ever found out you read Hawthorne Miller's dime novels, he would have a heart attack! He has his own view of the real Stuart Brannon, not as exciting as Miller's version. But thank goodness, Stuart didn't marry that Englishwoman. Oh my, what a disaster that would have been. Now, the widowed señora ... well, perhaps ... as long as she moves to Arizona.

The knock at the front door snapped her back to the two-story home on the corner of Musser and Nevada Streets. She peeked through the lace-curtained window on the side door. Levi Boyer rocked on the heels of his well-worn boots.

She swung the door open. "Levi, what a delight! Did you come for a visit?"

"Yes, ma'am." Then he shook his head. "I mean, no, ma'am. I'm jist deliverin' a telegram. I was down at the depot and Ben said this one came in last night and he didn't have a chance to bring it by. So naturally I said I'd be happy to run it over."

"Thank you, Levi." Judith opened the envelope and tugged out the folded paper. "It's from Marthellen. She hopes to be home on Tuesday. That's today! How splendid. I have certainly missed her."

"I was hopin' it was good news. Sometimes it seems telegrams is only bad news."

"Levi, would you like to come in and have some lemonade? But I'm afraid I'm all out of ice."

"Thank you, Judith, but it looks like you're goin' some-where."

"What makes you say that?"

"You've got your hat on, and your purse is strapped to your arm."

Judith looked down and sputtered, "Yes, well, that does look definitive, doesn't it? I forgot. How about walking me to the library and telling me how you and Miss Marcy are carrying on?"

He followed her out to the sidewalk and strolled with her on the boardwalk, across the street from the Presbyterian Church. "Who said we was carryin' on? Has someone been spying on us down at the river in the evenin'?"

Aha! Marcy and Levi sparking down at the river. Maybe I have more to ask from Duffy Day. I'm just joking, Lord. It's none of my business. "Marcy is certainly doing a fine job with the children at the orphanage."

Levi nodded. "Did you know she wants to have a large family herself? Six or seven kids of her own, and maybe adopt some more."

"No, I didn't know that. I don't believe she ever discussed her future with me in quite such detail."

"Oh, me and her talk about things like that all the time. She surely is a wonderful girl. You know what, Judith? When I'm around Marcy I jist keep trippin' over myself tryin' to do the right thing. You know what I mean?"

"Yes, I do. And how does Miss Marcy feel about you?"

"This is the most amazin' part of all. She thinks I'm just swell. She told me so herself."

"Down at the river?"

"Yeah, and listen, don't tell no one, but as soon as I can buy me a decent racin' horse and win some big money, I'm thinkin' about asking her to … you know …"

"To marry you?"

Levi beamed. "Yeah. Is that foolish thinking?"

"Asking Marcy to marry you is not foolish at all," Judith

assured him. "But basing your future happiness on finding a fast horse is very foolish."

"It is?"

"Why, yes. Now here's what I think you should do. Sell your string of horses and work full-time for Mr. Benton at the livery. Everyone knows you're the best horseman in town. Then put your money down on one of those nice little homes over on Fifth Street. That's only a block from the livery and a few blocks from the orphanage. Then you could ask Miss Marcy to marry you."

"Do you really think she'd do it?"

"Levi, I can't tell what's in another person's heart. But how would you feel the rest of your life if you never asked her?"

"Miserable."

"Then you're going to have to ask her one way or another, aren't you?"

"I reckon you're right."

"So you should make sure you've done everything you can to help her say yes," Judith said.

"Like the full-time job at the livery, and the little house on Fifth Street?"

"Exactly."

"You might be right, Judith. Do I need to talk to her daddy?"

"Eventually."

"He probably won't like me."

"Why do you say that?"

"He's a lawyer. I don't think they like anyone."

"Nonsense, the judge is a lawyer, and he likes you."

"The judge is a lawyer? I thought he was just a judge."

"He's a lawyer, too."

"Well, don't that beat all? That bucks me up all over. Think maybe I'll mosey over to the livery and see if Mr. Bennett wants me to work full-time."

"That's a good start, Levi."

"I ain't as interested in a good start as I am in a good finish, if you catch my drift." He whistled as he trotted across Carson Street toward the capitol grounds and took a shortcut to Fifth Street.

Judith watched him disappear among the cottonwoods and poplars. *Now, there's an enthusiastic, focused young man.*

She resumed her hike. Buggies and horses whizzed by her. Small groups of men and a few women stood in front of the businesses, most of them fanning themselves with newspapers and hats.

Daisie Belle Emory met her at the door of the library. "Judith dear, you'll never guess what happened. The governor appointed me to head up the committee for celebrating Nevada's twenty years of statehood."

"Twenty years? Well, that gives you four years to plan."

"Oh, I know it's not much time at all. How I wish the captain could have seen statehood. You never met him, did you?"

"No, we didn't come out until '63."

"Well, I do want you and the judge to serve on the committee with me. We've got lots of planning to do. I was thinking of a giant stage over on that property between Eighth and Ninth Streets. I envision a fifty-foot-high vertical gold pan with a door at the bottom that opens up on a gigantic stage."

"Are you still going to have the orphans dress as little gold nuggets spilling out across the platform?" Judith asked.

"Oh, yes. Yes! Judith dear, we certainly are kindred spirits, aren't we?" Daisie Belle clutched Judith's arm with her gloved hand.

How does she wear gloves on a day like this? I've never seen this woman ever break into a sweat. Or look anything but assured, composed, and cool. "I'll check with the judge's schedule to see if he can serve. I just can't commit us without consulting with him first."

"Oh, certainly, dear. I do remember what it's like to be married to a strong, decisive man. Sometimes the judge reminds me so much of the captain."

I trust you don't make the comparison too often.

"Oh, there's Mr. Huffaker! I want to see if he knows where we can rent a buffalo for this year's Nevada Days. Would you excuse me, dear?"

Judith stepped aside as Daisie Belle exited the library. *Rent a buffalo? You can actually rent a buffalo? Well, if anyone could, Daisie Belle Emory could.*

Judith left the library with #6 of the Stuart Brannon, Arizona Border Ranger Series, *Slashknife Charley's Fatal Ride,* tucked deep in her handbag.

She had finished all the chores on her list except buying the beef chops when she detected Duffy Day slouched on the front steps of the U.S. Mint.

She stopped in the shade of the massive brown sandstone building. "Duffy, you look comfortable."

An easy smile broke across the slim man's face. "Howdy, Judith. When the shadows hit these steps, they cool down. It can be quite pleasant until they run me off. It's been more crowded lately, swarmin' with politicians. Don't do 'em no good, though. I'm votin' for Winfield Scott Hancock, even if Garfield seems a mighty nice fella."

Judith brushed off the step next to him, then set her package and purse down. "It's been quite hot today."

"Yes, ma'am. My bones stay cold all winter, so I kind of enjoy it. But don't you go tellin' anyone, 'cause they all get mad at me when I say I like the heat."

Judith patted his arm. "I won't tell a soul, Duffy."

"Thank you, Judith. I knowed I could count on your discretion. Did you know you're the only woman in Carson who will sit and visit with me?"

"I'm sure most are just in a hurry. You know how busy city people are."

"'Favor is deceitful, and beauty is vain; but a woman that feareth the Lord, she shall be praised.' Did you know that's in the Bible, Judith? My mama taught me that. My mama read us boys the Bible ever' day we was livin' at home."

"I'm sorry I never got to meet your mother, Duffy. She must have been a wonderful woman."

"Yep. The Lord needed her in heaven, so he jist picked her up one day and took her home."

"What happened?"

"A tornado hit our place. Me and my brother, Drake, were in the root cellar. Daddy was in town and missed the storm, but Mama went out to the barn to let the horses loose. That's when it hit. It jist lifted her up with the barn, the house, and ever'thing. Right straight into heaven."

"That's quite a dramatic story."

"That's exactly what Wild Bill Hickok said when I told him about it. Say, are you headin' home? I could carry that bundle for you, if you'd like."

Judith kept her purse but handed the package to him. "Thank you very much, Duffy. Actually, I'm goin' down to the depot to wait for Marthellen. She's comin' home today."

"She is? Does that mean she'll be cookin' biscuits and gravy in the morning? If so, I might have to come to town early tomorrow."

"Well, I'm not sure of the menu ... but with Marthellen home, you won't have to put up with my cooking, that's for sure."

"Oh no, Judith, I wasn't complainin'. Why, I think you jist might be one of the three ... or four ... or five ... or six best cooks in Carson."

"Thank you, Duffy." *I'm glad you couldn't remember any higher numbers. I have some pride.*

"Miss Marthellen is number one, of course," he added.

"I couldn't agree with you more, Duffy."

"See, I'm right about some things. Some folks say I ain't right about nothin'."

"Who says that?"

"That milling company that wants to take away me and Drake's property. They say I cain't remember right and it's not my property. And the judge even showed 'em the papers."

"Are they still pestering you?" Judith probed.

"They don't come out anymore, no, ma'am. But did I tell you they sent Wild Bill Hickok to shoot me?"

"Was that the night several weeks ago, or has he been back?"

"I don't reckon I remember when it was ... but he was with a woman."

Judith led them across Caroline Street. "Who do you suppose that woman was?"

"It was dark. I jist seen her silhouette, that's all."

"What did the silhouette look like?"

Duffy Day stooped down in the middle of the street and scratched at the dirt with a horseshoe nail from his pocket. "That's what she looked like."

"She had a rounded nose and a pointed chin?"

"Yep, that's her."

"Do you think you could identify the woman if you saw her again?"

"If there was moonlight behind her head and I saw her silhouette."

Judith glanced back at the face in the dirt as they continued their trek toward the depot. *Lord, if Duffy's at all right, that is definitely not Audrey Adair. And if the disappearing rider on the other horse was Milton Primble, then who was that woman? I'll have Duffy draw that outline on a piece of paper.* "Duffy, could you draw a picture of the man's silhouette, too?"

"Shoot, Judith, ever'body knows what Wild Bill Hickok looks like."

The Carson City depot of the Virginia and Truckee Railroad was only half-crowded as they entered. There was a mixture of those who wanted to board and those waiting for passengers to arrive. Mothers held tightly to their children's hands.

Judith peeked in and waved to almost everyone there, but she and Duffy stayed outside and sat on a slatted wooden bench that faced the tracks. Its paint had long since been worn off by the backsides of countless passengers.

"Here she comes, Judith. Ain't that a wondrous sight?"

"Yes it is, Duffy." Judith looked west, tilting her head so the brim of her straw hat would shade her eyes from the afternoon sun. A thick cloud of steam boiled up from the stack as the whistle blew on the train's approach to Carson Street. Children and adults clapped their hands against their ears.

"Sometimes I sit down here all day jist to wait and see the train go in and out," he reported. "Sometimes it goes ten runs up to Virginia City. You don't never know who's going to be on it." His eyes looked anxious.

"Are you worried about Wild Bill being on the train?"

Duffy grinned. "No, ma'am. Wild Bill was shot down like a dog in Deadwood. I was there, and I had his aces and eights beat with three queens."

Movement at the door to the depot behind her caught Judith's eye. A red-haired man with a revolver strapped on the outside of his thin denim coat blocked the doorway.

Didn't I see that man and others ride through town last week? She glanced down at the east end of the building. A tough-looking man leaned against the depot. A third man, with his gun in plain sight, was guarding the west side toward Carson Street. *Obviously, they're waiting for someone. But I can't tell if they're going to pat him on the back or shoot him. I think it might be expedient to greet Marthellen and scurry us both out of here.*

Brakes squeaked and steam boiled as the Virginia and Truckee rolled into the station. An elderly man and woman slowly descended the first car. Judith glanced over her shoulder. The gunmen were gone. *Where did they go? I'm beginning to be as suspicious as Duffy Day. Maybe they greeted their friend and left. Relax, dear Judith. This isn't a scene from Border Ranger.*

She surveyed the people exiting the other train cars and saw several familiar faces, but not Marthellen's.

She was still staring west when a male voice called to her. "Judith! Are you lookin' for me?"

She jerked around and saw a young man in wrinkled vest and new flat-crowned California hat strolling toward her. "Bence, I didn't know you were coming back. Where's Marthellen?"

A pretty young woman with flashing eyes and a straight

brown dress scooted out from behind him. "Hello, Judith."

"Willie Jane? My, this is a surprise! I thought you'd be in Traver by now with your sister."

"I sort of changed my mind. I wanted to come gather my things. We decided to move to Sacramento."

"We?" Judith said. *Somehow, I didn't remember Willie Jane had a rounded nose and a pointed chin. Oh my, this is getting complicated.*

Bence rubbed his beardless chin, then stared at his boots. "See, me and Mama bought tickets. I needed to return to discuss some, eh, legal matters with the judge. I was hopin' to move to Sacramento to be nearer Charlotte and her family. Right at the last minute, Char talked Mama into stayin' a few more days. That left us with an extra ticket, so ..."

"So Willie Jane came with you?"

He blushed. "It seemed like a more pleasant trip to have someone to travel with."

"This is a surprise. Let's head up to our house, Bence. You can stay in your mother's room again. Willie Jane, we have a guest room for you upstairs."

"That's all right, Judith, I'll go back to the—"

"You most certainly will not!" Judith asserted.

"Miss Marthellen ain't comin' home?" Duffy asked.

"Not for a few more days," Judith said.

"Well, I'll be. Think I'll cook my own breakfast in the mornin'. In fact, I ought to hurry back to the river. I'm expectin' my brother any time now."

Duffy scurried down the tracks to the east, like a cat sensing lightning before it strikes.

Judith motioned toward Carson Street. "We can head this way. I need to stop by the meat market on the way home. Bence, would you carry my bundle?"

He plucked up the package wrapped in thick brown paper and twine. "I want to step inside first to send a telegram."

"To Marthellen?"

"No, to Murphys."

"Where?"

"I'll explain later."

As Bence led Judith and Willie Jane through the door, two shots rang out. Bence Farnsworth staggered into the depot and collapsed in the doorway.

Screams.

Curses.

Shouts.

People rushing everywhere.

Then, more shots.

Willie Jane stood frozen, staring at the bleeding body of Bence Farnsworth.

"Grab his other arm ... pull him back out of there," Judith ordered.

The depot was filled with black powder gunsmoke as they dragged the wounded man to the railroad platform. When they rolled him over, Judith saw two chest punctures. Deep red blood flowed out. Her head started to swim and she dropped to her knees beside the man.

"Put your hand on that one," Willie Jane shouted.

Judith gasped. "What?"

"Do like I'm doing. Press down hard with your palm, right on top of that bullet hole. We have to stop the bleeding," Willie Jane pleaded.

Judith quickly did as she was told. She could feel Bence's warm blood seeping through her fingers. *I've got to keep from passing out. Lord Jesus, help us. Don't let him die. Jesus, oh precious Jesus ... deliver us from evil.* She glanced up and saw pure panic in Willie Jane's face.

"He's going to die, isn't he?" Willie Jane moaned.

"I'm asking the Lord to spare his life. What are you asking the Lord for?"

Willie Jane kept her hand planted firmly against Bence's wound. She began to sob. "Oh, Lord Jesus, forgive me of my sins. And Lord, forgive Bence of his sins, too. Oh, please, Lord Jesus. Don't let him die."

Men were still shouting inside the smoky depot.

Judith recognized her husband's voice. She took her free hand and held it against Willie Jane's mouth. Almost on cue, both of them sucked in air and stopped crying.

"Judge Kingston? Dr. Jacobs? You get over here ... and you get over here right now!" Judith screamed.

From out of the depths of the dark gray depot, strong men appeared. One wore old duckings and a flop hat. He hugged Judith's shoulders and covered her small hands with his large, calloused ones.

Dr. Jacobs called out orders to the other men, but to Judith's ears his voice seemed to be fading.

Willie Jane looked at her and pulled back from Bence to slip her arm around Judith's shoulders.

The smell of blood, sweat, woodsmoke, and steam seemed to dissipate as Judith looked down at the sticky blood on her hands and tried to wipe it off. However, she had no feeling in either hand.

Her mouth tasted so dry her tongue stuck to the top of her mouth.

She started to fall to the right and expected to feel her head crash to the railroad station platform. Instead, she felt Willie Jane's sturdy shoulder. Then all turned peaceful and black.

CHAPTER SIX

Judith stood in front of a full basket of laundry and pulled out wet bedding to hang on the rope clothesline in the backyard. She had taken off her white high-buttoned shoes and was enjoying the crisp, cool grass that massaged the bottoms of her aching feet.

Willie Jane burst out the door wearing a simple navy blue dress buttoned high at the rounded white collar. "Let me do that," she called out.

Judith lowered her arms and let the blood circulate. "Thanks, I appreciate the help. How's the patient?"

"Still unconscious, but Dr. Jacobs wants to change the bandages and I didn't think I could go through that again."

The dampness felt good against their bodies as Willie Jane and Judith folded and hung a large white cotton sheet. "I was the one who fainted yesterday," Judith replied.

"I was too stunned to faint." Willie Jane reached into the basket and pulled out a green and mauve embroidered pillowcase. "Everything happened so fast. I don't think it was two minutes from the time Bence was shot until the judge and Dr. Jacobs got to us, but it seemed like such a long time. It was as if half my life went by."

"It's not exactly the same as reading about it in a book," Judith noted.

Willie Jane paused, a half-dozen unpainted wooden clothespins in her hand. "To tell you the truth, I don't read very well."

"Willie Jane, that's something you can learn quick enough.

You just need to practice a little every day."

"I thought about reading one of those books in your drawer."

"What drawer?"

"Your petticoat drawer. Remember? You said for me to borrow a petticoat for this new dress, and I happened to notice at the bottom one of those dime novels, and I figured ..."

Judith cleared her throat, "That's just a library book. That wouldn't be a good place to start. I'd suggest you begin by reading in the Bible every day."

Willie Jane stared across the clothesline at the empty cobblestone alley and took a deep breath. "Judith, I need to ask you a personal question or two. Is this a good time?"

That all depends on the question, my dear. "I think so. I've been wanting to ask you a question or two myself."

"Really? What is that?"

"You go first," Judith prompted.

"Well, I was ponderin' this all night as I sat beside Bence's bed. Do you really think Jesus wants to forgive me for all I've done?"

Judith felt a tension in her spirit begin to relax. *A personal question about the character of a holy, merciful God? I can handle that.* "Of course. That's why he came to this earth, to save sinners."

"Yeah, but here's the problem." Willie Jane rubbed her rounded nose with the palm of her hand. "I wanted to do all those things. Nobody forced me into this kind of life. No one kidnapped me and carried me off. I had chances to get out from time to time and I just didn't want to. Not that I ever intended to keep it up forever. It didn't seem to be any more important than choosin' to do sewin' ... or to clean rooms in a hotel. I never really felt that bad about it. It's like my heart had no say in the matter. I think my heart must be completely dead."

"That's not true, Willie Jane. When you and I hovered over Bence down at the station and our hands were pressed down on his chest to keep him from bleeding to death, we both prayed. Do you remember?"

Willie Jane's voice was soft and barely audible. "Sort of."

"Do you remember what you prayed?"

"Not really ... I mean, I was so fearful I was out of my mind."

"Before you ever prayed for Bence to live, you prayed for the Lord to forgive you of your sins."

"I did?"

"I think you did that because your conscience is still at work and you didn't think you should be asking God for anything when you lived such an unrepentant life. I believe he sincerely forgave you when you called out yesterday."

"Is it like the Lord's giving me another chance?"

"That's one way to put it."

"That's what scares me most."

"Why is that?"

"Well, what if I really mess up again? For the past few days I've felt like a person hanging from a cliff by my fingertips. I'm all right now, but any minute I might fall right back into it all."

"Perhaps your image is only half right," Judith suggested.

"How's that?"

"Perhaps, indeed, you are dangling over that cliff. But what if it's not your fingers that are keeping you from falling? What if it's the hands of the Lord gripping yours?"

Willie Jane sucked in her breath. She was quiet for a moment.

Judith noticed a new softness in her features when Willie Jane said, "Then, he won't let go, will he?"

"Never."

"I like that."

"So do I. Did you have another personal question?" Judith asked.

"Yes, but it can wait. It's your turn."

Judith stumbled to find the appropriate words. "Willie Jane, when I came to see you at your ..."

"My crib. That's OK, Judith. I know who I am."

"Yes, at your crib ... you were quite despondent about Milton Primble jilting you. Did you tell me everything about that relationship?"

"I don't remember all I said that day. I was mad."

"As well as drunk ..."

"And on morphine. I know it. I was horrible. Anyway, I'm sure I didn't tell you everything."

"Audrey Adair is a good friend of mine, Willie Jane. Some people in town seem intent on accusing her of killing her husband. I know she couldn't have done it, but I'm not sure about all that happened that night. I thought perhaps you could fill me in on other details between you and Milton."

Willie Jane's eyes grew wide. "You want to know everything?"

Judith raised her hands in protest. "No ... no, I don't want to know those things. But I would like to know all you did that evening."

"What kinds of things are you talking about?"

"For instance, did you go for a horseback ride with a man

down at the Carson River after dark?"

Willie Jane sighed, a look of longing on her heart-shaped face. "No, but it sure sounds romantic. Did someone say they saw me at the river with a man?"

"Duffy Day saw a woman riding sidesaddle with a man that night and the profile was similar to yours."

Her eyes lit up. "Did you say sidesaddle?"

"Of course."

"Then, it wasn't me."

"You don't ride sidesaddle?" Judith asked.

"Never. I like to straddle the horse and feel all that power and strength beneath me."

"Oh!" Judith's eyes grew wide and she covered her mouth.

Willie Jane laughed. "Judith, one of the advantages of being a crib girl is I don't have to do things the way every other woman does. No one expects me to be decent and proper."

Just then, Dr. Jacobs banged out the back door. "I'm all through, ladies. He's still mighty feverish, so one of you should go cool down his forehead."

"I'll do it," Willie Jane offered.

"Yes ... we can talk more later," Judith countered.

Willie Jane nodded. "I'd like that." She scooted through the side door that led directly to Marthellen's room.

Judith dropped the empty wicker hamper on the back porch, then went to the kitchen to pour herself a cup of lukewarm water. The judge, wearing coat and hat, stepped into the doorway that separated the kitchen from the dining room.

"Will you be all right here?" he asked.

"Oh yes, don't worry about me."

"I always worry about you."

"Well, don't worry needlessly. Bence is in the Lord's hands

now. All we can do is wait. Did any of those men say why they shot him?"

"Not as of last night. Of course, they were all feeling poorly. Perhaps the sheriff has more information today. I'm guessing it has something to do with the holdup and murders over in Murphys."

"You think Bence was in on that?"

"I don't know. It's not a very pleasant thought."

"Will you be extraditing them?"

"Eventually. We have to wait and see whether the Nevada charges will be attempted murder ... or murder. I'll telegraph the authorities in California and let them know we have the Kendalls incarcerated."

"And I think we'd better telegraph Marthellen."

The judge sighed. "I hope I know how to put that down in a few words and still be truthful and sensitive. What a blow this will be for her."

"Did Dr. Jacobs tell you anything about Bence's condition?" Judith asked.

He walked over and laid his hands on her shoulders, then looked straight into her eyes.

"That bad?" she said.

The judge kept his steady grip. "Doc said most every time there are wounds like these, the patient dies. However, once in a great while they pull through. He can never predict which ones will survive. He said he'd give Bence about one chance in ten."

"It puts things back into perspective," Judith said. "Sometimes we get caught up in such a shallow existence. A week ago my biggest concern was how to avoid being in Daisie Belle Emory's Nevada Days pageant. Now this situation with Audrey

... then Bence ... and we have very needy people living in our home."

"And dying in our home," Judge added. "Are you saying you'd rather be bored, Mrs. Kingston?"

"No. But I'd prefer my adventures spread out and not involved with deaths and beatings."

"One day Nevada will be different from this," he said. "It will be known for its moral and decent people and the quality of life, not for the greed and lawlessness."

"I know ... I know ... that's why we're here, Judge Kingston ... to see that the transition from wilderness to civilization is built on a legal, moral, and spiritual base. But I wonder if you're talking about paradise—about heaven—not the real world."

"Well spoken."

"Thank you, Your Honor."

His arm circled her waist and he lifted her off the kitchen floor with one arm, pressing his lips against hers. "Don't you 'Your Honor' me, Judith," he said with a grin, then set her down.

Judith caught her breath. "Oh, my ... you mean, that's what will happen every time I call you, 'Your Honor'?"

"That's the chance you'll have to take. Seeing young Mr. Farnsworth in there struggling for his life reminded me how short life is for all of us."

"That's why you kissed me?"

"I didn't want to miss any opportunities."

"Well, I like it."

"But I don't want to spoil you. Would you like me to pick up the mail this morning?"

"Please do. I think I should stick close to home. Will you be back for lunch?"

"Yes, I'll plan to do that."

"And do you also plan on spoiling me some more, Your Honor?"

"Definitely."

Sheriff Hill paced the judge's outer office after he arrived at the court building. "What about Farnsworth? Is he still alive?" he asked.

The judge was solemn, his eyes red and tired. "For the time being. But he hasn't gained consciousness. What about the Kendalls?"

"They've got blue lumps. And if that redhead doesn't get his blood poisoned from birdshot, he'll be pickin' lead pellets from his skin for months."

"Did they reveal anything to you?"

Both the sheriff's ears twitched as he forced himself to stand still. "They claim that Farnsworth whipped out a pistol when he entered the building and they were defending themselves."

"That's hogwash. Farnsworth didn't have a gun."

"They claim someone must have stolen it off the floor in all the confusion. They said he was hiding it in a bundle he was carrying."

"A bundle? That was Judith's bundle. There was no gun. There wasn't anything in there but flour, rice, and a couple jars of tiny pickled corncobs."

"What?"

"You know, those little miniature ears ... Cheney's was having a sale on them."

"Yeah, I can see why." The sheriff shoved his round bowler hat back and paced the room again. "So that's the Kendalls' story. They're a mean bunch. I'd be happy to send them off to

California. They're cursin' and swearin' they're gonna kill me and you and the doc ... and the mayor."

"You ever have second thoughts about the kind of work you've gotten into?" the judge probed.

"Ever' day, I reckon."

"So do I, sometimes."

A knock on the door spun both men around. The sheriff's hand went down to his holstered revolver. "Those Kendalls can make a man jumpy," he mumbled.

"Come in," the judge called out.

A slight man, wearing a tailored dark wool suit and vest entered, carrying a brown leather attaché case. His bushy side-burns extended to his full mustache. "Are you the judge?"

"Yes, and this is Sheriff Hill."

"How remarkable ... the two men who can help me. I'm Garrison Grimshaw, an attorney for Consolidated Milling. We're interested in purchasing the property of Mr. Duffy Day, among others."

"I thought Duffy already turned you down," the judge said.

Mr. Grimshaw gave a quick nod. "Mr. Day rejected a bid by my predecessor." He raised the leather case. "However, I believe I have a much better proposal."

"What did you want of me?" the judge asked.

"I had an appointment with Mr. Day this morning in the lobby of the courthouse, and he hasn't shown up."

"Did you go out to his place? I'm sure you know where it is," the sheriff said.

"I had a man from the livery drive me out there to no avail. I wondered if either of you might know his whereabouts. I really can't go back to San Francisco until I've had a chance to make him our offer."

"I suppose Duffy doesn't want to talk to you," the judge mused.

"But he agreed to meet with us."

The judge tapped his fingers on his desk. "He must have changed his mind."

"But why? What is the harm in presenting the man an offer for greater compensation?"

"Maybe he thought you sounded too much like Wild Bill Hickok," the sheriff said, chuckling.

"I beg your pardon?"

The judge tugged his shirt cuffs down below his suit coat. "Mr. Grimshaw, if Duffy Day wants to meet with you, he will. If he doesn't, there's no wide way on earth to force him. But here's what I'll do for you; if I see him, I'll tell him to meet you on the steps of the U. S. Mint about a half hour after the sun starts going down."

"On the steps, you say?"

"If Duffy's in town, he's always there in the afternoon shade. That's all I can promise."

"I'm obliged to you. That gives me some direction. I really do have a generous offer to make him."

The judge walked Grimshaw to the door. "I'm sure you do, Counselor. But knowing Duffy, I doubt if he would trade that parcel for a gold mine. At least not until his brother returns."

"How long has his brother been gone?"

"Nine years."

"Oh, my. Where is he now?"

"No one knows."

"But he might never come back."

"Well, don't tell Duffy that."

"And don't mention Wild Bill Hickok, either," the sheriff said.

Garrison Grimshaw shuffled out of the office, clutching his case with both hands. The judge shut the heavy door behind him.

"Where do you suppose Duffy is?" the sheriff asked.

"Hiding out, I surmise."

"Think maybe I'll ride out to the river. I wouldn't put it past Consolidated to try to pressure Duffy."

"Sheriff, are you accusing Mr. Grimshaw of high-handedness?"

Sheriff Hill clasped his hands behind him. "Maybe Grimshaw is just a diversion to keep you and me out of the way. Do you want to ride out with me?"

"I'm sorry, I can't. I've got to be in court at 1:00 and, besides, I told Judith I'd be home for lunch."

Judge Kingston had just strolled out of the post office, empty-handed, when Franc Penrose, wearing his double extra large butcher's apron around his rotund belly, stepped out in front of his shop and signaled to him. "Judge, have you seen Duffy today?"

The judge shrugged. "Duffy seems to have taken the day off, Franc. Others are looking for him, too."

Mr. Penrose wiped his broad hands over his apron. "I know he's hard to count on, but he's never been late on sale day. I told him I'd buy a hog from him and I expected him to herd it to town around daybreak."

"The sheriff rode out that way to check on him. Duffy probably just forgot what day it was. He was down at the station yesterday afternoon when the shooting broke out and you know how he gets disoriented when there's gunfire."

Penrose leaned closer, reeking faintly of raw beef. "Say, I

heard you and the sheriff captured a gang of train robbers."

The judge narrowed his eyes. "We just happened to be there at the time. But I don't think the Kendalls had in mind to rob the train."

"Makes a man jumpy thinkin' there's types like that on the loose," Penrose said. "A person can't even feel safe standing at the station."

"I can assure you, the Kendalls are behind bars today."

"Yeah, but who knows what others are roamin' around?" Penrose patted his pocket. "I've been packin' my pistol all day, just in case."

The judge waved good-bye and had sauntered east on Musser a few paces when a woman's voice hailed him.

"Judge Kingston?"

He tipped his hat to the woman. "Mrs. Conroy?"

"I need to know the legal procedure for removing my brother's belongings from that woman's house," she demanded.

"Oh?"

"My brother certainly had personal possessions when they married, and gained more over the years. I believe I'm entitled to them. How do I proceed to file a claim and enter the house to remove such items?"

The judge tugged off his hat and held it in his hand. "Mrs. Conroy, the only legal way I know for you to retrieve anything that belongs to Milton is for him or Audrey to give it to you."

Eliza Conroy glared. The nostrils on her round nose flared with each word. "But she has done away with my brother. He can't give me anything."

The judge rubbed his chin whiskers as if pondering a verdict. "At the moment, all we know is that Milton willingly left, and he is still legally married to Audrey Adair. Until any condition can be proved otherwise, all personal property belongs to Milt and Audrey. Only they can give it away."

"But she's not even in town. She perpetrated a heinous crime, then ran off. What more proof of guilt do you want?"

"Mrs. Conroy, all of this has been explained before. We have to prove a crime has happened before we can issue a verdict."

"You mean, I get nothing at all until I find my poor dear brother's body?"

"I'm sorry, I have other pressing matters to tend to," the judge declared. "I'm afraid this conversation isn't accomplishing anything for either one of us."

She pressed the end of her fringed umbrella against the judge's chest. "I will not leave Carson City until I discover the truth about my brother."

He firmly pushed the umbrella to the side. "Perhaps, Mrs. Conroy, you have already discovered the truth about him and refuse to admit it."

Judith met the judge at their white picket gate and wiped off the glass balls on top of the posts. She studied the scrolls of terra cotta trim on the white house for signs of peeling and was relieved to see the exterior of the house was in good shape.

"Is Bence all right?" he asked.

"Still unconscious. Willie Jane is with him."

"Did you get to talk to her?"

"Not too much. But I do think she has more to reveal about Milton Primble. I'll try to visit with her this afternoon."

The judge hugged her. "You look tired, Judith."

"I'm not used to running a hospital and a boarding house all by myself."

"Perhaps we should hire some help until Marthellen returns.

I expect her in a day or two after she receives that telegram. Meanwhile, I pray Bence will hang on at least until his mother arrives." He held the front door open for her. Inside, he removed his hat and coat and noticed the scent of fresh lupines. "There wasn't any mail today," he said.

"Yes, there was."

"Oh? Did you go get it?"

"No. Levi Boyer was at the depot when I got a telegram. He brought it to the house and, well, sort of swung by and picked up our mail too."

"Judith, does this entire town wait on you hand and foot?"

"Of course not," she protested.

A knock at the door brought the judge to the front of the living room. "It looks like Mr. Cheney. What could he want?"

Judith stepped to the door behind him.

Mr. Cheney's thick gray hair was tousled after his walk. He looked like he had been running. "Howdy, Judge. Don't mean to bother you, but I was on my way home for lunch and thought I'd bring these to Judith." He handed her a small brown sack.

"Oh!" Judith rolled her eyes. "Thank you, Mr. Cheney."

The grocer retreated toward the front gate.

"What is it?" the judge called out to him.

"It's a couple more jars of those pickled baby corn ears. I heard Judith's got busted in the shooting and I have to keep my favorite customer happy."

The judge grinned and shook his head as he closed the door. "You see, even Queen Victoria doesn't get as much service as you do."

She smiled brightly. "I'm glad to see you're in a good mood."

"Why's that? Did the pump play out again?"

"No. We received a letter from your daughter today," she reported.

"My daughter? My word, what did Roberta do now to alienate her mother?"

"She's coming home."

"At Christmas?"

"No, she's coming home by the first of October."

"She can't do that!" The judge began to pace the living room. "That will be leaving in the middle of a term," he fumed. "We aren't paying college tuition so she can walk away from her studies. I simply forbid it."

"She didn't ask if she could come home, she merely announced it."

"Announced it?"

"And that's not all." Judith caught up with him and held his arm.

"Do I need to sit down for this?" he asked.

"I'm not sure. She said something wonderful happened and she could hardly wait until she got home to tell us the news."

"What? What wonderful news? Good heavens, Judith, she's not getting married, is she? I didn't even know she had a boyfriend."

Judith folded her hands together in front of her narrow waist. "Perhaps she's already married."

The judge unfastened his tie as his breathing grew more rapid. "This is preposterous. A smart, attractive young woman who grows up in a good Christian home knows better than to go off to the university and marry the first handsome man she sees."

Judith tilted her head and batted her eyes. "Oh, you mean, like I did?"

"That was different and you know it," he blustered.

"Roberta's the same age I was when I met you."

"Yes, but I was five years older."

"Perhaps she met an older man."

"Ludicrous … you were … you were much more mature than she is."

"I don't believe my parents thought I was."

"Surely she's not married. I can't imagine Roberta falling in love and being courted by a young man and never letting us know anything about it."

"I can imagine it," Judith demurred. "But we'll just have to wait and see."

The judge plopped down in a leather chair and rested his forehead in his hands. Judith slipped behind him and began to rub his neck. "Oh, the joys of adult children," she murmured.

"She's hardly an adult."

"She is too an adult. Besides, she's also very pretty and very smart."

"But not very wise."

"That, dear Judge, will take time. Let's just relax and wait for her arrival. Then we'll find out what this is all about."

"Relax? I haven't relaxed about that child since the day of her birth."

"I know that. And she knows that. And I don't think she mailed this letter to torment us."

He sat back in the chair and took a deep breath. "When, exactly, do we relinquish this burden of child rearing?"

"On our deathbeds, I believe."

The judge pulled her hand around to his face and kissed her fingers. "You said Levi brought you a telegram. Was it from Marthellen?"

"No. She might not wire back. I would imagine she'll just get on the first train out of Sacramento. This telegram was from Audrey."

"Don't tell me she's decided not to return?"

"She's coming back next week. But she wanted me to take care of some things at her house."

The judge refastened his top shirt button and retied his tie. "What kind of things?"

Judith scanned the page. "She sent me a list of items to box up. It looks like she wants to purge Milton out of her house before she returns."

"That's a strange coincidence. Mrs. Conroy met me on the way home and asked how she could retrieve Milton's belongings."

"What did you tell her?"

"To ask Milton. It's still his home, and Audrey is still his wife."

"Well, Audrey wants me to discard everything. Perhaps I should just store them in our shed until the air clears on this. If Audrey later wants to give them to Mrs. Conroy, that's all right with me."

"Did Audrey say anything about buying a place in San Francisco?"

"No, but I believe she must have found something. She wanted me to do some banking for her."

"How are you going to do that?"

"She has some funds in the safe in her bedroom that she wants deposited in the bank—$15,000 according to this telegram."

The judge whistled. "She keeps that kind of money around the house?"

"Apparently."

"Surely she didn't send you the combination to her safe containing fifteen thousand dollars in a telegram!"

Judith rested her hands on her hips. "Audrey gave me the combination to her safe last year. She wanted someone else to have it in case of such an emergency as this. She didn't think it proper to give it to Mrs. Coffee."

"You have the combination to Audrey Adair's personal safe? I didn't know that."

"Dear Judge, I don't tell you about every safe I have the combination for."

"What?" He tugged her toward him. "There are others?" She leaned over and kissed his forehead. "How I do love to tease you." *There is no way, dear Judge, I would ever mention how many ladies in this town have their own private safes. Yes, they're sweet, domestic, and clever ... very clever.*

"That's quite a sum," he said. "Would you feel safer if I helped you transport it to the bank?"

"No, you have your court date. Besides, no one on earth would believe that I carried such a thing on my person."

"Please, be careful," the judge pleaded, then looked toward the kitchen. "Would you have a bite to eat for a teased old judge? I hear the court calling my name."

"I just happen to have a pot roast and onions and potatoes in the oven."

"And pickled baby corn ears?"

"Aren't those the cutest things you ever saw?"

"Cuteness has never been an important factor in my dietary habits."

"Well, Mr. Cheney just got some in and I thought I'd encourage him and buy a jar. Of course, I had no intention of their getting smashed at the depot."

The judge followed her into the kitchen. "Have you seen Duffy today?" he asked.

"No, but I didn't expect to. He was rather perturbed at Marthellen's not returning. He told me he'd just stay at the river. I do believe he's tired of my cooking. As soon as he spotted Bence and Willie Jane, he took off."

"Before the shooting?"

"Yes, actually. That is a little strange, isn't it? Why do you ask?"

"A couple different people have been looking for him."

Judith opened the oven door, using thick brown pot holders. The room filled with the aroma of meat spices and vegetable juices. "You know Duffy. He wanders off for days at a time. Normally, no one misses him."

"If you see him before I do, tell him a corporation lawyer wants to meet him down at the Mint."

"To buy his place?"

"That's what they say."

"No wonder he's in hiding."

Judith pried open the back iron gate to the Adair mansion and quickly ran up the winding brick pathway. She unlocked the back door and closed it firmly behind her, then stepped softly through the highly polished mudroom and out the side kitchen doorway.

Audrey Adair's home always felt sadly empty to Judith.

There were no pictures of children.

No frayed furniture from a happy family life.

No chipped paint from an errant tossed toy.

No scratches in the hardwood from rainy day hopscotch.

Even when Audrey was there, each room seemed more like a museum than a home.

But dear Audrey seems to enjoy it, and that's important. However, she never seems content.

Lord, what am I saying? Can a person be happy but not be content?

Judith took down the wedding picture of Audrey and Milton, plucked up the crystal swan, and proceeded to the library. She sorted through the shelves for several volumes, then stole back into the kitchen.

It's amazing how they could be married for four years and yet Milton had no more than a basketful of belongings to call his own. It's as if he was never thought of as a permanent fixture. He was just another expensive piece of furnishing.

I'm glad Audrey had Mrs. Coffee box up his clothing. I don't think I'd be comfortable sorting through some other woman's husband's clothes.

With the large basket of goods in hand, Judith hiked up the stairs to the master bedroom. Although it wasn't her first time in the room, the enormous size of the French canopy bed always amazed her. The ten-foot-tall white wood pillars, each pillar the girth of one-foot tree trunks, supported the floral silk draped canopy. Huge pastel satin pillows blossomed so thickly on top of the bed that the white silk comforter could only be spotted as a backdrop. The bed was a giant square, eight feet wide and eight feet long.

There are many rooms in this town that are not as big as that bed. It's luxurious, but not very friendly. A husband and wife could sleep in the same bed and never touch each other. How horrid. How lonely.

Judith thought about the judge's long arm that usually draped across her shoulder every night. I married that man to get close to him, not lose him in the covers.

Lord, forgive me for judging Audrey. Each couple discovers their own habits, their own relationship. How arrogant of me to assume others must be like the judge and me.

But, poor Audrey. I don't think she and Milt were ever very happy.

Judith placed the basket of belongings on the large tapestry rug. She entered Audrey Adair's personal walk-in closet. A sky window provided good interior light, and a floor-to-ceiling mirror at the back made the closet seem enormous.

Each dress hung on wooden hangers, and each had a small velvet bag attached. Judith peeked inside one of the bags.

My goodness, Audrey, you have matching jewelry attached to each garment? So many of these I've never seen you wear. Looking at your closet is like shopping in Paris.

At least, I think this is what Paris fashions would be like.

I can't even remember what a shopping trip to New York is like.

Judith shoved the long dresses to the front of the clothes bar and bent down to the two-by-two-foot cast iron safe. The brass dial glistened in the refracted sunlight. She stooped to her knees and leaned forward, scrutinizing the markings on the dial. She reached into her dress pocket and tugged out a small piece of lavender colored paper with pansies at the top.

L - 24, R to second 12, L - 16 ... then tug the handle with two sharp yanks down on the handle and ... voilá!

"The top box will have documents," she mumbled. *Deeds, mining stock ... a pressed poppy? Audrey, how romantic. Her Last Will and Testament ... then ...*

Judith glanced at the date on the will.

August 15, 1880? She made a new will just a few days before Milton beat her and fled? Did she know something was going to happen? Did Milt know about this? If he did, did he get upset when he read it?

Judith chewed on her lower lip.

She didn't say "Don't look at my will." Of course, it's none of my business. But … well, perhaps it will help explain things and clear Audrey of … but then that would be her decision, so I shouldn't.

Judith slowly unfolded the stiff paper of the legal document. The handwriting was definitely Audrey's. The lettering was text-book penmanship, but slanted to the right. She perused each line, most of which was standard legal jargon. The next to last paragraph stated that in the event of Audrey's death her assets should be divided equally among The First Presbyterian Church of Carson City, Nevada; The Nevada State Orphans' Asylum; and Miss Hannah Clapp's Sierra Academy.

It was the final paragraph that riveted Judith's attention.

> To Mr. Milton Primble, his descents and assigns, I bequeath the sum of one dollar ($1). Under no circumstance will he receive more than the specified amount. If he protests this will, he must forfeit even the above amount.

Judith read the page several times. *I'm not sure all of this is legal, but Audrey certainly thinks so. And if she wrote him out of her will, she certainly assumed he'd be alive.*

She must have known that Milton was leaving. I must talk to Audrey. She has to stay in town long enough to clear this up.

"It doesn't surprise me to see you are a common thief," a voice boomed behind her.

Judith dropped the will into the top drawer of the safe and spun around, still crouched on her knees. Eliza Conroy loomed in the middle of the master bedroom, pointing a very small ivory handled pistol at her.

"What are you doing here?" Judith demanded.

"My, isn't that a strange thing for a thief to ask?"

"I have not stolen anything."

"You have a basket full of valuable possessions right here in the bedroom and you are rifling the safe."

Judith stood awkwardly to her feet. "I am not rifling the safe. I am a friend of Audrey's, and she instructed me to transact some business for her. She has given me the authority to do so."

"Your audacity is exceeded only by your deceit, Mrs. Kingston."

"Mrs. Conroy, you are holding a gun on me. I presume you think that means you have the freedom to call my character into question. I am here under instruction of Audrey Adair and can prove that, if you'd care to summon the sheriff. However, you obviously would not do that because you can't explain what you are doing in Audrey's house with a revolver in your hand."

"I found the back door open."

"You knew Audrey was out of town."

"Yes, and I thought perhaps my brother had, indeed, returned home."

"I didn't hear you call out his name."

"Whether I called out my brother's name or not is not the point. Step aside; I want to see what possessions of my brother's you are pilfering."

"Everything that belongs to your brother is in that basket. Audrey asked that they be removed."

"I don't see any men's clothing."

"She told me those were removed before she went to San Francisco. She will be home in a few days and you may ask her about such items. Now, if you will please leave this house, I have work to finish."

"You mean, you have items to purloin?"

"Mrs. Conroy, if you don't call the sheriff, I will."

"I will not be bluffed, Mrs. Kingston. I am not leaving this house until I see what is in that safe."

"It's none of your business."

"It's my brother's business, and he's not here to oversee his affairs."

"I'm afraid his affairs were the cause of the problem."

"Move aside," Mrs. Conroy demanded. "Do not underestimate the resolve of a woman from the south side of St. Louis."

"Don't you mean Pennsylvania?" Judith corrected.

"I know what I mean. I will fire this gun."

Eliza marched straight at her. Judith scooted back deeper into the closet. *If she finds the will, she'll tear it up ... I've got to scream for help or get that gun ... or distract her with something.*

"What were you looking for when I came in?"

"I ... I had just opened the safe," Judith blurted out. "I was supposed to transfer some funds to Audrey's bank account."

The gun was still pointed toward Judith as Eliza Conroy glanced down at the contents of the safe. "I don't see any money."

"I suppose it's under the drawer of papers."

Eliza Conroy transferred the small revolver to her right hand, then squatted and lifted the metal drawer out of the safe. "I'll just make sure it's all still here."

Judith leaped forward and grabbed the barrel of the revolver, twisting it straight up.

Eliza staggered back, releasing the gun. Her face was contorted with anger. "What have you done with that fifteen thousand dollars?" she snarled.

Judith glanced back down at the empty safe as Eliza Conroy rushed out of the room.

CHAPTER SEVEN

I knew I should have gone with you," the judge said with a groan. He shoved open the stiff canvas curtains on his office window. A small boy with a stick was rolling a hoop in the dirt of Carson Street.

Judith slumped back in the leather chair, her eyes shut tight. "What difference would that make? The money would still be gone."

He turned around and tried to keep his voice calm. "It's always better to have two witnesses."

Judith opened her eyes and stared at the twelve-foot ceiling. Hanging all around the room above the bookshelves were pictures of government officials and friends, and a large oil painting of Abraham Lincoln. She made a mental note to have Marthellen come down to the office and dust the cobwebs. "There were two of us. But I can't figure out how Eliza Conroy knew there was fifteen thousand dollars in that safe. It doesn't make sense. Audrey said she had not even given the combination to anyone but me."

The judge tapped his fingers on top of the oak desk. "Which, in some minds, my dear sweet wife, will make you the chief suspect for rifling the funds."

"That thought has occurred to me, too. I do believe Mrs. Conroy is the type to noise it around that I took the money." Judith fussed with repinning her hair on top of her head. "There are risks in having the combination to someone else's safe."

"Quite so. But what are the possible explanations?" The judge began pacing the room. "Either you took the money, which is absurd, or Audrey forgot where she keeps the money. But who forgets about fifteen thousand dollars? Or maybe Audrey is deliberately trying to imply your guilt."

Judith sat straight up. "I don't believe that."

"Or someone else has gotten hold of the combination. What, for instance, if Milton snooped around and found it somewhere without her knowledge? Normally, you write down a combination somewhere just in case your memory fails."

"That's exactly why she wanted me to have it … so it wouldn't be lying around."

"Well, I've eliminated you as the culprit."

"Thank you, Judge. I trust others will be so kind."

"And for now, let's say Audrey isn't setting you up. That means she was wrong about where the money is, or someone has broken into the safe." He leaned his arms on the back of her chair. "I think you need to telegraph her before she gets home."

Judith leaned back against his hands. "But what if she's on her way? I don't want others reading such a note."

He walked around the chair and cradled her chin. "You have to tell her."

"But I want to do that face-to-face," Judith insisted. "Besides, that gives me a day or two to look around for the money."

He stood straight and stretched his back. "Look around where?"

"I want to do a thorough search of her house," Judith said.

"You think the money's lying around under a chair cushion?"

"Not necessarily, but who knows? Maybe I'll stumble onto some other clue about what's going on."

"In the meantime, we'll have to endure Eliza Conroy's innuendos," the judge said.

"I suppose."

"There's another concern. If Mrs. Conroy spreads the news that Audrey has piles of cash in her house, every drifter and bum in Eagle, Carson, and Washoe Valley will be trying to bust in."

Judith slumped her shoulders. "What are we going to do?"

The judge pulled a chair up beside her and sat down. "I'll stay over there tonight, just to make sure there are no visitors."

"You most certainly will not. There's only one place you will spend this night, Judge Kingston, and you know where that is."

The judge tried to look too concerned to blush, but it didn't work. "OK, then I'll ask around and see what Mrs. Conroy is telling people. Perhaps we're wrong about her. But even so, I'd feel much better if we'd hire a night guard for Audrey's house."

Judith yawned and stretched her arms. "How about hiring Levi Boyer? He's trying to earn extra money."

"To buy another racehorse?"

"It's much more important than that. I told you about him and Marcy Ciprio, the one who works at the orphanage."

"You did?"

"Never mind. You check on Mrs. Conroy. I'm going home."

The judge got up and helped her out of the chair. "On your way out I want you to dictate to Mr. Gabbs the entire sequence of events at Audrey's. If we ever need a deposition, it will be on file at an early date."

"This is getting complicated, isn't it?"

"I'm sure there is a logical reason for all that's happening."

"A reason, yes. A logical one? That remains to be seen." She waved from the doorway. "I'd better hurry so I can give Willie Jane a break. She hasn't left Bence's side all day."

A hot west wind blew down off the Carson Range and filled the city with a fog of dust as the judge finally left the courthouse. Even though the temperature hovered above eighty, he turned the collar up on his suit coat and tugged his hat down tight as he walked out into Carson Street. He could hardly see the capitol building right across the road.

The blowing dirt stung his face and hands and settled on his neck and ears. Dirt hung heavy even inside the Virginia and Truckee station, but at least it wasn't blowing there.

He took a blank telegraph form and printed the words.

Dear Roberta,
    Under no circumstances leave the university early. Finish your term. We'll discuss it at Christmas. Write to us about your good news. Mother is worried sick.

Sincerely, your father, H.A. Kingston

He hiked back out into the growing gale and down to Bennett's Livery. Levi Boyer lolled inside the barn on a sack of oats beside bales of hay. He was staring intently out at the dust storm. "Ain't that a mess, Judge? Could be a real Washoe Zephyr before it's done."

"It's been a dry summer. I suppose we should expect some days like this." The judge stomped his boots and shook his coat. "Say, I've got a job for you to consider."

Levi rubbed his eyes red. "I already got me a job right here."

"This is a temporary job. I'll pay you five dollars a night to house-sit over at Audrey Adair's. Just sleep on her porch for several nights and see to it that no one disturbs anything until she gets back."

Levi pulled out some hay and chewed on it. "You expectin' more trouble? I already heard Judith and that Conroy woman had a run-in."

"What exactly did you hear?"

"Well, Franc and Ruth Penrose came in about an hour ago, wanting a drive down to Genoa. They told me Milton Primble's sister was ranting down at Meyer's Hardware that she caught Judith stealing money out of Mrs. Adair's safe, and that Judith threatened her with a gun."

The judge felt an inner heat that had nothing to do with the zephyr blowing outside. He had to force himself to keep from shouting. "That's ludicrous!"

"Franc Penrose claims they laughed the lady right out of the butcher shop. What I can't figure is, what was that Conroy woman doing in Audrey's house anyway?"

"She said she was trying to find her brother."

"I thought Primble ran off."

"That's what we all assume."

"Well, that Conroy woman's got a lot of explainin' to do, then. She could get herself tarred and feathered for sayin' things like that about Judith. Around this town that's as serious as insultin' the Mother Mary. No blasphemy intended."

"I appreciate your support, Levi. But the truth is, some unscrupulous type might determine that Audrey's house is filled with sacks of gold. I'd like a couple men to watch over it at night."

"You got someone else in mind?"

"I was going to ask the sheriff for the loan of one of his deputies. Has he come back to town yet?"

Levi peered outside. "He ain't brought his horse in, if that's what you mean. Seems like he's been gone a long time for jist a jaunt out to the river."

"I was thinking the same. Perhaps I'll take a ride out there. You want to saddle me a horse?"

Levi jumped off the bag of oats. "You didn't pick a very purdy day for a ride."

The judge slapped his clothes. "I don't believe I could get any dirtier than I am now."

"I know what you mean. Do you mind if I ride along with you? I'm gettin' tired of being cooped up with nothin' to do. Not many calls for horses or rigs on a day like this. I can't even work them green-broke ones."

The judge rode a long-legged buckskin and Levi Boyer saddled up a wide-rumped gray gelding. They trotted along Fifth Street just out of town. "This wind will be the devil when we have to turn around and ride into it coming back," Levi shouted.

"Are you looking for an excuse to stop and rest at the orphanage?" the judge chided.

"I considered it," Levi hollered from under the red bandanna that kept dust out of his mouth. "But it's about suppertime. Ain't a good time for a social visit."

Just past the state prison the wind stiffened and swirled from the north and the west. The judge squinted his eyes almost closed. He opened them a tad to watch the shadow of a rider approaching. "Is that the sheriff?" he shouted.

"It's the sheriff's horse," Levi hollered back. "Can't rightly tell who's under that dirt pile."

The rider turned his horse around so his back bore the brunt of the storm. As the judge and Levi drew closer they heard above the roar of the wind, "You two lookin' for me?"

The judge pulled alongside. "I was worried you fell in the river and drowned, Sheriff."

"Can't drown in the Carson this time of the year, unless you're stone drunk and face-down," he retorted.

"Did you find Duffy?" the judge asked.

"Nope, but I spent an hour trying to chase down one of his hogs. It was wanderin' around lost out by the fork in the road. It kept to the brush and snookered me south for a couple of miles before I could herd it back to Duffy's."

"Duffy takes better care of those hogs than that!" Levi exclaimed.

"Yep, I agree with you there," the sheriff said, his voice raspy. "Duffy must be on a trip somewhere."

"Did you see any signs of Consolidated Milling?" the judge quizzed.

The sheriff cleared his throat, then spat far out over his horse's ears. "Didn't see a thing but pig prints."

"That might have been the hog he was supposed to sell to Penrose this morning," the judge hollered as the roar got worse.

"Could be. All of Duffy's hogs look the same to me: big, fat, and dirty."

The judge pulled his wide-brimmed hat even lower. "You didn't find any sign of him?"

"Nope. With the zephyr there won't be any sign left now. But I did find something about two miles south of Duffy's." The sheriff unrolled a brown wool suit coat from his saddle bag.

The judge surveyed the garment with squinting, dust-filled eyes. "Doesn't look like something Duffy would wear."

"Take a look at the inside pocket," the sheriff hollered.

"M.P.? Nice of Milton to label everything and then toss his stuff along the trail."

"That's near where Judith, Marcy, Jesse, and me spent the

afternoon lookin' for traces of Primble," Levi called out.

The judge raised dusty eyebrows. "When was that?"

"Last week," Levi announced, "right after Mrs. Adair got all beat up."

"It looks like Primble left town this way," the sheriff shouted.

"Or someone wants us to think he came this way," the judge hollered back. His mouth and throat were feeling sore and gritty. "I can't imagine tossing your coat to the ground on purpose."

"It's strange, all right." The sheriff's horse bolted forward. He backed it up to the others. "I do appreciate your coming out, but I could have made it back on my own."

"That isn't the only reason I needed to talk to you," the judge yelled.

"Them Kendalls didn't bust out, did they?"

"Not that I know of. Let's bite the bullet and face this dust storm. I'll fill you in back at the livery."

Judith stood at the kitchen sink and watched the dust swirl down Nevada Street. The tea in her cup was hot but tasteless. The air in the room smelled like dead flowers. Her shoulders were slumped forward, her smile sagged. Her eyes, drawn tight at the corners, were half-closed.

Judith Kingston, pilfering a safe and stealing money from her friend? Lord, I can't deal with this. I've struggled my whole life to do everything right, open, honest. I've never been perfect, Lord. You know that. The judge knows that. But I've worked so hard to demonstrate honesty and integrity, and now this crazy lady from St. Louis ... Pennsylvania ... wherever, charges into my life and casts doubt about me all over town.

I don't think I can handle this.

Maybe it's time to move back to Kentucky. We've been here seventeen years. That's long enough. Sure, pack up and leave. Then they'll really think you're fleeing a crime. I can't leave; I'll just spend the rest of my life indoors. "Poor Judith," they'll say, "she hasn't been out of her house in years."

She opened her eyes wide. *St. Louis? Why did Mrs. Conroy say she was from the south side of St. Louis? Milton's sister is from Pennsylvania. From Martinsburg, Pennsylvania. Audrey told me that much. She showed me on a map, last week.*

"Are you moping or meditating?" Willie Jane asked as she entered the kitchen carrying an empty teacup.

"Both, I suppose."

"Well, if you're worried about what that woman will say about you around town, you can't let it depress you. I should know. I've been talked about in every town I ever worked in. I decided years ago I wouldn't believe any of 'em. I am who I say I am, not who they say I am."

Willie Jane scooted her cup on the wooden counter. "'Course, there is a difference. What they said about me was usually true. No one in this town is going to believe you stole any money."

"But if I can't find out what happened to it, there will always be doubts." Judith leaned against the counter. "How's Bence?"

Willie Jane shrugged. "About the same. Ever since I thought he awakened, he just stares at the ceiling and doesn't say anything. He don't even follow the candlelight when I wave it in front of him. Dr. Jacobs says that's what should happen next. It's kind of spooky lookin' at a man starin' up like that. I think he went back to sleep, or at least shut his eyes. Do you think he can hear anything?"

"I'm not sure. I guess we should assume he does," Judith said.

"I brought the clothes in when this wind picked up."

"I noticed, and I appreciate that greatly."

"About Bence," Willie Jane began. "Me and him talked a long time on the train to Sacramento. We saw each other every day we was there. Then we talked all the way back to Carson City."

"You must have discussed a great number of subjects."

"We did. I never talked that much with a man before."

"Provided Bence pulls through, is this a serious relationship for you?" Judith quizzed.

"Serious?" Willie Jane laughed. "We ain't even kissed or nothin'."

"But does it seem to you like it could lead to something serious?"

"That's what I wanted to ask you, Judith. I'm a little confused."

"About Bence's feelings for you? Or your feelings toward him?"

"Both. Bence and me hit it off right away. Most times I don't have long conversations with men, if you follow my tracks."

"I understand."

"It was nice and friendly-like the whole time we was in Sacramento. So on our way back to Carson, Bence said it would be agreeable to have someone like me to visit with all the time. Night and day, he wanted someone there with him."

"And what did you say?

"I told him I never had someone like that and it sounded good to me. Then Bence said, 'Do you reckon we ought to just up and marry after I clear up this matter in California?'"

"What matter in California?"

"I'm not sure. He didn't explain."

"What did you tell him about getting married?"

"I told him I'd surely ponder the matter."

"Then what did Bence say?"

Willie Jane picked at her fingernails. "He said I'd have to quit workin' the cribs."

"You told him about that?"

"I told you we talked and talked. I told him almost everything there was to tell."

Judith turned away toward the sink and scrubbed on a pot. "How do you feel about quitting?"

"I could quit easy enough. I don't have the heart for it anymore. So I told him I'd give it up if he gave up drinkin' and fightin'."

"Was he drinking and fighting when you were in Sacramento?"

"No, but he was honest with me. He told me some history. Did you know he was in jail in Fresno City for eighteen months?"

"No, I didn't," Judith admitted.

"He's not proud of it."

"I imagine not. So, what was your conclusion? What did you two decide?"

"We hadn't decided anything. He said he had some things to talk over with the judge … and I wanted to talk to you. Then we stepped off the train and he got shot."

Judith wiped her hands with a cotton dish towel. "Willie Jane, what's it like for you now, all these hours tending to his wounds and needs? What do you think when you see him like that? What kind of feelings does he stir in you?" she challenged.

"Well, if he pulls out of it and still wants to get married, I suppose we will."

Judith wound and unwound the towel around her arm. "You don't sound exactly convinced."

Willie Jane's eyes had a pleading look. "That's why I wanted to talk to you. I never in my life had to worry about taking care of a man or being tied down by marriage. Bein' in the cribs is good that way. You just have some fun, make him feel good, and try to keep yourself from gettin' hurt. But you don't have to worry about nothin' else."

"What exactly are your worries now, Willie Jane?"

"I like to talk with Bence. I like being with him. I think we could surely make good friends. But I don't know if I love him." Willie Jane's eyes began to tear up. "I don't even know what love is. I've had hundreds of men tell me they love me, but I never believed a one of them. What do you think I ought to do?"

"Pray for him," Judith suggested.

"Pray for him to change?"

"Pray for him to live."

"I've been doin' that."

Judith wiped dust from the washboard and cupboards with the towel. "It seems to me you and Bence certainly have the makings of a good friendship. That's a good base for any marriage. Keep the friendship strong, then allow the Lord to lead you into something more."

"You saying we shouldn't get married?"

"My advice would be to postpone that commitment for awhile. Each of you needs some time to redirect things in your life."

"I know you're right. But if Bence pulls out of this and asks me to marry him right away ... well, I know I'll say yes."

Judith clutched the towel with both hands, squeezing it tight. "Why's that?"

"'Cause I might not get a better offer."

"But you're still young and attractive."

Willie Jane's pointed chin rested on her chest. "Judith, my youngness was used up years ago."

The man who appeared at Judith's side door looked vaguely familiar. He had the height, build, and exact posture of the judge. But the layer of dirt that covered every square inch of him was totally uncharacteristic.

"Go around to the back door, mister. That's where I feed transients," she ordered.

The judge wiped a clean circle around his eyes. "Have you ever seen anything like this?"

"Not on the Honorable Judge Hollis A. Kingston."

"It's a bit dusty out there."

"Willie Jane and I stuffed wet towels on all the doors and windows, but it blew in anyway. We've been coughing and hacking all day. It would be a tad more tolerable if it were cooler."

"Humans were not made to exist in this kind of weather," the judge announced in such a way that Judith could hear the gavel come down. "But it will probably die down at sunset," he added.

"There's a sun out there?"

"Somewhere behind that soaring grimy brown cloud."

"Shall I heat you a hot bath?" she asked.

"Don't you dare! I want that water as cold as possible."

"I was hoping you'd say that. I really didn't want to build a fire in the stove. I'm thinking of serving a cold supper."

"Is Willie Jane with Bence?"

"Yes. She hardly leaves his side."

"Has he spoken yet?"

"No, he doesn't seem to recognize anything or anyone."

"Well, I have a suggestion. You and Willie Jane go out to supper at the St. Charles. Let them heat their kitchen."

"Go out in that awful zephyr?"

"You wait. In a half hour the dust drift will be all the way out to Ragtown and it will be settled down quiet in Carson. I'll sit with Bence while you're gone."

"But when will you eat?"

"After you get home. Thought I'd take a late supper over to Tray and Levi at Audrey's house."

"So what did you find out? Is that woman making a big stink about me?"

"She is quite loquacious."

"Is she saying she caught me stealing Audrey's money?"

"And that you chased her off with a gun."

"It was her gun."

"She's not mentioning that part."

"What are people saying?"

"They laugh and chase her off. They seem to be insulted that anyone would cast a disparaging word on their queen."

"Queen? I think that's an exaggeration, Judge."

"I don't know, Judith dear. Levi compared you to the Madonna."

"That's absurd. We have nothing in common."

"I don't know … you both married older men." He slapped a dusty hand against the bustle of her dress.

She scooted out of the way. "You get that dirt washed off you, right now, mister. Don't you take liberties with me. How do I even know you really are Judge Hollis A. Kingston?"

At 6:31 P.M., the sun touched the top of the Carson Range. At 6:34 P.M., the wind stopped completely and the temperature dropped below eighty degrees.

Judith and Willie Jane left the Kingston home and strolled east on Musser Street.

"It feels so funny to be going out to supper at this time of night," Willie Jane remarked.

"Does it seem late to you?" Judith asked.

"No, I always eat late. But this is usually the time I start to work."

"Used to start to work," Judith corrected.

"Yeah. I hope so."

"You sound discouraged."

"It's a tough habit to break."

"Well, you have to break it tonight. You're with me, and I simply don't approve," Judith asserted.

"Yes, Mother," Willie Jane said, starting to laugh.

"What's so funny?"

"How old is your boy?"

"David's twenty-eight."

"See, you are old enough to be my mama. It's the first time I ever thought about it. I don't mean this as an insult, but you just sort of seem ageless."

"Like a precious antique?"

Willie Jane laughed. "No, no. See, I knew I'd say it wrong. But to most folks in this town you and him are Judith and the judge. Those are important roles. Age just doesn't matter."

Judith turned north on Carson. "Well, I can feel age in my bones."

"The St. Charles Hotel is south," Willie Jane said. "Where are we going?"

"To the depot. I need to send a telegram."

While Curtis, the bald operator with garters on the sleeves of his white shirt, waited impatiently, Judith filled out two telegrams.

Dear Postmaster, Martinsburg, Pennsylvania:

I am trying to locate Mrs. Eliza Conroy of Martinsburg with news concerning her brother, Milton Primble. If she can send me her address by telegraph I will pay the charges and mail a letter to her with details.

Yours sincerely,
Judith K. Kingston,
Carson City, Nevada

Willie Jane leaned over her shoulder. "How can she get a telegram if she's out here in Carson?"

"I'd like for the people in Martinsburg to tell me that."

"You mean, this lady might not be Milt's sister?"

"The thought has occurred to me. Did he ever mention to you anything about having a sister?"

"Yes, he did. He even showed me a photograph one night, which was sort of funny because we never did talk all that much and one night there was this big discussion about his sister."

"And did the picture look like Mrs. Conroy?"

"Oh, yes, that's her."

"I'm going to send this anyway."

"What's the other telegraph for?"

"I need to wire Roberta."

"Your daughter?"

"Yes. A letter might be too slow."

Judith leaned over the counter and printed each word with large block letters.

Dearest Roberta,

Darling, under no circumstances must you leave the university early. Please finish your term. Father is absolutely beside himself. We can discuss it all at Christmas. Write to us about your good news. I'm dying with curiosity.

Lovingly, Mother

"What's her good news?" Willie Jane pressed.

"That's what the judge and I would like to know."

"Maybe she's getting married."

"Don't even hint that idea around the judge. In his mind Roberta's still twelve and there is no man on the face of this globe good enough for his little girl."

"Wow! How does she get along with her dad?"

"Roberta thinks the judge can walk on water."

They waited at the corner of Telegraph and Carson for several riders to pass. One dusty man, wearing leather leggings and a leather vest, trotted up to them in the twilight shadows. "Willie Jane? What are you doing way down here? I came to town jist to see you!"

Judith stepped between Willie Jane and the man on horseback. "Young man, are you making insulting remarks to this lady?"

"Who are you?"

The buckaroo shoved his hat back as his friend rode up next to him. The man on the black horse tipped his hat. "Judith? I didn't see you over here. We just pushed a herd down from Oregon to the stockyards."

"Welcome back, Benjamin."

"Rowly, what are you doin' hasslin' Judith?"

"I was talkin' with Willie Jane," Rowly pouted.

"Boys, Willie Jane is staying with me for a while. I'll expect you to treat her just like she was my daughter."

Rowly groaned.

"Is that understood?"

"Yes, ma'am." Benjamin tipped his hat as he rode away, "Evenin', Judith."

The two ladies continued their stroll after the men galloped south.

"You sent them scurrying," Willie Jane declared.

"Yes, there's two down, four hundred to go."

"How do you get men to do whatever you tell them to?"

"I smile a lot and I never, ever back down. And they know it."

Judith and Willie Jane were seated in the southwest corner of the large dining room at the St. Charles Hotel. The table was large enough for four, so they took the two chairs with their backs to the walls, allowing them to watch the other guests.

"Do you always eat in the corner?" Willie Jane asked.

"Only when I don't want to be seen."

"Are you ashamed of me?"

"Heavens, no. I'm ashamed of me. Someone is going to wander in here and say, 'Judith, is it true you stole fifteen thousand dollars from Audrey Adair's safe?'"

"Nobody will believe that!"

"If it's said often enough, people will believe most anything," Judith said with a sigh.

They had just ordered salmon cakes and wild Delta brown rice with pickled asparagus when Daisie Belle Emory waltzed into the room. The azure blue satin dress with billowing bustle swished its way through the crowd.

"Judith, dear, what a surprise! I never see you out for supper without the judge. How is that dear man?"

"Dirty."

"Wasn't this dust storm simply insufferable? Oh, dear me, I don't believe we've met."

"I'm Willie Jane."

Daisie Belle reached out a gloved hand. "Jane? What an interesting last name. I knew a Colonel Jane ... isn't that wild? Some thought we had drafted women."

"She's a dear friend of mine," Judith announced.

"How delightful. Are the judge and some others joining you?" Daisie Belle glanced at the two empty chairs.

"No, they aren't. How about you eating with us?" Judith offered.

"What a marvelous idea. I'd be delighted." Daisie Belle pulled out a chair and slid into it, tugging off her white gloves. "Did you already order?"

"Yes, we're having the salmon cakes with rice," Judith said. *Daisie Belle knows everyone and everything in this town. And if she doesn't mind dining with Willie Jane, perhaps others will do the same.*

Daisie Belle called out to a waiter. "Peter, I'll have the same thing as Judith. But bring us an appetizer of those cute little pickled ears of corn." She leaned over the table. "Did you know Mr. Cheney said they have become the rage of Carson City?"

The jingle of spurs could be heard all over the room. Twig and Lester Washburn moseyed up to their table. "Judith, what in the world is this we heared about you over at Mrs. Adair's?" Twig began.

Daisy Belle Emory stared the men down with her best icy

glare. "I certainly hope that you heard how Judith was willing to defend her dear friend's possessions, even at the risk of her own life, even at the point of a firearm."

"Eh ... yeah ... " Twig stammered. "That's sort of the way we heared it, too."

"Well, that's our Judith, isn't it? Her loyalty and honesty are legendary, aren't they, Mr. Washburn?"

Twig scratched his dusty red and brown beard. "Yes, Mrs. Emory, you're right about that."

The two men stomped their way across the dining room toward the adjoining saloon.

Judith looked up at Willie Jane who winked back at her. Suddenly, Judith felt so ashamed. *Lord, I've heard it said that you don't know who your true friends are until some kind of test, when things don't look so good. Daisie Belle just stood up for me and for Willie Jane in the most public kind of way. Forgive my misjudging her. Continue to open my eyes to see this woman the way you see her. Help me to be a true friend to her.*

"Thank you for that splendid defense," Judith said.

"Nonsense! I will not have outrageous inferences about my Judith to be uttered anywhere in this town. And neither will anyone else with an ounce of decency."

"Daisie Belle, the judge and I would like to accept your invitation to serve on your statehood celebration committee."

"Oh, how splendid. How absolutely glorious!"

Daisie Belle Emory glanced over at Willie Jane. "And how about you, dear? Would you have time to serve on the committee with us?"

The words came out like an explosion in the midst of a silent night. "Did Willie Jane get shot, too?"

Bence Farnsworth's first words brought the judge out of a fitful nap. He leaned forward out of the velvet settee next to the bed in Marthellen's room.

"You took a couple of bad bullets, Mr. Farnsworth."

Bence's voice was weak but clear. "Willie Jane? Did she get shot?"

"No, you were the only one."

"What about the Kendalls?"

"They are all in jail."

"Good. I hope they hang."

"And we hope you get your strength back soon. I sent Judith and Willie Jane out to eat some supper. They will be back soon."

"Am I in Mama's room?"

"Yes, you've been here for a couple days. Your wounds are deep."

"I'm dyin', Judge."

"You hang in there, young man. You can make it. You've done well to make it this far."

"A man knows when he's dyin'. I don't reckon I can explain it, but I know. It's like a little tiny part of me is dyin' an inch at a time."

"Dr. Jacobs says you have a chance to pull through."

"Dr. Jacobs don't know what it's like to die neither. Is my mama here?"

"No, but I sent her word yesterday morning. I expect her to be here by tomorrow or the next day."

"I wish she was here now. Must sound funny for a man my age to say that."

"I don't see anything funny about it. Do you hurt? Dr. Jacobs said I could give you some of this purple stuff if you hurt."

"Nope. Ain't that strange? I don't hurt. I don't feel hardly nothin'. Sort of peaceful, really."

"That's good. It will give your body some rest. That way you can heal up faster."

"Can you give me a drink of water? My mouth is surely dry."

The judge lifted Bence's head with his left arm and brought the clear barrel glass of water to the injured man's chapped lips.

"Thanks, Judge." Bence closed his eyes.

The judge rubbed his chin whiskers, then brushed back the corners of his eyes. *Lord, Bence is about David's age. Our boy could get sick over there in India. Or injured. Or shot. Lord, I won't be there for him. And it scares me to death. Take care of our boy, Lord. And when and if it's his time, may there be someone there to put a glass of water to his lips.*

The judge walked over to Marthellen's old teak dresser and snatched a wet cotton rag from the white enameled basin. He wiped his own eyes, then came over and laid the damp rag on Bence's forehead. The injured man looked up.

"Thanks, Judge. You don't know how good that feels."

The judge sat back down and scooted his chair closer. "Do you feel like talking?"

"Sure. At least when I talk I know I'm alive." His chest heaved a time or two. "You want to know whether I'm right with Jesus, don't you?"

"Among other things. But that's certainly the most important."

"I ain't done a good job in this life, Judge, but I never, ever stopped believin'. Mama taught us right when we were little. I ain't gave up on Jesus. 'Course, he has ever' right to give up on me."

"That's against his nature," the judge said. "Your mama taught you that, didn't she?"

"Yes, sir, she did. But it's surely a whole lot more important now than it's ever been."

Neither man spoke for a moment.

"Did you want to ask me somethin' else?" Bence asked.

"Why did the Kendalls want to kill you? Were you in with them on that Murphys stage robbery?"

"I figured you knew. Yeah, I was drivin' the stage. They said they wanted to rob the strongbox, that was all, and no one would get hurt."

"How much did they pay you?"

Bence swallowed with some effort. "I was supposed to get five hundred dollars. I ain't never had five hundred dollars in my life, Judge. But, afterward, I refused to take the money. It all went wrong. They were only going to take the bank's money and leave. But oh, Lord, did it ever go wrong. They went crazy. They not only killed the men, they shot to death two women and one little child."

"What did you do?"

"What could I do? It was over before I even got down off the stagecoach. I went running out into the woods as fast as I could, carrying nothing but my shotgun. They trailed me clear across the Sierras. For two weeks I was only hours ahead of them, and that was because I traveled half the night. I lost them for a time when you and Judith sent me off to Sacramento to see Charlotte and Mama."

"So, why did you come back?" the judge quizzed.

"Because me and Willie Jane was gettin' mighty chummy and

I knew I had to go back to Murphys to testify against the Kendalls. I wanted to do it in such a way so as not to get myself hanged. I needed your advice and I thought they would have left Carson by now."

The judge rested a hand lightly on Bence's arm. The young man's skin felt hot and rough. "When the ladies return, I'd like to get my clerk, Spafford Gabbs, and have him write down your statement. It will greatly assist in seeing justice carried out against the Kendalls."

"You want to do it tonight?"

"Just to get it over with."

"You don't think I'm goin' to live long either, do you, Judge?"

"None of us knows the number of our days, Bence. But if your mother comes tomorrow, I don't want her to have to hear all you've just told me."

He closed his eyes again. "You're right. I'll talk to him tonight."

"Can I get you something to eat? Judith said this broth was good for you."

"I couldn't bring myself to eat yet."

Bence bent his head and stared across the room. His eyes cleared. "What's that on the table near the outside door? Is that my mama's belongings? Is she here?"

"Remember, I said we're hoping she'll be here tomorrow."

"What's in that basket?"

"Those are some things Judith was asked to remove from Audrey Adair's house."

"Her husband beat her, I heard."

"Yes, he did."

"I never met the man. Was he a big old boy, like Mrs. Adair?"

"Not really. Rather slight," the judge reported. "Slight, but violent. There's a picture of him right there. Let me show you."

The judge brought the oval framed, curved-glass photograph over by the lantern light next to the bed.

"That's him," Bence spit out.

"It's who?"

"The man in the barn."

"What barn?"

"The night before I got to Carson, a squall hit the mountains and dumped an inch of rain in an hour. I was coming down King's Canyon and found a broken-down cabin with a barn still standing. I crawled up in the loft. When I woke up in the night, some folks—a man and a woman—were campin' out downstairs. I wasn't about to reveal my hand, so I jist peeked down."

"It was Milton Primble?"

"It was this man in the picture, that's for sure. Only he was wearing old canvas clothes."

"And the woman. Who was she?"

"She was in the shadows. I couldn't see her at all. But I could hear her voice."

"Did it sound like Willie Jane?"

"Shoot, no. It was nothing like hers."

"How about Mrs. Adair? Could it have been her?"

"Judge, it was so dark in there it could have been Queen Victoria."

"Would you recognize the voice if you heard it again?"

"I reckon I would." He tried to raise up, then fell back. "When did you say Mama's coming?"

"Tomorrow. Hang on until then, Bence. You don't want to give up before your mama gets here."

"No, sir, I don't."

CHAPTER EIGHT

Judge Hollis A. Kingston, I can't believe this!"

The judge's strong hands circled Judith's waist as he lifted her up into the front seat of the carriage. The retractable awning had been shoved to the rear. "Amazing, isn't it?" he said.

She settled down on the black leather seat. It felt nicely padded, but firm. The judge tossed a green carpetbag valise in the back. "Do I get to know what's in the satchel?" she asked.

The judge swung up into the carriage and plopped down on the seat next to her. She scooted toward him until her dress pressed against his trousers. "A blanket, some towels ... and our bathing suits."

Judith's hand flew to her mouth. "Why, Judge Kingston, what a daring adventure!"

"That's me ... a dauntless vagabond." He tucked his old flop hat down in the front and slapped the reins on the rump of the lead of the two-horse team.

"Judge Kingston, in Mr. Webster's book of definitions, under the word *vagabond*, it says: the opposite of Judge Hollis A. Kingston."

"It wouldn't be the first time that book was wrong." He loosened his tie and unfastened his top button as they turned west on King Street in front of the Presbyterian Church.

"Oh, be still my heart. Is this the informal Judge?" She reached over and squeezed his arm, then kept her hand there.

"Are you going to lose control with some embarrassing

public act of devoted affection?" he challenged.

"I certainly hope so," she laughed. "After all, it's so sad to see a man of your advanced age beg for attention."

"Beg?" he blustered.

Judith threw her arms around his neck and kissed him. Her lips were still on his cheek when he reached up with his left hand and tipped his hat.

"Good morning, Miss Clapp ... Miss Babcock," he called out.

Judith opened her eyes and sat up quickly.

"Good morning, Judge. Good morning, Judith," Hannah Clapp called out.

Judith managed a meager, red-faced wave. "You set me up for that, Judge Kingston," she said under her breath. "You knew they were up there and you provoked me into kissing you. The only thing possibly worse would be to have the reverend walk by."

"Provoked? Posh." The tone of his voice was like a barrister's closing argument. "Besides, our new pastor is of the new school. He certainly wouldn't be shocked to see a happily married couple looking happy. Everyone knows you can't resist me."

Judith shrugged. "Well, that's true ..." She threw her arms around him again, and this time he turned his face. Their lips met.

Several workers lounging in the bright sunlight in front of the Carson City Brewery whistled at them. The judge turned and tipped his hat.

The men applauded.

"Well," Judith gulped. "This has already been a quite memorable morning and we've only gone as far as St. Teresa's." She glanced in the back of the carriage. "What's in the wicker basket?"

"Our picnic dinner, of course. I had the cook at the St. Charles pack something up for us. I made him promise not to include any tiny ears of corn or pickled artichoke hearts, or any other foodstuffs of questionable edibility."

"I'm sure whatever it is will be delightful. But I'm still in shock. You come home at 11:00 in the morning and tell me to get my hat because we're going for a ride. It's very romantic."

"Romantic? It's not like we've never taken a drive to Lake Tahoe before."

"Judge Kingston, you have never in your life canceled court on a weekday to take me anywhere."

"That's not true," he protested. "How about when Roberta was born?"

Although warm out, the slight breeze on Judith's face felt refreshing after the previous day's dust storm. "OK, this is your second time. I'm thrilled … delighted … a little puzzled … and I will be the envy of every other woman in Carson City for at least a week. But I must know what made you think of this."

"I suppose it's been building up. We've been running from one emergency to another for two weeks. Have you noticed we've hardly had time for a quiet visit?"

"Yes, I've noticed."

"And then, when Marthellen came in this morning … well, Bence has his mama, Dr. Jacobs, and Willie Jane to look after him. I decided we could slip out and they would hardly notice."

"I'm so relieved Marthellen made it home before Bence …" Judith looked down at her lap and fidgeted with her wedding ring.

"Before he died? I suppose that was the deciding factor. Like I told you, when Bence first came to, he talked incessantly about death and dying and all the things he regretted not doing in life. Most of them were things he would have liked to live long enough to do with his mother and sister. It gave me something to think about."

"About family?"

"Exactly." The judge leaned his shoulder against her. "Some day every one of us are going to be there like Bence. Maybe five … ten years away."

"Or twenty years," Judith inserted.

"I considered me being on that bed."

She shuddered. "I don't even want to think about it."

"I don't either. But once in a while it's good to review. So I said to myself, 'Judge, what are you going to regret never having done when you're on your deathbed?'"

Judith answered for him. "And it came to you in a flash: 'Why, I'll regret not taking my darling wife to Lake Tahoe for a swim on a hot August day in the middle of the week.'"

"That was one of many things."

"You mean I might have more surprises in store?"

"Could be."

"Oh, be still my anxious heart."

"Judith," he said, then cleared his throat. "I want you to know I love you more every day that I spend with you."

She bit her lip.

With the background clopping sound of horse hooves on the baked dirt road up Kings Canyon, he turned to look at her. "Did I make you cry? Those words were supposed to make you happy."

She clutched his arm as the tears bubbled down her cheeks.

She gulped a deep breath between sobs. "I've never been happier in my life."

The judge shoved his hat back and stared up the canyon at the tree-covered Carson Range. "My word, that's a rather strange way of expressing it."

Judith fumbled to pull the linen handkerchief out of the sleeve of her light gray cotton dress. She wiped her eyes slowly, then blew her nose. "Judge, I love you dearly. You know that. And I know how very much you love me. We were talking about deathbeds and regrets; I couldn't help but think of someday sitting at your bedside and how I don't think I could survive a day without your dear sweet love." Judith began to sob again.

"My word, Judith, if we don't change the subject, we'll be swimming in our own tears and have no need for Lake Tahoe."

She wiped her eyes again. "Yes, Your Honor."

"That's better. We need to add a little decorum to this journey."

"But not too much." She took a big, deep gulp of air. It tasted a lot like sage. "Are we really going swimming? I haven't gone swimming since the children were both at home."

"The water will be frigid, but a quick dip should be invigorating," he said.

"It won't be flocked, will it? You know I don't like to swim where there's a crowd."

"It's a huge lake. We'll find ourselves a vacant beach."

The horses slowed as the incline grew steeper. Judith settled back in the comfort of the black leather carriage seat. "What else did you and Bence talk about last night?"

"Besides the fact that he spotted Milton Primble in a barn with a woman on the night Audrey was beaten?"

"I overheard all of that last night when he gave that deposition to Mr. Gabbs."

"Then you also learned about the stagecoach murders?"

"Oh, yes. I can't even imagine the horror. Most times the evil one is subtle in his destruction. But that was Satan uncovered."

The judge slapped the lead line on the slowing horses. "Exactly what I was thinking."

"If Bence lives, could he be prosecuted as an accessory to the murders?"

"I'm sure the Kendalls will implicate him as well. But I think, with good representation, he could keep from hanging. But it might be a long prison term. No jury will have any leniency in such a matter where women and a child are involved. In fact, it will be quite difficult for the authorities there to prevent a lynching."

Judith rested her hands on the carriage seat. "Has the thought occurred to you that perhaps God allowed Bence to be mortally wounded as an act of divine kindness?"

"To keep him from getting hung by an angry mob in Murphys?"

"And to spare his mother that particular sorrow," she said.

"It's an intriguing thought, my dear."

They came to a bumpy place in the road. Judith hung on to her husband. "We have several intrigues, Judge Kingston."

"You're thinking of the disappearance of Milton Primble?"

"Not to mention Duffy Day, and the sudden appearance of Eliza Conroy."

"Do you think she's all she claims to be?"

"I don't know. But I've never in my life met a woman who could bring out the worst in me so fast. We're like two magnets when you reverse the poles. We're constantly at each other. It's like coming face-to-face with evil. I sent a telegram to Pennsylvania to get some background on her."

"My word, we've sent a lot of telegrams lately."

Judith folded her hands in her lap. *Does he know I telegraphed Roberta?* "Oh? Which telegraphs did you have in mind?"

"Why, eh ..." The judge gazed up the narrow dirt road, which was getting steeper. Pines clustered around them. *Did she find out I telegraphed Roberta?* "You know, to Audrey ... Marthellen ... over to the sheriff in Murphys ... those telegrams."

Judith loosened the tight grip of her own fingers and brushed out her skirt. "Isn't it a marvelous invention?"

"I certainly wish we could locate Milton Primble. There are so many loose ends to this matter until we do," he said.

Judith gazed through the forest, watching for signs of water. "I see it like a recipe."

"Oh? Like that mystery stew you make?"

She gave him a quick glare. "Just listen to me. We have all the ingredients on the counter," she explained, "but we don't know what it will make."

"Just what do you see as the ingredients?"

"First, Audrey is savagely beaten by Milton."

"Again," he added.

"Right. Then Milton runs off."

"But doesn't pick up Willie Jane, whom he has promised to take with him."

"But he does meet with some woman in a barn. Where was that barn, anyway?" Judith quizzed.

"Bence stumbled onto it at night. He said it was just on the north side of Kings Canyon."

"Do you suppose we could look for it on our way home?"

"We could loop over that way, if it isn't too dark."

"Too dark? Why, Judge Kingston, are you planning on keeping me out after sunset?" She tilted her head and batted her eyes.

He grinned at her. "It's sad to see a woman your age having to beg like that."

"Beg!" she protested. "Me, beg?" The shallow protest slipped into a wide grin. "OK, maybe it was a small beg."

"Let's continue with this case."

"Yes, Your Honor."

"Judith!"

"Relax, dear Judge ... we just mentioned the element of Milton Primble meeting with a woman in the barn."

"Perhaps he had more than one gal lined up to run away with him."

Judith clutched both the judge and the side of the carriage as they hit a rock. "But he didn't take the money he had embezzled and locked in his desk drawer."

"So what was funding his journey?"

"The fifteen thousand dollars missing from Audrey's safe?"

"Could be. But if Milt discovered the combination and took the money, why didn't he rip up that will that left him nothing?"

"I suppose he figured Audrey would just write another one. But how did Mrs. Conroy know the exact amount in the safe ... unless Milton told her?"

"Did Milt know what was in there before he took off?" Judge said.

"He certainly knew afterwards."

"Then why did he mention Mexico and then ride off to the

river and throw his things away?"

"In places where they would obviously be found," Judith added. "Not to mention the man and woman Duffy saw ride to the river and take a shot at him. When Duffy drew the silhouette, it looked somewhat like Willie Jane, but she claimed it wasn't her."

The judge pulled a red bandanna from his back pocket and wiped off his forehead. "And where is Duffy now? We haven't even brought up the most basic ingredient to your recipe concoction. Why were Milton and Audrey arguing in the first place? Did you ever ask her that?"

"No ... I didn't want her to have to relive it."

"I think we should ask her." The judge folded the bandanna and slipped it back in his pocket. "If Milton had the money arranged and a crib girl willing to flee with him, why did he bother beating up Audrey? Why didn't he just sneak out of town?"

"Talk about swimming ... my head is swimming. Is this what you have to go through all the time with court cases?" she asked.

"Most of the time I spend my day listening to two lawyers argue over whether something gray should be called 'light black' or 'dark white.'"

"Well, Mr. Judge, what have you figured out in the Milton Primble case?"

"I think we should toss the pieces of evidence all together in a pan and stick them in an oven."

"How do we do that?"

"Turn up the heat."

Judith scooted closer, raised up from the seat, and kissed the judge on the back of the neck.

"What are you doing?"

"Turning up the heat."

"You certainly seem full of public displays of affection these days."

"Public? There isn't another person for fifty miles."

"Nonetheless, you seem to be having a difficult time resisting my charms," he chided.

"Judge, are you bragging or complaining?"

He reached his arm around her and gave her a squeeze. "Bragging, actually. Wasn't this day trip a marvelous idea?"

She laid her head on his shoulder. "Absolutely splendid."

They took the wagon road north of the wood yard at Spooner Lake.

"We aren't going to Glenbrook?" she asked. "Daisie Belle says they have the finest bowling alley in Nevada and one of the best dance halls."

"She would know. But I thought you wanted privacy. Besides, we brought our swimsuits, not our dancing shoes."

Judith pointed through the trees. They could hear the sounds of timbering in the background from one of Glenbrook's four sawmills. "There it is, Judge Kingston. Lake Tahoe ... my favorite lake in all the world. It's always so beautiful up here."

"Or Lake Bigler, as some still call it, named after one of the California governors."

"I like the name Tahoe better," Judith replied.

"That's a word taken from the Washoe Indian language, meaning 'water,'" the judge reported. "But then, Captain Fremont called it Lake Bonpland back in the 1840s."

"After the French naturalist?"

The judge looked at her. "How did you know that?"

Judith bit her lip. "I read a lot." *Massacre at Zephyr Point ...
Stuart Brannon in the High Sierras, Volume 2 ... by Hawthorne
H. Miller.* She untied the blue and white ribbon that held on
her hat.

"What are you doing?" he asked.

"Relaxing. You did promise to find us a private beach."

"Yes, of course, but—"

"Good." Judith pulled the pins out of her hair and let the
natural streaks of sable and pecan brown wavy hair cascade
across the back of her dress and halfway down her back.

"You're taking this relaxing quite seriously," he remarked.

"You don't really think women actually enjoy having their
hair pinned up all the time, do you?"

"I never thought about it."

"Well, you should. There will come a day when women will
wear their hair any way they please."

"I always thought women pinned their hair up because they
wanted to," he said.

"They do."

"But you just said they didn't like their hair pinned."

"That's exactly right. What we want is to wear it any old way
we want, any old time we want."

"Sounds rather libertine."

"Yes, doesn't it? How about down there?" she pointed
through the Ponderosa pines to a patch of sandy beach no
larger than Audrey Adair's master bedroom. They could no
longer hear any sawing or fluming activity.

"We'll have to hike from here," he cautioned.

"That's fine. The horses will enjoy the shade."

The judge parked the carriage in a clearing next to the narrow wagon road and assisted her to the ground. "I'll get you

situated down at the lake, then come back and unhitch the team," he announced.

"What can I carry?" she offered.

"I'll get the lunch basket and the satchel. How about you grabbing my shotgun?"

"Do you plan on hunting quail?" she teased.

"My intention was to fight off the horde of ardent admirers, once you don your suit."

"Oh, definitely," Judith chided. "Admirers of a fifty-year-old woman."

"You're not fifty yet," he reminded her.

"It is only weeks, my dear Judge."

"You don't look a day over thirty-five and you know it."

"Mother was right. Always marry a man with poor eye-sight."

They hiked through the shade of the thick grove. The searchlight of the sun followed them through the trees, bumping against trunks, blazing around limbs. Small swarms of puffy white clouds drifted across the high Sierra sky. A slight breeze rolled off the lake and ruffled Judith's hair. "Isn't that the most marvelous cool draft of air?"

"Quite unlike yesterday's zephyr," he said.

"It's the first time I've really cooled off since May," she added.

The judge motioned. "I'll put the blanket down here and go tend to the team."

He had just gotten the green, gray, and mauve quilt spread across the sand when Judith signaled him from the water's edge. "We can't swim here!"

"Why? What's the matter?"

"It's not private enough," she announced.

The judge surveyed up and down the lakeshore. "What do you mean, it's not private enough?"

"They're looking at me."

"They? I don't see anyone."

"In the boat!"

The judge stepped down beside her. "That's just a little rowboat with a couple of fishermen. They must be a mile away."

"At any moment they could drift toward us."

"Aren't you going to wear your bathing suit?"

"Of course I am," she snapped. "But I will not have myself seen soaking wet from head to toe by strangers, especially men."

The judge threw up his hands. "What do you want then?"

"A more private beach."

He sighed and started folding the quilt.

"I'll help you," she offered. "What do you want me to carry back to the carriage?"

"The shotgun."

"Again?"

"Only this time point it at my back. That way the scene will be more accurate," he grumbled.

They discovered another small cove four miles north. No one coming along the road could see them or the unhitched team. A small creek flowed into the lake and deposited a long sandbar that only revealed itself above waterline in late summer.

A small lap blanket around her shoulders, wet hair tousled limp down her back, Judith stared into the hot flames of the driftwood fire. She inhaled the mixture of pine and smoke scents.

"That, without a doubt, is the coldest water I ever swam in," she announced. "But I loved it."

The judge stretched his long arms out and tried to relax the muscles in his neck. "It's been a long time since we dawdled like this."

"You're not very good at dawdling, Judge Kingston."

"I'm absolutely horrid at it. I've never had any practice."

"Not even as a child?"

"Certainly not. A young man on a Kentucky farm is expected to work."

"Do you know what Roberta said once? She asked if you had worn suits and ties and sat around reading law books all your life, even as a child."

"Of course not. I had no thought of becoming a judge until ..."

"Until when?"

"Until I watched them march the Cherokees through Kentucky on their way to the Indian Territory. I figured a judge in the right place could have come up with a more fair solution."

"The Trail of Tears? When was that?" she pressed.

"The winter of '38 and '39."

"You wanted to be a judge when you were thirteen?"

"Yes, and I didn't even own a suit at the time," he said with a laugh. "Are you hungry, my dear?"

"Oh, no. This was a delightful picnic. Turkey drumsticks, cheese, wonderful rolls, grapes ... and I just loved the Greek olives stuffed with almonds and pickled crabmeat."

"I'm glad you liked them. They gave me heartburn. I hoped we could avoid such delicacies, but Mr. Cheney brought them by my office this morning. He said he just got a whole case in and wanted us to be the first to sample them. I can't imagine why he thought we'd want to do such a thing. We always eat such plain food."

"Mr. Cheney is eternally enthused about new products."

"Well, he can't afford to be giving out dollar a jar delicacies to just everyone."

I assure you, dear Judge, he does not give them to just anyone. I think we're the only ones. Judith glanced out at the lake. "Do you know what I'd like to do before we pack up and go home? Go for one more swim."

"I thought you were freezing."

"I am, but this might be my last swim in Lake Tahoe, and I want to remember it."

"Your last swim? I thought we agreed not to talk so melancholy."

"When was the last time you and I swam in Lake Tahoe?"

"Let's see, about the time David was in high school," he suggested.

"He was still in grammar school. It was the summer he was twelve. That was fifteen years ago."

"Was it that long?"

"Yes, and if we don't have an opportunity to come back for another fifteen years, it will be 1895. And in 1895 I will be sixty-four, and you, dear Judge, will be seventy. Do you really think we'll come up here swimming at that age?"

He thought about it. Then, a rare, sly grin crept across his stoic face. "We might."

She burst out laughing. "You're right, Judge Kingston, we just might. But I'm not taking the chance. Build up the fire. Let's take one more dip."

She stood up and let the small blanket drop off her shoulders, then rubbed her hands together.

"Aren't you afraid fishermen on the other side of the lake might spot you?" he said.

"Since I can see no one on earth but you, I feel quite brave, even if my swimsuit is not very flattering."

"Oh, I don't know. Longjohns with a ruffle around the midsection is … cute."

"Especially wet. At least yours only goes to your knees and elbows. Come on," she motioned.

"I'll get this fire ready for a hasty retreat. You go ahead."

Judith plunged into the brisk waters of Lake Tahoe. Once again she felt like her heart and breath had completely stopped. *I think this is long enough. Why did I want to do this?* The water came halfway up her chest. She dipped her knees and let the water flow over her head, then splashed back up for a gasp of air.

She began to get used to the coolness and watched moving specks in the sky. Birds, far in the distance, swooped and swirled toward her. They got closer and bigger. As they sailed across the waters, she counted five of them and marveled at the immense wingspans. Then the huge bald eagles spread their glory over her head. She raised her arms high in response.

"Judith and the judge, boy am I glad to see you."

She strained to examine the shoreline. The voice came out of a thick stand of trees.

"Duffy?" she heard the judge call out from his spot by the blazing fire.

"Judge, bring me a blanket," she called out.

He turned toward her but didn't move. "Judith, it's just Duffy."

"I don't care if it's St. Matthew and the apostles, Hollis A. Kingston, you get me a blanket and get it over here right now."

"Yes, ma'am."

"The big blanket," she barked, sloshing out of the water.

She braced her arms full across her chest.

When the blanket was pulled over her head and dragging the sand, she trudged up next to the fire.

"Hello, Judith," Duffy called out as he approached.

She grabbed up her clothes and the shotgun and marched toward a thick grove of aspens.

"I said, 'Hello, Judith,'" Duffy repeated.

"Hello, Duffy. I will shoot anyone who comes near before I am completely dressed. Is that understood?"

"Boy," Duffy muttered, "I ain't never seen Judith so ..."

"Riled?" the judge offered.

"Ain't never seen her so blue, neither." Duffy squatted down and warmed his hands by the fire. "You two went swimming, didn't you?"

"Yes, we did."

"That's what I figured. I've got an eye for things that way." Duffy pointed toward the food basket. "Say, did I interrupt you at dinnertime? Mama said I should never do that."

"We're all through eating, Duffy."

Duffy stared at the leftovers in the basket. "All through?"

"Yes, and look at all we have to pack back to Carson City. You would do us both a big favor if you'd eat some."

Duffy reached over and snatched a turkey drumstick. "My mama said I should always help out friends whenever they was in dire need."

The judge pulled his trousers over his bathing suit. "Thanks for the help, Duffy."

"You're welcome."

"Now, you know why we're here. But we don't know why you are. All sorts of folks have been looking for you back home."

"I'm hidin' out," Duffy said between bites.

"Who are you hiding from?"

"That Wild Bill Hickok. Said he'd shoot me if I tried to go back. He liked to kill me yesterday." He licked his fingers. "Could I have me another of them rolls? I ain't et in two days."

A fully clothed Judith Kingston emerged from the aspen grove, her unpinned hair hanging wet against the back of her dress.

"Hello, Judith. You still ticked at me?"

"I'm sorry for my ranting. It wasn't your fault."

"I reckon you were just cold … what with nothin' on but that swimmin' uniform."

The judge could see Judith's eyes narrow and her lips purse.

"Yessir," the dauntless Duffy continued, "when a garment's wet like that you can see ever one of them—"

"Duffy," the judge roared. "The wrath of Wild Bill Hickok is nothing compared to what you are about to experience."

Duffy stopped eating and turned his blank, drawn face from one to the other of his puzzling friends. His eyes dropped to the roll in his hand. He began to pinch off pieces and make little balls of bread.

"Tell Judith about how you were shot at by Wild Bill," the judge said.

Duffy slowly warmed to the new subject. "It all started when Judith and me was at the depot. Wild Bill must have been on that train 'cause I had jist turned my back and headed toward the settin' sun when I heard some bullets shot at me."

"So you took off running?" Judith pressed.

"Yep. I ain't goin' to stick around anywhere I'll get shot, no ma'am. I ran out of town and right up into the foothills."

"But that's the opposite direction from your place," the judge commented.

"I figured to wait until dark to go home. But I, eh … well, to tell you the truth I kind of got lost. So I slept back in the trees and waited until daylight. The next morning I must have taken a wrong turn. Anyways, the sun was straight up and I was still in the hills when that zephyr hit."

"It was a bad one. What did you do?" Judith asked.

"I found me a broken-down barn."

"You actually went inside a building?"

"The broken-down part didn't have no roof, so I took a chance and huddled in a corner. Well, that zephyr didn't lighten up until the sun went down. As soon as it died, I spied a man in the shadows. Someone else had been in the other part of the barn all along and I hadn't noticed it."

"Who was it?" Judith asked.

"I'm a-comin' to that part. I was hungry and didn't want to impose on him at suppertime, but it was dark and I thought he might have some scraps left. So I asked him if he had something to eat."

"I'll bet that startled him," Judith said.

"He jumped straight up, pulled a sneak gun out of his vest, and waved it careless like at me. I looked him up and down. He looked sort of familiar, but it was mighty dark, so I didn't say nothin'." Duffy stuffed all the roll bits in his mouth and quickly chewed them. "Then he admits it right out. He says, 'I'm Wild Bill Hickok, and I've come to kill you, Duffy Day.'"

"He knew your name?" the judge prompted.

"I told ya, Wild Bill has been after me a long time. I told him not to shoot me, 'cause it wouldn't be right and he'd have a hard time lookin' his mama in the eye if he turned killer."

Judith squatted down to warm herself by the fire. "What did he do?"

"He told me not to come back to Carson for a week, then he let me go."

The judge pulled on his shirt and buttoned it. "So he just let you walk out of there?"

"I think it was just a scheme to shoot me in the back. 'Cause as soon as I left that barn, bullets started whizzin' over my head. I jist kept runnin' and runnin' and runnin'."

"You can go back with us, Duffy," the judge offered. "We'll see that you get home safe."

"I don't reckon I could go home for a week," Duffy declared.

"What a shame," Judith added, "you being up here at the lake with nothing to eat, now that Marthellen's home."

"Marthellen done came home?" Duffy gasped.

"Yes, she did."

"Judith, would you tell that Wild Bill not to shoot me?"

"I'll tell him."

"In that case, I'll go back with you." He beamed as he added, "Ever'body knows they have to do whatever Judith says."

"Why don't you show us that barn you stayed at on our way back," the judge proposed.

"What if Wild Bill's there?"

"I'll make him straighten up and mind his manners," Judith pledged.

"I ain't afraid, as long as you two is with me."

Duffy hiked out to hitch up the team, while the judge tied his tie and Judith packed up the baskets.

"Do you think it's the same barn that Bence told you about?" Judith asked.

"Sounds like it could be."

"But who chased Duffy off?"

"Someone who knew his name and that he was terrified of Wild Bill Hickok, and that he'd run away from the sound of bullets," the judge said.

Judith popped a stuffed olive in her mouth. "That covers most every man in Carson City."

"True, but who would play such a mean joke on poor harmless Duffy?"

"The Washburn brothers would," she said.

"But they live south of town."

"If Milton Primble was hiding in that barn, like Bence says, he would have a reason for chasing Duffy off."

"He certainly would," the judge concurred.

The sun was almost down behind them when they uncovered the broken-down barn several miles north of the Kings Canyon Road. Duffy insisted that the judge carry the shotgun. Duffy hid behind Judith all the way to the barn. He stayed outside with Judith while the judge entered.

"Is he in there?" Duffy called out.

"No, the barn's empty," the judge shouted back.

Duffy waved his hand at the adjoining forest. "He must be hiding in the trees, waitin' to ambush me."

"Duffy, did Wild Bill wing you? Did you get grazed by a bullet?" the judge hollered.

"Nope, I was too quick for him. He missed me ever' time."

"Well, someone got shot in here," the judge declared.

Judith peeked inside the barn door.

"There's dried blood on this center post that looks about one day old," the judge was saying.

"Could it be animal blood?" she questioned.

"Maybe. The lead balls are lodged in this post."

"You mean the bullets went clear through someone?"

"Looks like it."

Judith stepped back, away from the door, her hand to her mouth.

"Are you goin' to vomit, Judith?" Duffy blurted out.

"I just may," she murmured.

"Sit down there and put your head between your knees. That's what my mama always told me. I used to feel that way when she chopped the heads off of chickens."

Judith sat down and dropped her head. *Duffy, the cure is worse than the disease. I was doing all right until you mentioned headless chickens.*

"Are you ill?" the judge asked as he exited the barn.

"I'll be all right in a minute."

"Well, get a big deep breath. I've got something to show you."

"I trust it isn't a dead body."

"No. At least, not yet." The judge turned to Duffy Day. "Duffy, we've got jam rolls in that little gingham sack. You help yourself if you're hungry. I'll have to toss them out when we get home."

"Jam rolls? Well, there ain't no use for a man to have to toss 'em out. I believe I'll jist wait for you over at the carriage."

"What was that all about?" Judith asked as she watched Duffy jog back to the carriage.

"This." He showed her a bloody canvas jacket with two bullet holes in the chest. "Whoever was wearing this is the one who got shot near the center post."

"Whoever shot at this person probably accosted Duffy."

"Maybe. But it sounds like they just wanted to chase Duffy off, not kill him. Whoever pulled this trigger was aiming to kill."

Judith leaned her head between her knees again. "You think maybe Milton was hiding up here and shot someone who discovered him?"

"I don't think a man like Milton could do much more than punch a defenseless woman. My guess is, it's Milton who got shot."

"Why do you say that?" she asked.

"Look at the initials in the lining."

"M.P.—just like the other coat. Did he personally mark everything he ever owned?"

The gas street lamps were burning brightly by the time they rolled into Carson City. The judge let Judith off at home. Then he and Duffy drove the rig straight to the sheriff's office.

Duffy waited in the carriage.

"Judge, where on earth have you been? We've looked all over for you," the sheriff greeted him.

"Judith and I took a drive up to the lake."

"In the middle of the week? You missed all the excitement. Levi came tearin' in here not more than an hour ago sayin' he and that Marcy girl were out at the river spoonin', and lo and behold they hiked around a corner and stumbled onto the dead body of Milton Primble."

"Did he have two bullet holes right below the heart?" the judge asked.

CHAPTER NINE

J udith sat across the small pine kitchen table from Marthellen. Although there were only two years' difference in their ages, Marthellen at that moment looked much older. And because they had such similar small noses and thin mouths, they were often mistaken for sisters. The main difference was in the eyes.

Marthellen's graying hair was thicker and curlier, but today it was limp and straggly. She wore no makeup. Dark circles framed her weary gray-green eyes. "I'm so tired," Marthellen moaned. "I'm physically, emotionally, and spiritually wore out. Birthin', dyin', praisin', pleadin', cryin' … I don't think I can handle too much more. Why did this all have to happen in the same week?"

Judith sipped her orange spice tea. "I don't know. I can only guess that the Lord thinks you can handle it."

Marthellen crumpled on the table, her head in her hands. "When Bence took a spell for the worse last night, I actually thought about running out into the street and screaming, 'Why, Lord, why are you doing this?'"

Judith felt her heart race. "I wouldn't blame you at all."

"I haven't seen my son in years. Now he's home and I have to watch him die." Marthellen raised up and rubbed the wrinkles in the corners of her eyes. "I know it's better this way. I'd rather he be with me than out on some lonesome trail all by himself and I just heard about it after the fact."

Judith glanced down at an age spot on the back of her hand

and absently grabbed a piece of raw potato from the sink and rubbed it, as if it would go instantly away. "He needed you with him. He watched that door for two days waiting for you to walk through. No matter how old he is, you're still Mama."

"I know. The only way I made it through last night was to look over and see the same concern on Willie Jane's face. It's like her appointed task was to be an angel in the last days of Bence's life." Marthellen stretched back in the straight-back pine chair and closed her eyes. Her features relaxed into a brief semblance of peace.

Willie Jane peeked into the kitchen. "I think I need a cup of coffee."

"Come on, dear," Judith urged. "Pull up a chair with us."

"I hate to leave Bence. He seems to be hurting a lot," Willie Jane reported.

Marthellen stood, taking a porcelain teacup with her. "It's my turn."

"Here, you take the teapot, too," Judith offered. "You'll need it worse than I will."

By the time Willie Jane sat down, Judith had her coffee poured. "You look tired, young lady. You should go upstairs and sleep a little. I've already made your bed, but you could just lie on top of the comforter."

Willie Jane gripped the clay mug with both hands and let the steam warm her face. "I can't sleep. Not today. I don't think Bence will make it through the day, do you?"

"It doesn't seem like it, but what do I know? I surely didn't think he would last this long," Judith admitted.

"What were you and Marthellen talking about?" Willie Jane asked.

"About Bence ... and about you."

Willie Jane's face turned wary. "What about me?"

Judith smiled and rubbed her hands with the potato again. "Marthellen thinks that maybe you're an angel sent to take care of Bence and to bring a little happiness to him in his last days."

Tears coursed down Willie Jane's round cheeks. Her dark eyes look startled and confused.

Judith reached over to the sink and snatched up a clean tea towel and handed it to her. She tried to console the young woman whose harsh edges seemed entirely melted. "It's difficult to sit and watch him die."

Willie Jane wiped her eyes. "That's only half of it."

Judith scooted out to the dining room. She returned carrying a wide-brimmed straw hat. "I'm sorry, but I have to go soon to meet Audrey at the train."

She fussed with the tie on her hat, then she clipped the gold filigree butterfly pin to the collar of her tan dress. The full lace cuffs on the long sleeves billowed slightly as she brushed off the small bustle at the back.

Willie Jane sipped her coffee and watched. "Judith, did you tell Marthellen about me?"

"What about you, Willie Jane?"

"You know, the kind of work I do?"

"You mean, the kind you *used* to do?"

"Yeah," Willie Jane said and sighed.

"No, I don't believe we've discussed the subject."

"If Bence has to die, I'm hopin' it happens before she finds out about me. She'd run me off if she knew."

"So you two haven't discussed your past?" Judith quizzed.

"Oh, no." Willie Jane glanced back toward Marthellen's room and talked in hushed tones. "In Sacramento she was very kind and friendly to me, but that's part of the problem. I didn't tell Marthellen about me bein' a crib girl and all. I told Bence I just couldn't say those things to his mama. He said she would understand, but I just couldn't do it. All his mother and sister knew was that I was a friend of Judith Kingston's."

"You've been a faithful friend to her son, day and night, for the past several days. That means more to Marthellen than anything about your past," Judith assured her.

Willie Jane's large, coffee bean-rich brown eyes pierced into her own. "You and the judge are the two greatest people I've ever met. You give me a chance to be someone different. You completely ignore my past and make me want to be a better person. But not everyone in this town's that way. Most won't even glance at me when I walk down the street, let alone talk to me. I can't expect Marthellen to treat me like you do. I can't expect anyone to treat me that way this side of heaven."

"You're selling Marthellen short. Let me tell you something about Marthellen you don't know." Judith led Willie Jane over to the wall shelf next to the cookstove. She pulled down a battered gray book. "This is our cookbook. It's filled with recipes and it's divided into days of the week."

"You mean, what to cook on Monday, Tuesday, Wednesday, and like that?"

"Precisely. Marthellen and I like planning specific meals on certain days. I've used this old book for years." Judith handed the volume to Willie Jane. "Look up Wednesday and read the names penciled in on top."

Willie Jane flipped through the pages. "I told you I don't read real well."

"You'll be able to read this. Go ahead, read the names out loud."

"Willie Jane, Adelia Haven, Martha Ann, Stone Julie, Fidora, Pokey, Irish Sue, and Mercedes Barega." Willie Jane looked up, wide-eyed. "That's all of us down at the cribs. Why on earth are our names in your cookbook?"

"Because that's where we keep our prayer list, right there in that cookbook, so that we know who to pray for each day."

Willie Jane stared down at the table. "You were prayin' for us girls even while we were sinnin'?" she murmured.

Judith adjusted her hat. "Perfect people don't need our prayers."

"What do you mean, our prayers? Who prays with you about us girls?"

Judith stood behind the chair and put her hands on Willie Jane's shoulders. "My prayer partner, Marthellen."

Willie Jane's eye widened. "Bence's mama knew who I was all along?"

"Yes, she did."

"And she treated me nice anyway?"

"She said you were like an angel."

Willie Jane's shoulders quaked and she began to sob. "Why are you doing this to me?"

Judith stepped aside. "Doing what?"

"Treating me so much better than I deserve."

"Everyone needs somebody to treat them well or else how can they ever know how to treat others?"

"I don't ... I really don't," Willie Jane sobbed and wiped her eyes. "Maybe a little nice sometimes ... but not like this. I can never repay you."

"You already have by the way you're taking care of Bence and Marthellen," Judith assured her.

"I haven't done much."

"Well, I'm going to leave you in charge of them right now. Mrs. Adair is scheduled to be on the morning train. It will take some time getting her situated and settled in at home. Then I have to tell her about Mr. Primble's death."

"You ever notice how I ain't very lucky with men?" Willie Jane blurted out. "Milt jilted me, and now he's dead. Bence and me was just gettin' chummy and now he's dyin'. That ain't a good record."

Judith hugged Willie Jane. "I have a feeling things will be different. Right now, I need to go to the depot. I'm a little nervous to tell Audrey about Milton. I don't know if she will laugh or cry. And I have no idea what she'll say when I tell her the fifteen thousand dollars was not in her safe. You and Marthellen go ahead and fix yourselves some lunch. It might be a while before I return." At the door she paused and turned around. "Be sure and pray for me."

"Me?" Willie Jane gulped. "You want me to pray for you?"

"Can you do it with a sincere heart?"

"Eh … yes, ma'am. I reckon I can."

"Then I definitely want you praying for me."

The coffee at the sheriff's office was cold and bitter as the judge swirled it in his tin cup and took a swig.

"I figure Primble probably met his just desserts," the sheriff mumbled, "but I've got a murder to solve just the same. I've just got too many suspects, and most all of them women. There's Audrey, the crib girl, and this woman who claims to be Primble's sister. If Primble was up in that old barn, I surely wish I knew who was with him."

"You've got two witnesses who were up in that barn, too. Bence, who is dying … and he didn't see the woman anyway.

And then there's Duffy." The judge could feel the coffee sour his stomach. "He saw a man in the barn, but you know Duffy; he'll stand up in court and say it was Wild Bill he saw. And even though the coat with the holes in it belonged at one time to Primble, there's no proof that Milton was wearing it. Or that the blood on the post was his. His clothing has appeared all along the river."

The sheriff took another deep gulp of coffee. "Having only Duffy Day as a witness is almost worse than having no witnesses. The truth of the matter is, Audrey Adair is the last person we know who was with Primble and she had plenty of reason to fight back." He offered to refill the judge's blue tin cup.

Judge Kingston covered his cup with his free hand. "But that doesn't fit, Sheriff. If he was beating her, and she shot him, that would be self-defense. No jury in Carson would have convicted her. She knows that. Besides, how does a severely injured woman tote a grown man out to the river, unseen?"

"You aren't much help in this, Judge." The sheriff wiped coffee drips off his chin. "All I'm sayin' is most folks in town think Audrey did it and most folks are glad she did."

"I think Primble disappeared, but he was hiding out when his sister came to town," the judge offered. "I don't know if they ever got together, but I don't figure Eliza would shoot her brother."

"We could blame it on a bushwhacker passin' by, ridin' the highline, if Primble's body was found in that barn," the sheriff said. "But if he was moved to the river, someone wanted him to be found there."

"And if someone wanted him found there, then they're still playing out their hand, which leads back to Mrs. Conroy." The judge swigged the last of his coffee, half of it grounds. "If I have to drink another cup of this sludge ..."

Dr. Jacobs pushed open the door, a thick, short cigar pinched between his lips. The room filled with a smoky tobacco aroma. "You two solvin' a crime?"

"No, we're discussing the merits of the sheriff's coffee," the judge said.

"I've declared it a health hazard on numerous occasions," the doctor hooted, "but I can't get anyone to enforce the ruling."

"No one has to drink what they don't want to drink. I been cookin' good coffee like that ever since I left home at age twelve," the sheriff blustered.

"Which is another good reason why a lad should stay home until he's twenty," the doctor said as he flipped cigar ashes into an old milking bucket that served as a trash can. "I just came from Kitzmeyer's. He's got Milt all laid out in his Sunday finest. He wants to know if Audrey's payin' for the funeral, or is it a county job?"

"Audrey's coming home this morning, and Judith is going to talk to her about that." The judge patted his chest, trying to relieve the heartburn.

Levi Boyer burst through the door and strolled straight for the woodstove and the coffee.

"You get Judith and Mrs. Adair delivered?" the judge asked.

"Yep." Boyer tipped his hat. "Sheriff, Duffy Day's out on the steps waiting for you. Say, do you mind if I have me a cup of this here coffee? You know what, Judge? The sheriff makes the best coffee in town." He inhaled deeply, "And the doctor smokes the finest smellin' cigars that Jacob Tobriner sells."

"You see, Honorable Judge Kingston!" the sheriff boasted. "Mr. Boyer is obviously a man with discriminating tastes. Now, how about you and the doc coming with me and Duffy?"

"Where are you headed?" the doctor asked.

"Down to Kitzmeyer's." The sheriff pulled on his hat. "I want to see if Duffy can tell me whether this was the man he saw in that old barn."

"I think I'll stay here," Levi said, smiling from behind a tin coffee cup. "I've already seen him dead."

The three men meandered out into the courthouse hall.

"Duffy won't go into the building," the judge reminded them.

"Don't matter," the doctor reported. "Mr. Kitzmeyer has Primble propped up on a board and peering out the window of his furniture store. He's chargin' a nickel a look. It's provin' a good draw for their closing-out business sale."

The sheriff led the procession to the southeast corner of Carson Street and Second Street, to Kitzmeyer's Furniture and Undertaking.

The Washburn brothers loitered at the Second Street window. "Hey, Judge, ol' Primble sure does look peaceful, don't he?" Twig Washburn called out as the ensemble approached.

"I reckon his ol' lady shot him in his sleep, don't you?" Lester Washburn added.

Duffy Day shuffled behind the judge, making sure he didn't come in contact with the Washburn Brothers. The Washburns finally sauntered across Second Street toward the state capitol.

The judge stopped short of the display window. "Duffy, you understand what I want you to do?"

"You want me to look at a corpse and see if it's Wild Bill Hickok," Duffy stated.

"That's not what I said," the judge corrected. "I want you to tell me if this is the man you saw out in that barn, the one that chased you off into the Sierras."

Duffy rocked back and forth on his heels. "Yep, that's what I said."

The sheriff raised his long, thin eyebrows. "I don't think you got a credible witness here, Your Honor."

"Well, I'll believe him," the judge retorted.

"Me, too," Dr. Jacobs said, pulling the stubby cigar out of his mouth and waving it in front of him. "Duffy, step up there and take a look at that corpse."

"Is it goin' to cost me a nickel?"

"You get to do it for free," the sheriff informed him.

A wide smile broke across Duffy's face. He stepped to the window, cupped his grimy hands around his eyes, and peered in.

When he turned back, the look on his face couldn't have been more joyous if he had discovered mother lode gold at the Comstock. He threw his flop hat on the wooden sidewalk and began to dance a jig and sing. "'I'm Captain Jinks of the horse marines, I feed my horse on corn and beans … '"

"Is that the man, Duffy?" the judge prodded.

"That's Wild Bill, all right! They done shot Wild Bill!" Duffy continued his sidewalk jig. "'… escort young ladies in their teens, I'm a captain in the army.'"

"Is this the man you saw at the broken-down barn?" the sheriff said again.

Duffy didn't stop dancing. "I said it was! ' … Oh, I teach the ladies how to dance, how to dance, how to dance, I teach the ladies how to dance, for I'm a captain in the army.'"

"This is the one who shot at you, Duffy?" the judge repeated.

"Yes, sir … yes, sir … yes, sir … he shot at me by the river and he shot at me by the barn. Now, he's dead ... he's dead, and I'm alive. Ain't that somethin'? Ain't that somethin'? 'Oh, I'm Captain Jinks of the horse marines, I feed my horse on corn and beans, I often live beyond my means ... a captain in the army.'"

The judge grabbed Duffy by the shoulders and held on until he stopped dancing. "Duffy, listen, did you say this man shot at you down by the river?"

"That's him, all right. I seen his shadow in the moonlight. A big old harvest moon was hangin' over the hills that night, and I seen him."

"I thought it was dark and you didn't know who it was," the sheriff questioned.

"I didn't know for sure until today. Look at that shadow." He pointed toward the corpse behind the window pane.

"You mean the shadow on the wall caused by Mr. Kitzmeyer's gas light?" the judge offered.

"Yep. That's the exact outline of the man that rode out to the river that night and took a potshot at me. I never forget a shadow, no sir. Now maybe everyone will believe me. I was right, it was Wild Bill Hickok." Duffy hummed his song and continued his jig.

"What do you think, Judge?" the sheriff asked.

"I believe Milton is the man Duffy saw in the barn and I believe he's the one who rode out of town that night with a woman," the judge replied.

"So do I," Dr. Jacobs concurred. "Duffy may be touched, but he's not dumb."

As Duffy continued to sing and dance, the sheriff stepped closer to the judge. "Is there any way we can use Duffy's testimony in a court of law?"

"Absolutely not. Even a novice lawyer would shred him. They'd have Duffy seeing Kit Carson, Major Ormsby, and old Chief Winnemucca, himself."

The sheriff exhaled deeply, his shoulders slumped. "So where do we go from here?"

"Back to my office to do some contemplating," the judge said. "There's something missing in all this and I haven't figured out what."

They watched the jubilant Duffy, who showed no signs of slowing down. The judge chuckled. "I am glad to see all of this has made one man happy."

Audrey Adair arrived at the Virginia and Truckee Railroad Station looking rested and determined. Her speech was limited because of her sore jaw. She walked slowly because of bruised ribs. Her arm was still in a purple silk sling. But the steady eyes and firm chin defined a matriarch who ruled the roost of the mansion on West Robinson Street.

Levi Boyer helped load Audrey's luggage into the two-seat black carriage.

"Judith, it is so nice to see you waiting at the station for me. You've helped to make Carson feel like home. I'm afraid I will miss it and you very much," Audrey gushed.

Judith lightly kissed Audrey's wide cheek. The older woman's skin felt soft, like a young child's. "You really are moving to California?"

"Oh, yes, it's inevitable. Mr. Ashley Fitzgibbon turns out to be the most fascinating and capable fellow. He found me just the place I wanted and could afford."

"Eh … Audrey, I need to tell you some important things," Judith began, as they climbed up into the sleek carriage. The black leather seats were much softer than the carriage she and the judge had ridden to the lake.

Audrey held up her hand. "Not nearly as many as I need to tell you. Not another word until we are having Chinese green tea at my house." Audrey nodded to the front seat where Levi Boyer sat. "I like my conversations in private, dear," she whispered, then so all could hear, "Isn't this a delightful day? I can see by the load of dust on the trees we had a zephyr this week."

"It was quite horrid."

"I will not miss those, of course."

"I'm surprised Mrs. Coffee didn't return with you," Judith said. "I presume she's preparing your new home in San Francisco?"

Audrey Adair leaned close to Judith, holding a gloved hand to her mouth and nodding at the driver again. "I let her go, dear," she whispered.

"Oh, my."

"I'm afraid there will be no more servants for me," Audrey declared.

"Why?"

Audrey sat up straight and dropped her hand to her lap. "That is only one of the things I must tell you."

Judith boiled the tea while Audrey tried to get herself comfortable. "That long ride stiffened me all up," she said.

They sat in the huge living room. Audrey lounged on a crimson velvet couch. Judith perched on the end and took a deep breath. "Audrey, I opened your safe exactly as you instructed ..."

Audrey's hands went to her mouth. "My word, it was empty, wasn't it?"

"Well, there were some papers, but ..."

"But no money!"

"Yes." Judith held back her emotions. "Did you know that?" *I can't tell if her eyes show anger or delight. But it is absolutely the first time I've ever seen Audrey's hands without one ring on any finger.*

"Oh, my, I can't believe I could forget. It was not until you said those words that it all came back," Audrey exclaimed. "That night ... that horrid night when Mr. Primble attacked me and fled, before I even sought Dr. Jacobs, I crawled over to the safe and took the money out. I was so worried Milton would come back and find out the combination, one way or another. It's as if I blanked that totally from my mind until this moment. Oh Judith, you must have been frightfully upset with me."

Upset with you? I thought I would be imprisoned for grand larceny. I thought I would have to take a job at the hotel and work for thirty years to pay you back. I thought we would have to sell our home and live in a tent to settle the debt. Judith wiped imaginary crumbs from her mouth with a rose pink silk napkin. "Oh no, I wasn't upset with you, Audrey. But if the money's not in your safe, where is it?"

Even though they were entirely alone in the massive home, Audrey Adair leaned over and whispered. "In my bloomer drawer, dear. No man would ever look there. Would you run upstairs and check for me? I'll pour us some more tea."

When Judith returned, Audrey was standing by her large carved teakwood and glass hutch, staring at the varied sizes of glasses and china. Judith admired the set of Hungarian blown crystal goblets in tones of emerald, ruby, amethyst, amber, rose, and sapphire.

Audrey turned around. "Did you find it, Judith?"

"Yes, it was all right there under your—"

"Yes, yes, under my bloomers. I can't believe I went to California and left money lying in a dresser drawer."

"You were understandably disoriented," Judith said.

Audrey continued to stare at the hutch.

"Would you like me to get something down for you, Audrey?"

"I was just wondering which things I will take to California and which I will sell off."

"You're selling your good dishes?"

"That's an understatement, my dear. And thank you for ridding my house of Mr. Primble's things. I'm grateful for that. There is one thing I'm glad about, and that is, I will never have to see that man again."

Judith studied Audrey's eyes, almost as deep blue as the sapphire in her goblets. *Why is she so certain she'll never see him again?*

"I know what you're thinking, my dear."

"You do?" *You know I'm wondering if you killed your husband?*

"You're wondering how I can be so sure that Mr. Primble will stay in Mexico. Well, my first husband, Mr. McKensie, has been down there for years. I'm sure Milton can—"

"Audrey, I've been trying to get up the nerve to tell you. Mr. Primble is dead." *What ever happened to subtlety? Sensitivity? Caring? You just beat her over the head with it, dear Judith.*

"Dead?" Audrey gasped.

"They found his body yesterday by the river. He was shot twice in the chest. I didn't have time to telegraph you."

Audrey's expression was stoic.

No tears.

No laughter.

Just a dull, blank stare.

"It doesn't surprise me, of course," she finally said. "I tried to tell him that night that his behavior could only lead to ruin and destruction. He didn't listen to me. Judith, have you ever spoken hours upon end to someone and then realized they haven't paid attention to one word you said? That's the way it always was with Mr. Primble and me."

Both ladies sat down on the couch. This time Audrey sat straight, feet on the polished rosewood floor. Judith sipped the tea slowly. *What I'd like to know, dear Audrey, is whatever in the world attracted you to Milton Primble in the first place?*

"He was wild that night, like a mad man. His death doesn't surprise me in the least. The fact that I didn't die, too, is the biggest surprise. Who shot him?"

"The sheriff doesn't know."

"I presume I am a suspect?"

"I suppose. Audrey, if you feel like it, why don't you tell me all about that evening? What was it that so aggravated Mr. Primble?"

"Money, of course." Audrey tapped her sturdy fingers on the table. "That's something both my husbands had in common. They loved my money. At least, McKensie did at first. But later he seemed to be bothered by it. I thought he tired of me. Now I wonder if I didn't run him off. But with Mr. Primble, when he learned the money was running out, he got quite upset."

"Running out? But your fortune …?"

"Why do you think I have to sell everything and move to a modest home in San Francisco?"

"But what about the money upstairs?"

"That will provide the home. And what I can get out of this mansion will provide my only income. I am much too old to open up a bookstore again. Besides, I never could make a living at the first one."

Judith felt all the blood draining from her face. "But I don't understand."

"Well dear, there is some old proverb that riches easily gained are easily lost. So true, so true. Besides the fortunes that were spent by my husbands, I lost most of the rest of it on my own."

"How did that happen?"

"About a year ago, a former banker of mine who is now in the Black Hills, wrote to me about the opportunities for making a bonanza in gold mine speculation there. I succumbed to greed and did a little investing."

"And you lost the money?"

"I lost over $170,000," Audrey reported.

"Oh, no!"

"Mr. Primble had a similar reaction."

"You did the investing without his knowledge?"

"Indeed. My money was all within my control. I had a legal document to that effect drawn up before we were married. I did not intend to repeat the same mistake twice."

"And Mr. Primble was extremely upset, I take it?"

"Oh, yes. Audrey Adair is not much of an attraction without her fortune."

"He beat you because you lost your fortune?"

"He beat me because I would not open my safe and give him my last fifteen thousand dollars."

"He knew the money was there?" Judith asked. *His sister knew it was in there as well.*

"He watched me put it there and was always resentful that I wouldn't tell him the combination."

Judith felt her neck and chin tighten up. "Did he know I had the combination?"

"Oh, no. I wouldn't have divulged that."

"So he attacked you to get the combination?"

"Yes. You see, he had this little peccadillo arranged with one of those appalling crib girls," Audrey announced.

"What kind of peccadillo?"

"To take my money and run off to Mexico."

"How did you know that?"

"He told me. It's surprising what a man says while he's busting your jaw and cracking your ribs. That's why I knew he wasn't coming back. There is no more fortune to plunder. He certainly isn't going to return to my arms. Not that he was ever in them very often."

"So, this move of yours to California was planned even before the beating?"

"I'm afraid so, Judith. I have no intention of being pointed at in this town as the lady who used to be rich but now is selling cabbages on the street corner. I waited until the last minute to tell Mr. Primble. Perhaps I shouldn't have told him at all."

"Audrey, I'm so sorry."

"About the money? Or Milton?"

"Everything."

"My dear, Mr. Primble was probably shot by the crib girl he could no longer afford to take to Mexico with him. I don't blame her. I had thought about it once or twice myself. And the night of the beating I would have done it, if I had a gun."

"But you've lost your money."

"For the first forty years of my life I survived on very little.

For the past twenty, I've been incredibly wealthy. And what has it brought me? An empty house of unused luxury, broken bones, and I can't count the buckets of tears. Being wealthy is overrated, my dear."

Audrey yawned and leaned back against the crimson fringed pillows. "Now I'm simply exhausted from the travel. I think I'd like a nap. Would you send word that I need to visit with whomever the new bank manager is? I think it's Sam Tjader. I'll need to forward these funds to California and make arrangements for the sale of my things. Please don't pity me, Judith. Even after I sell most of my treasures, I will have much more now than I ever did twenty years ago. And please, let Mr. Kitzmeyer know I will provide for the arrangements for Mr. Primble. Whatever else may be said about that wretched man, he was still my legal husband at the time of death."

The judge and the sheriff were hiking back toward the courthouse when Sam Tjader, the new bank manager, popped his shaggy head out of the tall, narrow doorway of the Ormsby County Bank and boomed out, "Do you have a moment?"

The sheriff and the judge followed the bank manager into his private office. Tjader closed the eight-foot-tall mahogany door. "Gentlemen, this is a most discreet matter. Was there any money found near where Mr. Primble was murdered?"

"I thought you accounted for the bank's money with the five thousand dollars in Primble's desk," the judge said.

"This is frightfully embarrassing. But the truth of the matter is, that money, while certainly embezzled, was only a decoy."

"What are you talkin' about, Sam? Come right out with it," the sheriff demanded.

"We believe Mr. Primble used that money to throw us off in

our investigation," Mr. Tjader replied.

The judge straightened his tie, then rubbed his chin whiskers. "You mean, the five thousand dollars was easy to locate in the books because he figured you'd be satisfied, then not look deeper?"

"Exactly. But I couldn't sleep last night. There was something about the operation of this bank that kept disturbing me. I've been down here since 2:00 A.M., poring over every account, every penny."

"And just how much is actually missing?" the judge questioned.

Sam Tjader lowered his husky voice, giving a try at a whisper. "Fifty thousand dollars."

"What?" the sheriff shouted.

Sam Tjader waved his arms up and down. "I'm sure you two will appreciate that I need to keep this quiet."

The sheriff spoke in a quieter voice. "No wonder Primble was shot. He must have had the money on him. This could be a basic case of robbery."

"But it doesn't make sense," the judge said. "If Primble had that much money, why did he linger at the barn for several days?"

"Maybe the funds were hidden someplace," the sheriff suggested. "Maybe he was lyin' low."

"Perhaps he had an accomplice," the bank manager added. "Sheriff, I've already wired my superiors about this and they are sending some Pinkerton men to try and retrieve the funds. But if I can turn up any more clues before their arrival, it will be important to me. I wonder if you might take me to where the body was found so I can have my own look around."

"Even better than that," the sheriff offered. "I'll take you to a place he was hiding out between the time of his disappearance and his death."

Judith was surprised to find Levi Boyer and the black carriage waiting outside of Audrey Adair's house when she strolled out to the sidewalk. "Levi, you haven't been waiting for me all this time, have you?"

"No, ma'am." He tipped his hat and waited for her to crawl up into the carriage. "I went down to the sheriff's office for a bit, then I had some folks to pick up at the depot and take to the capitol. But while I was there, Curtis said he had two telegrams for you and the judge. I thought I'd swing by and deliver them to you."

"Thank you, Levi, you certainly are kind to me."

He handed her the telegrams. "I ain't begun to pay you and Judge Kingston back for all the times you've helped me."

Judith unfolded the telegrams on her lap. *Lord, I never like to read telegrams in public. I always want to run into the house and read them in private and decide how I want to react.*

"Do you know what Curtis told me?" Levi called to her over his shoulder. "He said the only one in Carson City who gets more telegrams than you is Governor Kinkead."

"This has been quite unusual the past couple of weeks."

Levi turned east on Musser Street. "Guess who's coming to Carson next month?"

"I have no idea."

"Marcy's mama and daddy, all the way from Placerville."

"Is that because of you and Marcy?"

"Do you reckon?" Levi said.

"She's mentioned you, hasn't she?"

"I believe she wrote and said we was courtin'."

"Then they're definitely coming to see you," Judith said.

"I wonder if I ought to buy a new suit."

"That might be a good idea."

"I ain't too good at pickin' out nobby clothes."

"Perhaps Marcy will help you."

"I don't want Marcy to know I'm buying new clothes. She would feel bad if she knew I was makin' such a fuss about her folks comin'."

"Would you like me to go with you to Koppel and Platt's, across from the St. Charles?"

"Would you do that for me? I heard they got a new stock of merchandise."

Levi pulled up at the Kingston home.

"You just let me know when, Levi."

"Yes, ma'am, I surely will. Thank you, Judith."

She climbed down from the carriage. *A man picks up my telegrams ... waits for me at Audrey's ... gives me a ride home ... and then thanks me? Lord, I'm not sure I can live up to this legendary Judith Kingston image. But I do thank you for the kindness people show me.*

Judith went straight to Marthellen's room to check on Bence. She found Marthellen standing outside the door.

"Oh, dear ... is it Bence?"

"The Reverend Thomas Fraser is visiting with him now."

"Where's Willie Jane?"

"Upstairs trying to clean up. Bence said he wanted to talk to Reverend Fraser by himself."

"Does he seem to be ...?"

"There's no movement or feeling below his neck. His breathing is so shallow, it scares me. It's like every breath will be his last." Judith could see now that Marthellen was weeping.

Judith threw her arms around the slightly older, slightly taller, slightly heavier woman.

"I can't help thinking," Marthellen said between sobs, "that if I had provided him a better life ... if I had kept away from sin when I was younger ... if I could have kept his father from running off ... if I would have tried to find him these past years he wouldn't have gotten connected with men like the Kendalls and he would never be in this horrible situation."

Judith held on tight. "Dear sweet, sweet Marthellen, we are all responsible for our own lives. Your Charlotte made some good choices and she had the very same upbringing. Bence made some poor ones. We reap the consequences of our own decisions."

"But I could have done things better." Each of Marthellen's words came out with a guttural halt in her crying.

"All of us could do things better, Marthellen. Now is the time to entrust Bence into the loving arms of the God who created him. Forget about what you could have done. Think through what you are willing to do now. Besides, I'm sure Bence doesn't blame you for this."

"Oh, no." Marthellen wept all the harder. "He just keeps saying 'I'm sorry, Mama ... I'm so sorry, Mama.'"

The tears in Judith's eyes kept her from seeing Marthellen at all. The sobs in her own heart kept her from speaking. The two women just held each other and rocked back and forth.

Several moments later, Willie Jane entered the hallway. "Oh, no," she moaned as she saw the ladies. "He hasn't—?"

"No," Marthellen assured, "not yet."

"We're just practicing," Judith added.

Willie Jane's voice was so faint it was almost a purr. "Do you mind if I practice a little?"

Judith and Marthellen opened their arms and welcomed her into the circle.

After a season of hugs, the ladies retrieved their handkerchiefs.

"You can't imagine how nice it is to be hugged by someone who really cares about me," Willie Jane confessed. "I've spent so much of my life in a very phony world. I playact night and day until I can't even remember which emotions are real."

The Reverend Fraser opened the kitchen door. "Bence wants to talk to Marthellen and Willie Jane now."

They scurried quickly into Marthellen's room and Judith walked the Reverend to the door. "Thank you for coming, Thomas," she said.

"I'll be in my study, Judith. Send someone across the street to fetch me if I can be of any more service."

"Do you think Bence is trusting the Lord Jesus?" Judith asked him.

"Yes, he is. He has squandered his life, but he hasn't squandered his eternity."

Judith slipped her hands into the deep pockets of her dress as she watched the Reverend Thomas Fraser cross Nevada Street toward the church.

My telegrams!

The first came from the postmaster in Martinsburg, Pennsylvania.

> Concerning Mrs. Eliza Conroy. I am informed that she moved to St. Louis, Missouri, two years ago.

Judith stared at the beige-colored paper. "St. Louis?" she mumbled. *Milton's sister really did live in St. Louis? Mrs. Conroy really is his sister? Lord, I just knew she was a phony. In fact, I was kind of counting on it. Oh my, what is happening here?*

She quickly opened the other telegram.

Dear Mother & Father,

Two telegrams in one day? I get the point. I'll stay at the university this term. No, I'm not going to write my good news. I want to tell you in person. You'll have to wait.

Your obedient, twenty-year-old daughter,

Roberta

Judith reread the note. *Two telegrams? What does she mean two telegrams? Did the judge wire her, too? He didn't tell me a thing about it.*

Of course, I didn't tell him either.

Marthellen walked out of her room with bloodshot eyes but no tears. "Bence wants to talk to the judge and Dr. Jacobs right away."

"I'll go get them," Judith insisted.

"No, no, I'll—"

"Nonsense, Marthellen. You get back in there with your boy right now."

Although it was only midafternoon, the room was dark. There were no lanterns on, no curtains pulled wide. No windows were open. The air was stale, heavy, like a fog in December that shows no sign of lifting. The aroma of death seemed to settle into the room.

But the motionless man on the bed was not dead.

The tall man in a crisp suit with perfectly straight posture sat on the side chair beside him.

"Judge, I ain't got long. I know it. The doc knows it. Mama knows it."

"What did you need to talk to me about, Bence? How can I help you, son?"

"I need two big favors of you. And I don't have no right to ask either."

"What are they?"

"First, would you take care of my mama for me? I know you've been doin' a good job, and I've been neglectin' her. But it's my responsibility and I've known it ever since I was twelve and my daddy run off. Now that I'm willin' to do something about it, I'm just up and dyin' on her."

The judge dabbed at his eyes. "Bence, your mother's place is in this home for the rest of her life. As long as she wants to stay here she'll have a home with us."

"Thanks, Judge. I knew you would, but I had to ask. You don't know how good it makes me feel inside knowin' that Mama has you and Judith."

"What else can I do for you?"

"I want you to perform a marriage service."

"You and Willie Jane?"

"Yessir. Can you do that? I mean, I know it's legal. I talked to the Reverend and he said it was perfectly legal for you to do it. I know he could do it, but I don't know him much, and I'd like you to."

"I don't understand, Bence. Why marriage now?"

"I know this is hard to decipher, Judge. I explained it to my mama. She understood. I think Willie Jane understands, too. It's very important to me."

"You two love each other that much?"

"It's a whole different thing than love. I like Willie Jane a whole lot. I wish to God I had met her when I was eighteen and she was eighteen. But that wasn't what happened. I figure, if I had the time, me and her would fall in love and get married and straighten out our lives and maybe even live to make folks proud of us. But I don't got that time."

"So, why the marriage?"

"It's all my idea. But it seems to me it gives us both something to hold onto."

"What do you mean?"

"Well, sir, Willie Jane gets a new name. From this day forward she could be called Mrs. Farnsworth. Now, that ain't much of a name, I know, but in this town it takes her out of the cribs and gives her a family tie. She's got kin here. She's got a mother-in-law. She's got you and Judith. I ain't promisin' nothin'. But that could be just enough of a break to help her start over."

"I see your point. It's a noble gesture," the judge said, "but what do you get out of it?"

"Maybe I'll have one puny little jewel in my crown when I stand before my Maker."

"You know that getting to heaven isn't based on good deeds."

"I know it, Judge. I'm trustin' in Jesus and in him alone. But the Reverend said that when we get there, we'll cast our crowns before the feet of the Savior. And I ain't done much in my life to ever put even one jewel in that crown. I'd surely like to meet the Lord and hear him say, 'You done good right there at the end, Bence. You done real good.'"

This time the judge didn't bother brushing back the tears.

CHAPTER TEN

Marthellen poured the judge some hot, black coffee, then sat down to his right at the large mahogany dining table.

The judge turned to the young woman at his left. "Mrs. Farnsworth, how did your day go?"

Willie Jane looked startled. "It was busy, Your Honor."

Judith laughed. "Willie Jane, you are not allowed to spoil him and call him Your Honor. You may call him Judge, or you may call him Mr. Kingston, but he's still the one who splits the wood, buries the garbage, and burns the trash."

"I'm sorry, I just got flustered when he called me Mrs. Farnsworth." She glanced at Marthellen. "Don't get me wrong, I'm extremely proud to have that name. I just have to get used to it."

"Willie Jane and I were busy making arrangements for Bence's funeral," Marthellen added. "I didn't know there were so many details."

The judge glanced across the table at Judith. He noticed the loose wisps escaping from her usually neatly pinned hair. "I suppose you scurried about with preparations for the other funeral, Mrs. Kingston?"

Judith winced. "It was memorable, to say the least. Mrs. Conroy barged into Kitzmeyer's while Audrey and I were there. She said she didn't want Audrey to have anything to do with the service for Milton. She threatened to hire armed guards to keep Audrey from the cemetery. Then she screamed and cursed, accusing poor Audrey of killing her brother. I truly thought she and Audrey would come to blows."

"Does it strike you that she accuses too loudly?"

"Yes, and she's accusing the wrong person," Judith said.

"The only thing they agree on is they both want to settle the matter quickly," the judge replied.

"Audrey was too upset this afternoon to know what she wants. She swells up like a red beet when she gets angry. I do believe she was close to a heart attack today," Judith commented.

"My word, what happened next?"

"Audrey hollered that Milton was her husband and that no woman on earth could make her stay away from the funeral."

"This has the elements of a Euripides Greek tragedy," he said.

"Or an Aristophanes comedy. Anyway, it calmed down after that."

Willie Jane and Marthellen shrugged across the table at each other. The judge took a slow sip of coffee and nodded in appreciation. "What happened?"

Judith tried to stuff her falling hair back into the combs. "Audrey told me to make whatever arrangements necessary, then fumed and stormed out of the store."

"And the Conroy woman?"

"She said she was going to see the sheriff about preventing the 'murderess' from attending Milton's funeral. She also said I should go ahead with whatever plans I wanted."

"She did? She let you organize things?"

"By default, I suppose," Judith said.

The judge set the empty mug down. Marthellen got up and poured it full again. "But it does give you a chance to set things up the way you wanted," he said.

"I hope I remembered everything." Judith fussed with the tiny abalone buttons on her dress. "By that time my head was spinning so, I had a strong desire to run home and crawl in bed and hide under the blankets."

Willie Jane blurted, "I know how you felt. Sometimes I pull the blankets over my head, too."

Marthellen gazed into her empty teacup, "What's Audrey going to do? Is she going to the service?"

"At this point, I'm not sure. She's afraid if she doesn't go, there will be more rumors around town. On the other hand, she doesn't want to be where the Conroy woman is."

"And," the judge added, "I would suppose Audrey doesn't exactly like someone telling her what she can and can't do."

"Yes, I'm sure that's part of it."

"I do believe we'll have an exciting Saturday," he said.

Judith stood and begin to clear the dishes. "I am very glad Bence's service is earlier in the day," she said.

Marthellen scooted her chair back. "Mrs. Kingston, would you please put down those dishes? That is my job, and you know it."

"Oh, I don't mind, I can—"

"Well, I mind," Marthellen insisted. "The quicker I get back into the routine of things, the more I will feel at home. Besides, I have a wonderful helper tonight. Us Farnsworth women are in charge of the kitchen. Isn't that right, Willie Jane?"

Willie Jane took one last sip of coffee and stood up. "Yes, it is. Until I get a job and can have a place of my own, I intend to do my part around here. On Sunday Marthellen promised to teach me how to cook beef pasties, green tomato chutney, and corn chowder."

"You have the best teacher in Nevada," the judge assured

her. "Be sure she includes her Apple Charlotte. That's her daughter's specialty too." He glanced at Judith, standing near the hutch. "Well, Mrs. Kingston, after such an ordeal today, shall we go for a little stroll and try to quiet your spirit?"

"That sounds peaceful, Judge Kingston. I'll get my hat."

The sun had just set on the Carson Range to the west of town. The sky was sea blue, the mountains a silhouette of two dimensions—height and width—like a cardboard cutout. The random pattern of mountain peaks had no seeming order, no sequence, but Judith sensed a design and purpose in them as they tucked around the Eagle Valley. There was a soft, reassuring breeze, like one of the judge's kisses on the back of her neck.

They hiked across Nevada Street and strolled up Musser toward the Methodist church. Judith's left arm was looped in the judge's; her right arm held a small conical parasol that rested on her shoulder.

"Does our house seem crowded to you?" the judge asked.

"I suppose. It might take a few weeks for Willie Jane to get situated in her own place." Judith twirled the parasol slowly as they crossed Division Street, just ahead of Governor Kinkead's surrey.

They both waved, then the judge patted her gloved hand. "She and Marthellen seem to sincerely hit it off. Of course, they have the business of Bence's funeral to work on together now. It could be more difficult later."

"I think they'll do fine." Judith stopped next to the Methodist church and sniffed a large pink rose. "I think I'd like some perfume like this."

"Why? Doesn't your present perfume work?"

"Work?" Judith tilted her head and held her hands under her

chin. "Why, Judge, whatever do you mean?"

"You don't think I'm just some simple little Kentucky farm boy, do you?"

"Oh no, Your Honor," she feigned. "I think you're a simple, big Kentucky farm boy. May I buy some rose perfume?"

"Of course."

"Would you like to turn down Minnesota Street?" she asked.

"No, let's go on up to Phillips."

"Well, both Mrs. Farnsworths think you did a wonderful job with the wedding," Judith announced. She recalled the grim groom being nursed by his mother on one side of the bed, his hand clutched on the other by a pensive Willie Jane. The judge and Judith stood at the foot. The bride held yellow rose buds, wore a yellow shawl over Judith's brown dress and a small yellow hat on top her black hair. There were no cake or punch or presents.

The judge, sensing Judith's need to scurry to catch up, slowed his long stride. "I don't believe I ever married a couple who knew their marriage wouldn't last much more than an hour," he said.

"It seems like Bence just gave up after that. He's now in the care of God's mercy and justice. Perhaps he's better off than the Kendall gang. They have to answer an angry mob's justice and then come face-to-face with God."

The judge tipped his hat to several passersby.

"I think Bence finally released his spirit and quit fighting the inevitable," Judith added. She was beginning to perspire, but the leg stretching of the walk felt good.

The judge pointed across the intersection. "Let's go south on Phillips." They meandered across the vacant street. "Yes, my dear Judith, I sincerely hope this charade at the cemetery works."

"Did you get Duffy bathed, shaved, and clothed?" she asked.

"I sent Tray and Levi out to scrub him up. They came back grumbling and covered with mud," the judge reported. "But Duffy is clean."

"And his hair?"

"Mr. Matthews set him on a box on the sidewalk out in front of his barbershop. That's where he cut Duffy's hair and gave him a shave. You should have seen the crowd he drew."

Judith tried to imagine a bathed and clean-shaven Duffy Day, but she had absolutely no reference point. "How does he look?"

"He looks about twenty instead of forty."

"How old do you think he is?"

"As far as any of us can remember, Duffy should be about thirty." The judge reached up and loosened his black tie just a little, then unfastened the top button of his boiled white shirt.

"How about a suit?" Judith asked. "Could you actually get Duffy to try one on?"

"That was a farce."

"Duffy wouldn't go inside the store, would he?"

"The clerks at Koppel and Platt's strung a couple of blankets across the alley toward the ice house and made an outdoor changing room."

They waited for several men on horseback to ride west on King Street. Then they cut over to Thompson.

Judith flipped a gray hair off the sleeve of the judge's coat. "Did you find a suit that would fit him?"

"It needs alterations, but it will be finished Saturday morning."

"How does he look in it?"

"Like a different man. It's quite remarkable. Duffy wanted to wear the suit back to his place."

"Did you explain it to him?"

"Oh yes," the judge said. "Several times. He knows he has to show up clean on Saturday in order to get to wear the suit."

They stopped to watch a very pregnant black cat strut past the judge, then rub up against Judith's shoe, purring.

"You haven't promised to take in that tabby's children, have you?" the judge questioned.

"No, of course not." *But if they showed up at our door . . . well, what else could I do?* "Do you and the sheriff really think Duffy can pull this off?"

The judge's strides lengthened again. "As long as he stands in one place and doesn't talk, he might be mistaken for a credible witness."

Judith was now almost trotting. "I've never in my life seen Duffy stand still and not talk." She tugged on his coat sleeve.

He immediately dropped back to a slower pace. "That, my dear Judith, will indeed be a miracle."

"What if it doesn't work?"

"What have we lost? But how about young Mrs. Farnsworth? Does she think she can do her part?"

Judith brushed her curly bangs out of her eyes. "Willie Jane is confident. She says she has spent her whole life acting. This will be no different. I presume you've cued the sheriff?"

"The sheriff, Mayor Cary … the cast is complete." The judge led them east on Fourth Street.

"It is a clever plan you've devised, Judge Kingston."

"Oh no, you don't, dear Judith. This plan was totally your idea. I am still a bit surprised that I'm going along with it."

She grinned. "Then you know how shocked I was when you agreed in the first place."

Judith and the judge passed the silent monuments of the humble and great in the Wright Cemetery on the flanks of Lone Mountain. They stopped a moment by the Jennie Clemens stone marker and surveyed the city. In the foreground was the massive train yard of the Virginia and Truckee Railroad. Directly behind it loomed the brown sandstone United States Mint. Far to the south was the gleaming silver-colored dome of the Nevada State Capitol building.

A line of carriages and wagons pulled up Roop Street.

"It will be a larger funeral than Bence's," Judith said softly.

"That's because Judith Kingston has solicited the services of most every resident in town," the judge commented. "I presume they all know their parts?"

"We'll find out soon enough. I don't believe I've ever been to two funerals in one day," Judith declared. "At least, not since the war. Where shall we stand?"

"This will be fine, for now," the judge instructed.

"You're in charge of coaching Duffy," she reminded him.

"Yes, but I still can't believe that anyone would be threatened by the testimony of Duffy Day."

"But this is a sophisticated-looking Duffy Day. And if you are guilty enough, almost anything will intimidate you," she instructed. "And if you've killed a man, guilt will overwhelm you like a grieving mama bear."

"Where did you get that bit of advice?"

"Oh, I believe I overheard someone say that one time. Stuart Brannon in *Last Hanging in Paradise Meadow*, to be exact. While you lead Duffy to examine the shadows, I'll distract the subject."

"Do you plan to yell or just pick a fight?"

"I will be much more subtle than that," she said.

"This plan is not going to work," the judge insisted.

"It most certainly will. We're just doing exactly what you said we should do on that trip to the lake. We're turning up the heat."

"If the heat's up too high, someone could get injured," he cautioned.

Judith retied her hat's black satin ribbon under her chin. *Just scald that Conroy woman, Lord. Don't injure her ... yet.*

A black covered carriage pulled up and out stepped Daisie Belle Emory in a tiered, embroidered black tulle lace dress trimmed with black satin roses caught at the bustle and shoulders. *She could have worn that to Bence and Willie Jane's wedding. Even the black would have been appropriate,* Judith surmised. *But she would have out-dressed the bride by far.*

"I believe that's Mr. Kitzmeyer's rig coming up now," Judith said. "He's bringing Audrey."

"You said Marthellen's coming with her?" the judge asked.

"Yes, I didn't want Audrey to come alone, and I needed to be here early."

The judge peered over the heads of the other mourners. "It's Marthellen, all right, but there's no Audrey Adair."

Judith scooted around in front of him where she could signal Marthellen and pull her aside.

"Where's Audrey?"

"She decided she just couldn't be on the same hillside as that Conroy woman," Marthellen reported. "I do believe poor Audrey would move to San Francisco tonight if there were a train. I've never seen her so provoked. Does this ruin your plan?"

"Perhaps not. All we need is Mrs. Conroy," Judith explained, "and Duffy Day to recognize her shadow and make an accusation. Surely that will draw a confession out of her."

"It sounds a little too … ah … too simple," Marthellen admitted.

"You are sounding like Judge Kingston. You've got to trust the power of a guilty conscience."

"Judith, there could be a flaw in this plan," Marthellen cautioned.

"Not everyone has as sensitive a conscience as you," the judge interjected.

"It will work." Judith pointed to the street. "Look, here comes Levi. But he's too early. That Conroy woman isn't here yet."

"Maybe we should have them drive slowly around the block and come back later," Marthellen suggested.

"This is getting chimerical," the judge intoned. "We do have a man to bury here this afternoon."

"It's all right," Judith insisted. "Duffy can be standing here all gentlemanly like when she walks up."

Levi Boyer drove Benton's fanciest carriage, carrying Willie Jane Farnsworth and a scrubbed and suited Duffy Day.

Judith stood on her tiptoes and whispered in the judge's ear, "Duffy looks wonderful."

The judge nodded and rubbed his chapped lips. It seemed as if all the people on the crowded hillside examined Duffy's every step. He climbed down and held out his hand for the black-garbed Willie Jane. When she reached the ground, she quickly slid her arm into Duffy's. His smile was self-conscious. He kept looking up at the faces then down to the ground.

Willie Jane fussed over his tie and straightened his new black hat. Then they strolled up the hill toward the waiting congregation.

"They're doing grand," Judith whispered. "Too bad Mrs. Conroy can't see this performance."

"I trust after she arrives, he won't break into a dance and sing a few bars of 'Captain Jinks,'" the judge said.

When the somber Willie Jane and the grinning Duffy Day reached the Kingstons, Judith stepped closer.

"Where is she?" Willie Jane asked.

"I presume she's going to be fashionably late."

A clean-shaven, fresh-smelling Duffy Day leaned forward. "Do I get to keep the suit, Judge?"

The judge kept his eye on Roop Street. "Yes, Duffy, you can keep the suit."

Duffy started rocking back and forth, but Willie Jane's strong grip on his arm kept him from stumbling.

Everyone's attention was focused on another carriage spewing dust as it raced up to the cemetery.

"Is that her?" Judith asked.

"No, it looks like Sheriff Hill and his deputies."

"But ... but they can't come yet! Mrs. Conroy isn't here," Judith sputtered.

"That does present a problem," the judge grumbled.

"What are we going to do?"

"We're going ahead with the service."

"What about the sheriff?"

"Busting in to arrest a confessing Eliza Conroy is quite difficult when that woman isn't here," the judge said.

"Hurry," Judith nudged, "Go tell the sheriff to ride toward Moundhouse. If he returns in about ten minutes, that Conroy woman will be here. I just know it."

She watched the judge hike past the concrete and marble tombstones toward Roop Street. He and the sheriff talked, then the carriage pulled out, heading east. The judge's steps back were slow and deliberate. Judith knew the walk. It was the same he used when he came up Musser Street at lunchtime after deliberating a case all morning. She called it his "moment before the verdict" stride.

But his pace quickened as he hiked up the dirt trail past the tall spiral obelisk in memory of Mrs. Francine Pauline Doyle, consort of Captain William H. Smith.

He didn't stop until his face was in hers. "Judith, feign sickness. We're leaving."

"What?"

"Trust me," he ordered.

Judith slapped her hand to her forehead and collapsed in his arms. The crowd gasped and moved away as the judge gently laid her on the dirt.

Doctor Jacobs rushed to his side. "What happened to Judith?"

The judge spoke under his breath. "Tell me to take her home to get some rest, Doc."

"I say, let me at least look at—"

"Do it," the judge barked.

Doctor Jacobs stood up and said loudly, "Judge, you better get Judith home right away. She needs rest immediately."

The judge scooped Judith up in his arms. She fought to keep her eyes closed. *Judge Kingston, you had better have a tremendous explanation for this.* She relaxed in his strong arms and tried to go limp. Through the narrow slit of a not quite closed eyelid, she could see Daisie Belle's face. *Full of concern? Or is it envy? Longing? Eat your heart out, Daisie Belle Emory. I didn't mean that, Lord. Not too much, anyway.*

"Sorry, Reverend," the judge called out. "I'm going to take

Judith home. Please proceed with the service."

"What about me?" Duffy shouted.

"You stay right there and see they do a good job of burying Wild Bill," the judge hollered as he carried Judith toward the carriage. "Levi, you bring Marthellen, Willie Jane, and Duffy home after it's over."

The judge laid Judith across the carriage seat. He climbed up front and drove the horses south on Roop.

"Can I sit up, Judge Kingston?" she mumbled.

"Wait until I turn west."

"I will wait to sit up, but I will not wait for an explanation. What is all this about?"

"Your plan isn't working," he informed her.

"What do you mean, it isn't working? We didn't wait long enough for Eliza to show up. It will work."

"Judith, the sheriff and his two deputies are on their way to Moundhouse. Meanwhile, half the town is at the cemetery."

"All except Audrey and that Conroy woman," Judith added. She sat up and began to brush dirt off her dress.

"Did you hear what you just said?"

"Eh, what?"

"That the only ones who aren't there are the only two people who should be there: Milton Primble's wife and his sister."

Judith's mind was agitated. She tried to see up and down the streets, looking for anyone, especially a sign of Audrey or Eliza. "Do you think …?"

"I think it's possible Eliza Conroy purposely made Audrey so angry that she refused to attend the funeral. Then, while all of Audrey's friends are at the cemetery … "

"Oh no, what could she be plotting against Audrey?" The

carriage was rolling so fast, Judith grasped the rail. "But why the fainting act?"

"I didn't want to alarm anyone. Perhaps I've miscalculated. We don't even know where they are or what's going on. Besides, even Milton Primble deserves a decent burial."

Judith felt her stomach churn. She clutched his arm as they raced up Carson Street.

When they turned west at the U.S. Mint on Robinson, she could feel the right wheels lifting off the ground. But the team kept galloping toward Audrey Adair's.

They had just crossed Division Street when they heard a gunshot. Then two more.

Judith held back a scream. "Hurry! Surely, Audrey … that Conroy woman wouldn't … Why did I think my dumb plan would work? What did I do?"

"You did precisely what we said we needed to do," the judge reminded her. "You turned up the heat."

"But it was supposed to boil over within the confines of the cemetery. I didn't want Audrey to be the one who got burned."

"That's a risk we took. Perhaps there are more ingredients in the pot than we counted on."

"Some others are here," Judith called out. "There are two saddle horses in Audrey's drive."

"And one has a sidesaddle," the judge added.

Several people crowded on the sidewalk across the street in front of the Montgomery house as the judge pulled up next to the Adair mansion.

"Be careful, Judge," someone yelled. "There's shootin' goin' on inside."

"Who's in there?" he called back.

"I don't know," the man shouted back. "They rode up at different times."

"They?" the judge called.

"A woman arrived first, then a man."

Judith took the judge's hand and climbed down. "A man?"

"Maybe she hired an assistant."

"Or an assassin," Judith shuddered.

The judge pulled his shotgun out from under the carriage seat.

"Do you always carry shotguns to funerals?"

"Always," he said. "You stay out here. I'll investigate . . . carefully," he added.

"I'm going with you," she insisted.

"No, it's not safe."

"If you wanted me safe, you could have left me at the cemetery."

"Let me prowl around first, Judith. Then I'll come get you."

"I can't be of any help sitting outside, not knowing what's going on." She tagged close behind him as he approached the front door.

The door was ajar about an inch. The judge squatted down on his haunches and shoved the door fully open with the barrel of his shotgun. Judith crouched back on Audrey's front porch and backed into a prickly bush. She felt her dress catching on it.

"Audrey?" the judge hollered.

"What do you see?" Judith whispered.

"Nothing, but I hear voices upstairs."

Her dress ripped as she scurried to his side. He cautioned her to stay back and crept into the living room. Judith stole in behind him and found him in the middle of the entry, still crouched on his haunches, surveying the wide staircase.

"Which one's Audrey's room?" he whispered.

Judith swallowed hard. Sweat trickled down under her bangs. "The one at the top of the stairs with the door closed."

"Get behind her piano," he ordered. Judith scampered behind the upright, but banged her toe on some object.

The voices stopped and the bedroom door opened.

"Audrey, are you up there?" the judge shouted.

The barrel of a carbine poked through the door.

"Who wants to know?" a man's deep, raspy voice bellowed.

"I'm First District Judge Hollis Kingston. I demand to speak to Audrey Adair."

Audrey's voice sounded weak, yet somehow resounded with authority. "I'm up here, Judge."

"Are you all right?"

"I am now."

"Who's that up there with you?" the judge kept his shotgun aimed at the carbine barrel that still protruded from the door.

"My husband," Audrey yelled back.

The judge felt the hair on the back of his neck raise. He turned to Judith. Her face looked almost as white as the keys on the piano.

"Audrey, Milton is dead," he shouted. "They're burying him right at this moment."

Suddenly, Audrey Adair flew out across the hall and leaned over the veranda, her arm wrapped around the carbine-toting man's suit-covered arm. "No, no," she called down. "I meant my first husband."

It was close to midnight before the judge got home from the sheriff's office. Judith had pulled on a cotton nightgown and was sipping a hot drink. "Would you like some hot chocolate with me, Judge Kingston?"

"Yes, I believe I would." He hung his coat and hat on the rack by the back door, strolled across the kitchen floor, and kissed his wife.

Judith poured thick gooey chocolate into a ceramic mug, added hot milk from a pan on the stove, and briskly stirred it.

The judge plopped down at the pine breakfast table and loosened his tie. "How's Audrey?"

"Giggling like a schoolgirl."

"Over C.V. McKensie?"

"It appears so."

"Has she had a change of heart with him?"

"Perhaps. It's quite an amazing story." Judith handed the judge his chocolate, then sat down beside him.

"So, C.V. McKensie rode all the way up here from Arizona just to see Audrey and arrived just in time to coldcock Eliza Conroy, who was shooting up the house and threatening to kill Audrey if she didn't give her the fifteen thousand dollars which is now in the bank anyway?"

"Oh, the story gets much better," Judith insisted. "It turned out that C.V. has been living in Mexico all this time, after all."

"So Audrey was right about that?"

"Yes, she was. But very few in this town believed her."

"Why in the world did he pick this afternoon to show up?"

"Judge, just wait until I present the evidence," she insisted.

"Yes, ma'am." He pulled his tie completely off and folded it on the table.

"C.V. got word down in Mexico from his sister in Tucson that there was a package for him at the post office from his former wife."

"Audrey sent him something?"

"No, it wasn't Audrey. But he thought it was from her. When he got to Tucson, there was a brown bundle that was addressed to: 'The Husband of Audrey Adair.'"

"That's all?"

"Apparently it was sent by Mr. Primble to himself."

"Perhaps he had planned to change his name by the time he reached Arizona," the judge suggested.

"Good deduction, Your Honor. Now," Judith beamed, "guess what Milton Primble mailed himself?"

"My word!" the judge exploded. "Was it the fifty thousand dollars?"

"Yes. Can you believe it?"

"Tonight, I can believe anything. So what did C.V. do when he discovered the money?"

"This is the most astounding and romantic part."

"Romantic? This is the first husband who deserted her?"

"He never beat her or embezzled her money. He seems like a changed man," Judith replied. "He said his first thought was to take the money and go right back to Mexico and live a swell life."

"And he resisted?" the judge quizzed. "I'm impressed. What caused him to come here?"

"C.V. said he knew for a fact that Audrey would never send him that money unless something was terribly wrong. Over the years he's had a lot of time to think, and he regrets how he treated her. He says he'd love her whether she was rich or poor. Besides, he's made money in his own right, in Mexican mines. So he stuffed the money in his saddlebag and rode north with it, day and night, until he got here."

The judge slowly rubbed the back of his neck. "This is beginning to sound like one of those dime novels you hide in the bottom of your drawer."

Judith almost dropped her cup. It clanked against the saucer. "You know about …?"

"You know you can read whatever you want. But don't believe everything Miller writes about Brannon. Most of it is fabrication. That's my only objection."

"Well, C.V. got in last night and camped down at the river. At daybreak, Duffy Day wandered up to his fire and told him they were burying Wild Bill Hickok today."

"Which must have left C.V. in confusion."

"He didn't think much of it, and came to town to get a bath and clean up. When he found out it was Audrey's present husband who was to be buried, he was torn about going to see her."

"I suppose he didn't want to look like he was moving in on her grief."

"Exactly. But C.V. said he still couldn't figure out why she had sent him the money, so he decided to return it to her before the funeral. When he arrived, he spotted the sidesaddled horse and figured Audrey was about to go for her afternoon ride. He was standing at the front door, trying to figure a civil way of announcing himself, when he heard several gunshots. He ran in and found that Conroy woman waving a gun and screaming at Audrey. So he just marched up and hit her over the head with the barrel of his revolver."

"That's an incredible scene," the judge said.

"A tender, devoted one," Judith countered.

"He's still C.V. McKensie," the judge retorted.

"Maybe he's served his time and deserves another chance, Judge Kingston."

"Is that what Audrey thinks?"

"The thought has crossed her mind. Especially after he had to return the money to the bank and found out her fortune was gone, and yet he offered to stick around and help her move and get settled in San Francisco."

"What do you think his motive is? If he knows Audrey is broke ..."

"Perhaps he really cares for Audrey, now," Judith said.

"No, really, what do you think he's—"

Judith's glare halted him.

"Well, wouldn't that be an amazing turn of events?" he muttered into his mug.

"Audrey seems delighted to give him some kind of a chance. He certainly still is a handsome man." Judith sipped at her chocolate and found it tepid. "Now, Judge Kingston, what happened when Doctor Jacobs' smelling salts brought Mrs. Conroy around?"

"The woman absolutely turned maniacal. She was crazed, almost demonic."

"That, my dear husband, is what I tried to tell you the first time I met her. There was something about her. Did she admit killing her brother?"

"Yes. She ranted and raved about the good deed she had done. She actually thinks we should thank her for it."

"Good heavens, why?"

"In her words, 'I shot Milton because he deserved it. He always was a scoundrel. He was born a scoundrel. He lived a scoundrel. He died a scoundrel.'"

"So much for sibling affection."

"She said that after their mother died, Milton sold everything in the estate, kept the money for himself and came west, leaving her destitute. She moved to St. Louis and didn't hear from him for two years. He wrote to her last month and said she could make an easy five thousand dollars by showing up in Carson with a sob story about sick and dying children. He claimed Audrey was so bighearted she would reach into her safe and pull out the cash."

"But what would Milton get out of that except helping his sister, whom he hadn't spoken to in years?" Judith asked.

"She said, once the safe was open, he planned to help himself to the other ten thousand dollars."

"What happened to the plan?"

"His sister was five days late in arriving, and Milton panicked. He decided to beat the safe combination out of Audrey. But when he ran out of the house that night, there his sister was. They decided to concoct a story of Milton's death so that Mrs. Conroy would get a hold of a portion of Audrey's fortune and they'd split it."

"But why would Primble stick around if he already had fifty thousand dollars waiting in Tucson?" Judith asked.

"Mrs. Conroy didn't know about that money. I can only guess that Milton Primble had succumbed to the ultimate greed. He wanted every last penny he could lay his hands on."

"So why did she shoot him?"

"She said when things didn't work out quickly, she went back to the barn to talk over with Milton a different plan. Instead, he grabbed her horse and her funds and said he was going to ride off without her."

"Leaving her destitute once again?"

The judge nodded. "That didn't sit well, of course. She pulled out her sneak gun and threatened to shoot him if he tried to desert her. He tried."

"And she shot."

"Twice."

"How horrid."

"She doesn't seem to have much regret. But then, instead of getting out of here, she tried to keep working the scheme on her own, moving his body to the river."

"That's unbelievably gruesome."

"And when that didn't get her instant results, she went over to Audrey's with a gun."

"I'm glad that woman is in jail."

"Audrey should be safe now. Is C.V. staying at her place?"

"She said she'd make him sleep downstairs."

"I'm too tired to figure all of that out."

"I think it's time for bed, Judge Kingston."

"Go on. I still have a sermon to write. Remember? The Reverend Fraser has a Presbytery meeting in Sacramento this weekend."

"What is your topic, Lay-Preacher Kingston?"

"The snares of greed."

Judith, Marthellen, Willie Jane, and the judge sat in white-painted wooden lawn chairs after Sunday lunch.

"It is so nice here in the shade compared to the heat of the house," Judith remarked and stretched back in her chair. Swirls of white fluff from the cottonwood trees floated around them.

Marthellen fanned herself with a Chinese bamboo fan. "It has been a hectic two weeks."

"Lots of changes," Judith added.

"My head hasn't stopped spinnin' yet," Willie Jane said.

"I still marvel that Primble stayed around to try to pry Audrey's last fifteen thousand dollars, when he already had a sure fifty thousand dollars," the judge mused. "After over thirty years on the bench, I still can't understand why some men do the things they do."

"It's the greed," Willie Jane replied. "Just like you mentioned in your sermon. That was a very good talk, Judge. Of course, I haven't been in church in a long time."

"Yes, it was," Judith said, "but I believe the judge stifled a yawn several times."

"I was happy I didn't fall over asleep on the pulpit," he admitted.

"So was I," Judith said. "You had some challenging thoughts. It's difficult not to give in to greed when the whole state is caught up with silver and gold claims."

The judge laid his chin on his chest. "Greed seems to be the adhesive that holds our old nature together," he mumbled.

"And it sticks to our soul," Judith added. "It's so troublesome to get rid of."

All four turned their attention to the man walking up the sidewalk from the east.

"Mr. Cheney," Judith called out. "How's my favorite grocer?"

"I heard about your fainting spell at the cemetery, Judith. I thought I should check on your health."

"Thank you for your concern. I'm doing quite well today."

"Come on in the yard and sit with us," the judge called out.

Mr. Cheney opened the picket fence gate to the side yard and strolled toward them, carrying a small bundle. He tipped his hat, then glanced at Willie Jane.

"This is a very dear friend of ours … Mrs. Farnsworth," Judith said.

"Eh, yes, I believe we've met before. Didn't know your name was Mrs. Farnsworth."

"Hello, Mr. Cheney," Willie Jane said.

"Mrs. Farnsworth is a recent widow," Judith declared.

"I'm sorry to hear that." Mr. Cheney turned to Judith. "I have something for you."

"Say," Judith exclaimed. "Don't you have an opening for a clerk at the store? Mrs. Farnsworth will be needing a job. Perhaps you could consider her."

"I'm used to long hours," Willie Jane said.

"Oh, … I eh … well, you see, Judith … to be honest, I don't normally hire … eh," he stammered.

"You don't normally hire attractive women?" Judith chastened. "Perhaps the right ones just haven't applied."

"It isn't anything personal. I hope you understand. She's just not … well, not exactly what I was looking for in a clerk."

"Oh, we understand," Judith insisted.

Obvious relief flooded across his face. He turned to Willie Jane, "Good luck in finding a job, Mrs. Farnsworth."

"Don't worry about her," Judith added. "I'm sure she'll find something."

"Besides checking on your health, the other reason I stopped by was to show you these." He handed Judith the bundle.

She slowly unwrapped it. "My goodness, look at this." She held up two jars containing odd-shaped green chunks of fruit. "What is it?"

"That's mint pineapple straight from Rio de Janeiro, Brazil," he boasted.

"Mint pineapple?" Marthellen took one of the jars and stared at it.

"As I explained the other day, Mr. Cheney," the judge commented, "we eat plain food around here."

"I thought perhaps Judith would want to try these before

anyone else in town," Cheney insisted.

"Why, thank you. That is very thoughtful," Judith hummed. "But I think I'll pass."

"What?" Mr. Cheney gasped.

"You see, Willie Jane will probably get a job at Mason's. He seems to be willing to hire … women. So naturally Marthellen and I will be doing all our business over there. I hope you don't take it personally, Mr. Cheney. But we would want to patronize whichever store where Mrs. Farnsworth works." Judith smiled, nodded, and handed both jars back to the stunned grocer.

"You're saying you're going to do business wherever this young woman works?" he asked.

"This young widow," Judith corrected.

Mr. Cheney looked out at the street, then back at Willie Jane. "Eh, when did you say you could come to work?"

"Tomorrow," Willie Jane beamed.

"Can you work mornings from six until noon?"

"Yes, I can."

"Six days a week?"

"That's no problem."

"Then I'll see you in the morning." Mr. Cheney turned to trudge back toward the sidewalk.

Judith leaped from her chair and scooted up beside him. "Mr. Cheney, wait. You forgot to leave me my mint pineapple chunks."

"Oh, yes, indeed."

As he exited the yard, Judith hiked back. "I imagine we have the only two jars of mint pineapple in Carson City."

"Not for long," Marthellen grinned. "The word will be out by morning."

"I can't believe you just blackmailed him to give me a job," Willie Jane exclaimed.

"I most certainly did not!" Judith countered.

"Well, what do you call it?" the judge demanded.

"I merely helped him see clearly the obvious result of his own decision. Sometimes people don't think things completely through."

"And it's your duty to assist them?" the judge asked.

"Yes, it is." Judith handed the mint pineapple to Marthellen. "I don't suppose we have a recipe that uses these?"

"No, but I'm sure we'll assign them to a Wednesday lunch," Marthellen said.

Judith studied the green chunks in the glass jars.

"What do you think those things taste like?" the judge ventured.

Judith shrugged. "Probably something like guava or papaya, only mintier."

"Like what?" he asked.

Judith noticed sprightly movement out on the sidewalk. "Here comes Daisie Belle." *With no hat, no parasol, and her hair down.*

"She probably wants to check on your health," the judge suggested.

"I'm worried about her health," Judith said, beginning to fume.

"What's wrong with Daisie Belle?"

"She's going to faint."

"You can tell that as she walks up the sidewalk?" he asked.

"Trust me, Judge Kingston. She will faint. And you are not going to pick her up in your big strong arms and carry her home. Is that clear?"

The judge leaned his head back on the wooden lawn chair and gazed up at the thin blue August sky. A slight grin curved his lips. "Yes, Your Honor," he murmured.